THE SENTINALS
AND OTHER STORIES

by
Wayne Kyle Spitzer

THE SENTINELS

Statement of Mrs. Casey Marie Dunn (March 5th, 9:30 AM, interviewed by Detective Lamar Shaw)

Detective Shaw: Okay, now, I want you to focus, and tell me exactly what happened—starting with the landing of the canoe. Can you do that for me?

Dunn: Sure—yeah, I think. (sniffling) I ... we were taking on water, like I said. Not enough to sink—I'm not sure you can sink a canoe, can you? But enough so that we'd become extremely uncomfortable, and wanted to know where it was coming from.

Detective Shaw: So you landed the canoe near the Pyreridge Wind Farm. To inspect it.

Dunn: Yes. Well, we didn't know about the wind farm, not yet. There was only a thin width of beach—or whatever you'd call it—before the cliffs, which climbed straight up and sort of plateaued—and that's where the turbines were, still out of sight.

Detective Shaw: Out of earshot, too?

Dunn: You know, it's funny you should ask me that. I mean, yes—but ... but no, too. Because I remember sensing—a kind of pressure—like, like something heavy was laying on the air itself. Like, you know that feeling you get when you go up in elevation and your ears need to pop? —like that, only softer, more elusive. I honestly thought I was imagining it—at least until Bobby turned the boat over and we saw the hole in its bottom, at which the pressure seemed to increase (to double, actually), though only for a moment. Then it subsided and we were just standing there, looking at that hole. That funny little hole.

Detective Shaw: That's a curious way to describe it ... 'that funny little hole.' Was there something unusual about it?

Dunn: Well—yes. I should say so.

Detective Shaw: What? What was so unusual?

Dunn: It—it was shaped like a spiral. A perfect, proportionate little spiral, just as smooth and perfect as if it had been molded into the boat.

Detective Shaw: You mean drilled into the boat, surely?

Dunn: No. I mean molded. Or—I don't know—melted, maybe. But definitely not drilled.

Detective Shaw: And you'd never noticed it before?

Dunn: No, of course not. If that were the case, we'd never have embarked on the trip—much less without our phones.

Detective Shaw: Yes, I've been wondering about that. Help me understand, could you? It seems irresponsible to have left without them, even on such a wide, lazy river. Weren't you concerned about, say, an unexpected weather event? Or having a medical emergency? Being doctors, I can't imagine that—

Dunn: Mr. Shaw, please. You have to understand, the on-call nature of our jobs was precisely why such an excursion had become necessary in the first place. Surely it's the same in police work? No, this once, for our sanity and for our marriage, we were going commando, as they say. No cellphones, no iPads, no anything but nature and each other for the duration of the trip. That—at least that much makes sense ... doesn't it?

Detective Shaw: Of course, Mrs. Dunn. I suppose it does. But, my God, being so far from the nearest town, and not even knowing precisely where you were at, that must have been terrifying. What on earth did you plan to do?

Dunn: Well, the only thing we could do, which was to right the boat and continue on—while doing our best to bail, of course. And that's when I first noticed it: way up there beyond the ridge; something moving, swinging, like the tip of a giant sword—only black against the sun—something which, after we'd scaled a nearby rockfall, turned out to be the blades of an industrial wind turbine—just one out of what seemed an endless array, spread out across the scrublands for as far as the eye could see, casting long shadows, like Cyclopean sentinels.

Detective Shaw: Cyclop—cyclopean—what is that? Is that Latin?

Dunn: Huge, Detective. Massive.

Detective Shaw: Right. And then, what? You returned to your boat?

Dunn: You know we didn't return to the boat.

Detective Shaw: Yes, I understand that, just as I understood they found a spiraled hole exactly one inch in diameter in the bottom of your canoe. But it's better for the record if I pretend I know nothing, okay?

Dunn: Okay. No, then we began walking, because we'd figured out where we were at—the Pyreridge Wind Farm just north of Edgerton, as you said. And we knew, also, that they gave tours there and even had a visitor's center; a center which might still be staffed even though it was extremely late in the day, and which would have a telephone.

Detective Shaw: A wise move.

Dunn: Yes, it was as good as any. Or so it seemed—until we came to the wind turbine with the white service truck parked at its base; and saw ... where we saw ...

Detective Shaw: Yes?

Dunn: You've seen the pictures, Detective.

Detective Shaw: But I need to pretend I have not. And I need to hear what you, personally, saw with your very own eyes. For the record, Dr. Dunn. Please.

Dunn: Where we saw a man, a service technician, by his clothes, hung by his neck from his own safety line ... from the back of the wind turbine's nacelle. Just ... just sort of swaying there, in the wind. A man who was missing one shoe. And who ...

Detective Shaw: Go on ...

Dunn: And who had no discernible face. Okay? (inaudible) He had no face. Isn't that good enough?

Detective Shaw: I didn't mean to upset you. Still, talk about that a little. You say, 'he had no face'—what does that mean? Had it been mutilated or disfigured in some way? Was he wearing a nylon? What?

Dunn: No, no, nothing like that. It was just, dark, somehow. Smudged out. The truth is we couldn't tell; it was like the whole world was in focus except for that one spot, which was blurred, unlit. That's when I noticed all the little holes in in the truck, like it had been riddled with bullets—except on closer inspection they turned out to be spirals, like the one in the boat. I say 'I' because Bobby's attention had drifted to the blades of the wind turbine, which were directly above us, going woosh, woosh, woosh. And it was the strangest thing because it was almost as if he'd become hypnotized—as if they were a great swinging pendulum—to the point that he completely ignored me when I pointed out the visitor's center and only continued to watch.

Detective Shaw: Well, that is strange. Was he in shock, you think?

Dunn: My husband? The emergency room doctor? (laughter) No. No, this was something—different. Something more meditative. Almost as if—

Detective Shaw: Something spiritual?

Dunn: Yes! As though he were having an epiphany. To the extent that I had to physically drag him away; at which he came out of it and was just Bobby again—just everyone's favorite life-saver.

Detective Shaw: And that's when you went to the visitor's center and called the police.

Dunn: Yes. It—it was unlocked. We just walked right in. But no one was there, even though there was a utility truck out front. And then I called the police but the dispatcher had bad news: they wouldn't be able to get there for a half-hour, at least. And that's when I just, well, broke, for lack of a better term, and the next thing I knew I was waking up while Bobby dabbed at my temples with a moist cloth and the phone rang incessantly and he began telling me to answer it, that it was 911 calling back, and that he'd searched for the keys to the truck out front but hadn't found them and was going to go back to the first truck—the truck with all the holes in it—to see if its keys were there.

Detective Shaw: And how did you feel about that? About him returning to the scene? Or you being left alone in the visitor's center, for that matter?

Dunn: Oh, I thought it was a terrible idea! I didn't want to let him out of my sight. There was something so strange about him all of a sudden— so out of character—like he was high on marijuana. And his eyes, they were so distant, so unfocused. I practically begged him not to go. But then he had gone and I was answering the phone, and the dispatcher kept me busy with questions for I don't know how long ...

Detective Shaw: You say he wasn't himself and that his eyes were blurry; was there anything else? Was his speech slurred, for example? How about his color?

Dunn: He—he kept scratching himself, like he was covered in insect bites. And he was pulling at his clothes, especially his collar, as though they were suffocating him. It was all so very unusual, and I would have dropped the phone and ran after him if not for ... if not ...

Detective Shaw: If not for what, Dr. Dunn?

Dunn: If not ... for the blood. The blood on the glass case.

Detective Shaw: I'm afraid I don't—

Dunn: Stop. Just, stop, please. You know as well as I do that—

Detective Shaw: But the tape recorder doesn't, Mrs. Dunn. Now, please. Tell me what you saw that prevented you from pursuing your husband. Describe it to me.

Dunn: There—there was a large glass case in the center of the foyer ... it ... it contained a miniature of the wind farm., as you know. And it—someone had written something on top of it. Some kind of a message. In blood.

Detective Shaw: I see. Thank you. Now tell me: what did this message say?

Dunn: It ... I don't remember exactly. It was mostly gibberish. Something about 'the Wind' and 'the Way,' and going in to 'Them.' Something about how 'They' had attached themselves to the turbines—whatever 'They' were. And finally just a long scrawl, followed by a warning, all in caps, GET OUT OF HERE AS FAST AS YOU CAN.

Detective Shaw: I see. And I guess it needs to be asked: Did you? Or did you continue to field the 911 operator's questions?

Dunn: No. I dropped the phone as fast as I could and ran out the side door, the one Bobby had went out. And the first thing I saw was Bobby's pale-blue windbreaker, just thrown aside in the dirt, and further out, his T-shirt, white against the sage.

Detective Shaw: It's like he was burning up. Was it hot out? What was the temperature, you think?

Dunn: It was cold! No, like I said, it was if the clothes were suffocating him, cutting off his circulation. All I know it that when I reached the T-shirt I saw his belt further out, and beyond that, his shoes, just lying amidst the cheat-grass. That's when I knew something truly terrible had happened, was happening, and that if I didn't find him quickly he might genuinely hurt himself; though I'd scarcely had the thought when I noticed someone crumpled face down in the sage—not Bobby, this man was fully dressed—and ran to him.

Detective Shaw: The other turbine technician.

Dunn: Oh, are we done with the ignorant act?

Detective Shaw: It was a slip; I'm starting to think about lunch. Okay, and, seeing this, what did you do?

Dunn: He wasn't breathing and so I rolled him over. And ...

Detective Shaw: Yes? And what?

Dunn: Jesus, gods, you know what!

Detective Shaw: What did you see when you rolled him over, Dr. Dunn?

Dunn: I saw that he had no face. That it ... that it had just spiraled in, like the hole in the boat. That there was a gaping funnel where his eyes and nose and upper lip should have been—mottled red and black, pink and gray—just twisted cartilage and brain tissue. And then his body spasmed, as though by a reflex, and the funnel seemed to burp, spitting up blood.

Detective Shaw: Jesus.

Dunn: After which, dear God, I can't say, because I was running away as fast as I could; past Bobby's shoes and toward the wind turbine (the one with the truck parked at its base), as well as past a few dozen new funnels in the ground—which grew in size as I approached from an inch or two across to ones the size of manhole covers. Until I came to the turbine and—and stopped dead in my tracks. Because there was Bobby kneeling prone in the dirt, like a Muslim, I suppose, or a Buddhist, but completely nude—bowing before the turbine, the hatch of which was open, seeming almost to pray.

Detective Shaw: But ... but all right, in spite of his behavior.

Dunn: No, Mr. Shaw, not 'all right.' Because when he sat up again I saw that his back was ... It was riddled with those same spiral funnels. There were even some in his arms. But—but that wasn't all. Because, after he'd stood with some difficulty and turned to face me (he must have sensed my presence; that or saw my shadow), I realized something else. And that was that his eyes had gone completely white—rather they had rolled back in his skull enough so that only the whites were visible—at which moment he spoke and said, calmly, "The turbines, don't look at them. They eat your eyes."

Detective Shaw: The turbines ... they ... what did that mean?

Dunn: I'm sure I don't know. All I know is that my husband had become something hardly recognizable ... and that I was terrified. So much so that I began backing away as he approached— which seemed to anger him, enough that when he resumed speaking he sounded vicious—alien—full of disdain.

Detective Shaw: Good lord—what did he say? Think, Mrs. Dunn. This is the most vital part of your testimony ...

Dunn: He said that he was taking the way of the wind and the sky, and that he was going in—to Them—by which I presume he meant going into the tower and scaling the ladder. And he said other things: That our thoughts made patterns in their world—left 'prints,' as it were—as did theirs in ours; and that that was how they'd found us, by listening to our thoughts, zeroing in on our patterns. And he said that Bobby was merely a bundle of sensory organs wrapped in a skin of decaying matter and so wasn't important, wasn't needed. That only they mattered—they, the beings attached to and inhabiting the turbines. And that ... that ...

Detective Shaw: What, Mrs. Dunn? Say it.

Dunn: But ... don't you see? It doesn't matter what he said, because it wasn't him speaking, not really. Bobby would never have described a human being as just a bundle of sensory organs; he truly believed, with every fiber of his being, that we were more than that—more than just the sum of our parts—it was what inspired him to become a doctor in the first place. And knowing what I knew, knowing what kind of man he was, I pressed him, telling him that Bobby did matter—that he mattered to his patients and that he mattered to me—more than I would ever be able to describe. And then I approached him and embraced him and told him I loved him—feeling, for the briefest of moments, the spirals beginning to close on his back—and he smiled, his eyes returning to normal, after which he said, or started to say, "I love ..." (room tone)

Detective Shaw: (inaudible) He—he told you he loved you?

Dunn: No. He ... his eyes rolled back ... and then his face, it ... it simply imploded. In a spiral. Like someone had flushed a toilet full of blood and brains.

(room tone)

Dunn: And then his body, which had become light as a feather, like a papery husk, came apart in my arms—and simply blew away. Like so many dandelion seeds.

(room tone)

Detective Shaw: I ... I have to ask. It's—it's my job, you understand. Did—did you ever feel like ... I mean, did—

Dunn: Did I ever feel like I was being targeted myself?

Detective Shaw: (inaudible)

Dunn: Yes, right after that. I'd—I'd turned my palms up, see, because I couldn't comprehend that he could be there one minute and just ... gone the next. And there were spirals in both of them. Not deep, just, just impressions, but it was enough to snap me out of whatever I was feeling and to open the door of the truck, where I found its keys right there in the ignition.

Detective Shaw: And that's when you drove onto the highway and—

Dunn: And didn't stop until I reached Edgerton. Not even when the squad cars started passing me going the other way, their lights flashing.

Detective Shaw: Yes, well. When they got there they found things much as you described ... and photographs were taken. The other men, the turbine technicians, they ... when we tried to move them they, too, were lost to the wind.

Dunn: And the turbines? Have they been inspected?

Detective Shaw: (inaudible) Just turbines. Nor has there been any reports of ... strange occurrences. It would seem, then ... that this was an isolated event.

Dunn: An isolated event ...

Detective Shaw: Yeah.

Dunn: Are—are we done, Mr. Shaw?

Detective Shaw: Yeah. For now. There's ... there's a car downstairs; they'll, ah, take you home.

(inaudible shuffling)

Detective Shaw: Oh, and Mrs. Dunn? Thank you. I know ... it couldn't have been easy.

Dunn: Goodnight, Detective.

Detective Shaw: Goodnight.

(end of recording)

It's tempting to say, looking back, that it began with that warped wall—the wall in the basement garage which had been flat and firm when I'd first bought the house but had morphed into something misshapen and hideous. But in truth, it started with her voice, Mia's, a voice I would fall in love with—although, at the time, it existed only in my mind—a voice that had captivated me from the very first moment I heard it.

That would have been March 5, 2019, the day after they'd begun digging for the pool, when I'd taken to the deformed wall (which had been water damaged, I presumed, and was not part of the concrete foundation anyway) with a pickax—hacking away at it mercilessly until both the sheet rock and studs (which had been corrupted, as well) lay in ruins, and I was sitting on an inverted 5-gallon bucket, recovering, just staring at the exposed earth.

At least, until I heard that voice, which said to me, weakly, faintly, and yet somehow clear as a bell, *Please, Dear God. Help me. I have been buried alive.*

It's funny, because the first thing I thought of was a TV movie from the '70s—*The Screaming Woman*, about a girl found buried alive on a rich crone's property, and it's possible I mistook the voice for a memory of that, at least at first. But then it came again (once more managing to be faint yet clear as day), and I realized, finally, that it was not only real but emanating somehow from my own mind, as though I were not so much hearing it as transcoding it into a form I could understand. And what it said was: *Please ... there isn't much time. I'm not far, but as I have awakened, so have they. Now, use your pickax—I won't be hurt—and dig, dig!*

And, because I was captivated, that's what I did, approaching the earthen wall and swinging the ax again and again, grunting each time the blade struck the sediment, feeling the shock in my hands and arms whenever it hit a rock, until at last she cried, *Stop!*—and I stopped, wondering what had come over me that I should throw myself at the stones with such total abandon, or that I should suddenly feel as though I had the strength of twenty men rather than one. At which instant the voice said, *Now, look. See.*

And I did, see that is, and realized that something was glinting, ever so slightly, through the dirt—something metallic, something man-made. Something which revealed itself grudgingly as I dropped the ax and began clearing away the moist, black earth ... until at last I was looking at a State of New York license plate, its blue and yellow colors seemingly vibrant as the day it was pressed, its characters personalized to read: BRN 2 KILL, and its black and white tab dated 3— for March—1966.

As it turned out, we finished our excavations—me and the pool guys—at about the same time; in no small part because they'd lent me their conveyor belt over the weekend, which enabled me to move earth from the garage into the payload of my truck as fast as I could dig it out. Not that I couldn't have managed without it—I felt *strong,* as I said, stronger than I'd felt in years, as if the car and the voice had somehow infused me with super-strength. Nor had my new vitality gone unremarked, especially at Home Depot—which I'd been haunting like a wraith, primarily for support beams—where I was asked more than once what supplements I'd been taking.

Regardless, 48 hours (and several dump loads to my friend's farm) later, it was done, and I was hosing off what a web search had told me was a 1966 Corvette Stingray hardtop, black and red, with a 435-horsepower/5,800 rpm V-8 engine and a sterling Peace symbol—which hung from its rear-view mirror like a charm. Nor was that all, for dangling from its ignition was a set of keys—one, presumably, for the trunk—along with a maroon rabbit's foot, or possibly a cat's, affixed to a silver chain.

Here I pause, in order to better render what I was feeling and what had carried me through the last couple days. For while it is true I began digging (beyond the wall, that is) in response to the girl's cry for help—believing, as I did, that a living person might yet be saved—it is also true that that conviction faltered upon uncovering the 52-year-old plate, to the point that, considering the voice had fallen silent, I no longer expected to find a survivor—but a skeleton. I tell you this plainly so that you will understand why I didn't open the trunk immediately, and why, to be frank, I feared doing so. Rather, I believe it was the car itself that goaded me on during this time, growing as it was in power and actively suppressing Mia's attempts to communicate with me. Whatever it was, she must have at last found a way to break through, for as I opened the driver's side door and seated myself in the cockpit, I once more heard her voice, which said, as clearly as if she were standing next to me: *Hurry. Please. The keys. The trunk ...*

I paused, my fingertips kissing those very keys. The interior smelled of death, and decay, and something else—oily, pungent, like cilantro or burning tires, or a black beetle crushed underfoot. The truth is, I was terrified—what could the voice have been if not the ghost of someone buried with the car? And there was something else too, a completely different reason why I was so hesitant. And that was that—

I closed my thumb and forefingers on the keys, pushing in the clutch.

Don't do it! came the voice. Mia—their specimen. The butterfly they'd intended to collect. *That's what they want; what it wants. What the previous owner gave them. Resist—and open the trunk. We have work to do.*

But I hesitated.

And then came another voice—several others, actually, one after the other—which said, in a language older than words (but which I could understand): *Start it, James ... turn the key.*

Yes, yes, James. Continue the process.

Do it, James!

And I turned the key.

The truth was, I hadn't noticed how much attention my little digging project had garnered until I backed the rumbling, sputtering 'Vette up and out of the garage—and found half the neighborhood looking on. I shouldn't have been surprised; there were piles of dirt and stone everywhere—some of which had spilled onto the Merton's lawn (and the Diller's, too) and made tempting obstacles for boys on BMX bikes, not to mention that the conveyor running at 3 am would have undoubtedly stirred Miss Harper, who had once called 911 because a dog was barking. It's hard to credit, in retrospect, how I'd avoided a visit from the cops. Maybe *they* had something to do with it. The bugs. Who knows.

Regardless, the kids waved and hollered as I backed onto the street and put it into gear, and I gave them a rev or two before easing up on the clutch and moving down the road, the radio giving me a start as it came on without warning (and without my having touched it) and began playing "Fortunate Son" by Creedence Clearwater Revival.

Then I was off, cruising the streets of Schenectady as though I hadn't a care in the world, relishing it every time I drew alongside some kid in his Honda, speeding up a little as I handled corners, tapping the horn as I rumbled past female joggers. The truth of it is I was under the car's spell, and didn't think to question why the girl had fallen silent (again) or who—what—the other voices had been or how a car that had been buried for 52 years had simply rolled over and leapt to life. I felt young again, vibrant, strong, as though nothing could touch me and nothing could hurt; as though the logical part of my brain had simply turned off, as it does when you smoke a good blunt; as though I were in the clouds and nothing could bring me back. Indeed, I felt free of all human constraint and concern—at least, until I saw the Lyndon B. Johnson campaign sticker on the clean, chrome bumper ahead of me, and, realizing that both it and the Beetle to which it was attached were in as perfect condition as the 'Vette—"Black Betty" it said on the 'Vette's door, I'd nearly forgotten about that—began to come out of it.

That's when I really noticed it, the fact that the landscape immediately around the car had changed; that it had—*reverted,* somehow. I can only describe what I saw, which was that *none* of the vehicles at the light could have been newer than a '66, and that the *light* itself looked decidedly retro, decidedly quaint, at least compared to the one only a block away. More, the storefronts alongside had changed, so that a Kinney Shoe Store now stood where a Taco Bell had just been, and a Woolworth had replaced an Indy Food Mart. Likewise, the pedestrians had changed—yoga pants giving way to miniskirts, athletic shoes giving way to go-go boots and winklepickers, short hair giving way to long. And it was as I observed these things that I noticed something else—the Stingray's reflection in the Woolworth's front windows, or rather, the reflection of something which was not the Stingray but which stood—hovered—in its place: a long, translucent, green-black thing, like an enormous wine decanter, only laid on its side, which glowed slightly from within its bulbous body and seemed to warp the very air around it, to bend it, to curl it like burnt paper.

What you see is the car's true form, came the voice, the girl's voice, Mia's, startling me with its clarity, seeming at once to be both inside my head and without, causing me to turn instinctively— revealing her to be sitting beside me, right there in the passenger seat. *"... and the field in which it operates. That field is weak now but it will grow. And the longer it remains free—the car, the artifact—the stronger it will become, until the world itself becomes threatened. Now do you see why I tried to warn you?"*

But I could only stare at her, even as the late afternoon sun caught her auburn hair—which was styled in a flipped bob—and seemed to set it on fire. *Beautiful,* I remember thinking, even though her eyes and skin were all wrong: bluish-gray, almost green; deaden, but in a very specific way, as though she had drown. "Look at yourself," she said (actually said, it seemed, not communicated silently, like a specter), "Although its passengers are immune to the field it has already affected you—in other ways."

I adjusted the rearview mirror to look at myself, and saw that she was at least partially correct: my skin was sallow—almost greenish—and there were dark spots beneath—

That's when I saw them. *The bugs.* Three of them, to be precise, scrunched up in the storage area beneath the fastback, each about the size of a chimpanzee, and each a kind of hybrid between a locust and a mantid.

It was all too much—the car that had been buried for 52 years yet started right up, the flashback to the 1960s and the ghostly girl, the bugs the size of dogs whose stench filled the cab and caused me to wretch. I gripped the door handle instantly—even as the little chrome knob dropped, locking me in. Then we were accelerating— abruptly, powerfully— whipping around the cars in front of us and blasting through the intersection: the girl vanishing, just winking out of existence, the bugs making a sound like crickets but magnified a hundred fold—the V-8 (or whatever it was) roaring.

Yes—yes, James. Want this, we do ...
Want it! Want it!
Right there, James. The infestation. Do it!
But I wasn't driving—

No, I could see that wasn't true: my foot was on the peddle just as sure as my hands were on the wheel. And that foot dipped suddenly even as the skateboarder came into view—his eyes widening, his free leg kicking—so that he disappeared into an alley even as we exploded past— fishtailing to a halt in the middle of the road, where the high-compression engine sputtered and the glass packs rumbled— before my foot once again hit the gas and we tore after him, burning rubber.

And then we were bearing down upon the kid, as he kicked and kicked furiously and glanced at us over his shoulder. As I looked in the rear-view mirror and saw the bug-things leaning forward (as though in anticipation). As I fought whatever impulse had taken oven my limbs and partially succeeded—too late.

There was a *thud-crunch!* as he vanished beneath the hood—and the car bucked violently, as though I'd driven over a curb. I ground the brakes, glancing in the mirror—saw him tumble after us like a bag of litter. Only then, after I'd come to a complete stop, did it occur to me: I could see out the back window. The bugs were gone. The kid, meanwhile, was still alive—good God!—and thus it wasn't too late; I could still help him, still *save* him.

Yes, yes, James. Save him.

We're not finished yet, James.

Finish, finish!

I felt the gearshift in my hand—saw that I'd already put it in reverse and was stepping on the gas, letting out the clutch. And then the car launched backward—reversing straight as an arrow—until it bucked and rolled up onto the kid; and stopped.

"Please, mister," came the kid's voice—muffled, garbled—through my partially open window. "Please, God—"

But then my hand was shifting and the engine was roaring—the wide tires were spinning—and I saw through my side-view mirror that his blood was fanning the nearby bricks and a window—spraying them like rifle shot, spattering them with entrails, hurling pieces of bone against, and through, the glass—until the positraction gripped bare asphalt and the car leapt forward: roaring down the alley, skidding back onto the road, releasing its control over me.

At which moment Mia reappeared, like an apparition, and, rolling her milky eyes to face me, said, "Now will you listen? Now will you open the trunk?"

And then promptly faded away.

The key slid in smoothly and I paused, looking at the abandoned drive-in theater: at the rusted, canted speaker posts (the speakers themselves had long since been stolen) and the weeds bursting through the concrete berms; at the dilapidated concessions bar and the partially-collapsed steel fence. *Do it,* I told myself, and turned the key, hearing sirens in the distance as the trunk popped open, trying not to think about the kid. As it turned out, it wasn't that difficult, considering what I found myself looking at.

They were arthropods, of course, and so appeared in death much as they'd appeared in life, although their eyes had long since rotted out and their shells had become gray as tombstones. But that's not what interested me so much as what was beneath them—which, having shoved them all to one side, I realized was a kind of—well, *egg,* for lack of a better term. A huge, glass egg—built into the car and full of a greenish, glowing liquid—within which, curled into a fetal position, floated a naked woman. A woman I recognized as Mia her-self.

Now do you understand? she asked, speaking directly into my head, directly into my mind—again, as though she were standing immediately beside me.

"No. No, I don't," I said, shaking my head in the dimming twilight. "Maybe you can explain it to me."

Get in the car, she said. *And I will. All of it.*

That's when I looked over the trunk lid I saw that she was back, just sitting in the passenger seat like a zombie, staring straight ahead at the screen. A screen, I might add, which had been restored—and over which danced images of hot dogs and fountain sodas and fresh-popped corn; of cotton candy and licorice twists.

For the drive-in, you see, had *warped*—just like the streetlight, just like the storefronts—and was operational once again. Operational and rapidly filling up—with cars, that was a given, old yet somehow brand-new—but also with people, at least some of whom would have been dead, or so it seemed likely to me, only a few scant moments ago.

"Talk," I said, shutting my door, settling in. "Starting with why you encouraged me to unbury the car—when you knew full well what could happen." I glanced at her in the dark. "And you *must* have known."

"I knew that their spirits—which are fused with the car, as is mine—would attempt to influence you, yes. What I did not know is the extent to which they'd succeed, how easily you'd succumb!" She seemed to shift gears: "It's not important. What is important is that the car gets reburied—deeper, further away. So that it may never threaten the surface again."

"But, what is it ... and who are they? Who are you, for that matter?"

"The car? Why, it's a spacecraft, of course. A *time*-craft. It has been matter-cloaked to mimic an automobile, that's all—of a make and model that was popular in the year they came. It was their way, I suppose, the bugs, of moving amongst us; of observing us at close range—at least, until they decided we should be exterminated. That's where I come in: their specimen. The sole butterfly they'd planned to harvest as an example of what they'd wiped out—for that's precisely what they'd initiated before a flu strain killed them all."

She laughed suddenly and what looked like the green fluid from the egg gurgled up out of her mouth. "The Common Cold, I suppose. Like in H.G. Wells. At least that's what Crowley thought, when he found them, that is."

"Who—"

"Crowley, the man who first discovered the car, full of bugs and rolled over in a ravine near Schenectady, in 1966. It was his theory that the foreigners had taken the appearance of humans while piloting the cloaked craft, but reverted to bugs after they'd died—either way, he knew right away that the 'Vette was no mere car. As for me and my egg, he hadn't a clue what to make of that. But the bugs spoke to him just as they've spoken to you; and before he knew it he'd stuffed them in the trunk and towed the car home and applied for title—he even had a personalized license plate made, 'BRN 2 KILL,' something to do with his service in Vietnam—as well as commissioning someone to paint 'Black Betty' on its door. But by November of that year he was done, and wanted nothing further to do with it, even going so far as to bury it in the landfill he worked at, the Copperhead Earth Works, where he plowed it 6 feet under with his bulldozer and—"

"Copperhead?" I interjected, and thought instantly of Copperhead Farms, the name of the housing project which encompassed my new home. "How do you know all this?"

"I began to, project myself—sleepwalking, I call it—shortly after being preserved in the back of the ship. Nor do I know how that is possible. I only know that it is, and that I was able to monitor Crowley as he interacted with the car—although I could not yet communicate with him as I have with you. And it was during that time that I became aware of *them,* the bugs, but in spirit-form. I even learned how to intercept their thoughts, as I had Crowley's. All of which brings me to why I reached out to you when you began to dig—"

"You wanted to be free," I said, feeling as though I suddenly understood her, suddenly got it. "Either by death or by rescue ... you wanted to be free."

"In part, yes. Of course. But also because the car was insufficiently buried, insufficiently interred. It was bleeding through the sediment, you understand. Because what the bugs started before falling ill is still underway—an exponential charge, using the ship's warp field as a weapon of mass destruction. And as I've said, the longer the car remains free, the stronger it will become ... until at last all life on Earth will be threatened. And before you ask, the answer is no, it cannot be destroyed, not without detonating it at its present charge, which would still be enough to destroy half the planet."

I moved to speak but paused, letting it go.

"That's what I meant when I said we had work to do. We *have* to find a way to re-bury this car. And re-bury it for good. And for that you're going to need help—real help, not a disembodied voice. Or a ghost. And so I am asking you to at least try to set me free. But in order to do so you'll have to *see,* and I mean see in a way you've never seen before. I'll show you. I—I have faith in you, James. I know you can do it."

And then she placed her hand over mine and it faded into my skin, and I got out and went to the trunk.

I'd just told her that, because of her help, I could see— actually *see* the alien-looking control panel (which before I'd missed), when a youthful male voice said, behind me: "Excuse me, sir?" —and I spun around.

What is it, James? What's going on?

And found myself facing a security guard—one right out of 1960s—peaked hat, whistle, Billy club, and all.

"Y—yes?" I stammered, easing down the trunk lid, stepping away from the car. "Can I help you?"

He aimed his flashlight, a ribbed, chrome thing which looked positively primitive, into the empty cab.

"It's just funny," he said, "because I could have sworn I heard you talking to someone—in the trunk of your car. Just now, as I was coming up the aisle."

He paused, sizing me up. "You know, a lot of people seem to think that ripping us off by sneaking people in through the trunk is just good, clean fun." He unhooked the radio from his belt and placed it near his lips. "But 3.50 a carload means just that—*3.50 per carload.*" He keyed his mic. "K-91 to K-54, where are you?"

"Look, can't we just—"

Get in the car, James.

"I mean, I'm a little old to be sneaking—"

Get in the car, James!

"Stay right where you are, sir. K-91 to K-54: Request back-up in section A. *Excuse me, sir ...!*"

But I was already getting in the car, turning the ignition— revving the engine as Barney Fife rushed to my door and began yanking the handle—which I'd locked—putting it in gear.

"Get us out of here," said Mia, having re-appeared in the passenger seat. *"Go, go, go!"*

And then we'd backed up and swung around and were beginning to launch forward, the 'Vette's engine roaring, its rear tires spinning, until we blasted between the rows and I began searching for the exit, the skinny guard gradually giving up the chase, people running helter and skelter out of our way.

Yes, yes, James! Infestation!

Kill them, kill them!

Wipe them from the Earth ...

The bugs again—reaching into my mind, seizing control of my hands—as the radio sputtered to life and the Beatles began singing: *Well, shake it up, baby, now (Twist and shout)*

Come on, come on, come on, baby, now (Come on and work it on out ...)

My hands jerked the wheel as a man in a suit ran out in front of us and we struck him like a hammer—causing him to tumble up over the hood, splay against the windshield, where his bloodied face pressed against the glass. *Well, work it on out, honey ...* The wipers activated even as I slammed on the brakes and he slid off, then we were accelerating again, rolling over the top of him, as Mia screamed and the bugs ticked and cackled, as the Beatles sang, *You know you got me goin' now (Just like I knew you would ...)*

"Fight it, James! Resist them!" cried Mia—even as the car bounced up and over a berm and the Peace symbol hanging from its mirror swung. As it targeted a woman with an enormous beehive and rammed into her at full speed— knocking her at least twenty feet, trampling over the top of her, leaving her a bloody ruin.

"Get it together, man! Concen—oh, no. *Oh, no!*"

I followed her gaze as we fishtailed around the end of the front row and accelerated toward the screen, saw the children begin to scatter as we bore down upon the playground.

Do it, James, do it!

Faster, faster!

I fought the wheel but it had taken over completely— steering for the running kids, seeming almost to growl at me, jerking against my grip. The cab shook as we piled over the railroad ties at the edge of the playground and began tearing through the sand, aiming at a little boy even as the headlights popped up and drowned him in harsh light, as the glass packs roared and the Peace symbol swung.

"James!"

And something just—kicked in. I still can't explain it. But for a fraction of a second I was able to just, *merge* with the car—with the ship. All I know is that for that fraction of a second we were one: one entity, one organism. And as I applied the brakes and swung the wheel the car responded, fishtailing and skidding to a stop in the sand ... where it idled roughly as I looked at Mia and she looked at me. And it was at precisely that moment that an idea came to mind—an idea I thought just might work. If we could get there in time. If I could maintain control of the car.

It wasn't easy, communicating with the car, ordering it to lower its warp field; nor was it completely successful—the family we'd left twisted and mutated at a stoplight, partially fused with their car, was proof of that. Nor did we stop anymore after that but instead rumbled straight for my house, ignoring every sign and limit, rushing against the clock, praying we could make it before my concentration finally gave out and we were back in the '60s—back where we'd killed so many and the cops were surely looking for us. Back where the bodies lay scattered and broken everywhere we'd been.

"Hang on!" I shouted as we broke through the fence and hurtled toward the pool excavation—forgetting, for the moment, that Mia was yet a kind of ghost, and that if anyone need worry about the coming impact it was me. And then I was throwing open the door and rolling upon the ground—as the 'Vette which was not a 'Vette launched off a dirt berm (left over from the pool dig) and crashed into the pit, its steel frame seeming to howl like a wounded beast and its fiberglass crunching and breaking, its windows shattering ...

Hurry, James. The cement truck ...

"But you're still in the car!"

And it's possible I'll remain there. The world, James ... The world comes first.

I cursed, staring into the pit. At the Stingray, which had begun to glow and to morph. At *Black Betty* ... a bitch if ever there was one. Then I hurried to the cement truck and, to my great relief, found the keys still in the ignition (we'd become friends, after all, the contractor and I, nor was it a bad neighborhood). But I was not alone as I started it up and activated the mixer, for in addition to Mia the bugs were still in my head, louder than ever and seeming to sense what was at stake. *Angry,* for that was their nature, but terrified, too. Vulnerable at last.

Don't do it, James. You mustn't do it ...

Return, return. Drive us some more.

The girl, James. You must save the girl!

I looked at the pit as it began to fill up with concrete, frowning, then scrambled from the truck and into the hole, my shoes squelching in the cement, my heart racing, as I opened the door and retrieved the keys. As I hurried to the trunk and popped it open.

But the alien control panel was no longer there, which is to say I could no longer see it given the maelstrom in my head, the energy I was expending to thwart the ship's warp field. And it *was* becoming a ship again, that much was clear, as though the bugs' fear and vulnerability had weakened it and compromised its ability to multitask. As though their hatred of us and of the human race had trumped every other single thing. The charge had to be perpetuated; I could practically hear it in the air. The purge had to continue—even if it was from beyond their own graves!

And then a miracle occurred, one Mia and I talk about to this very day, although really it was just the result of the green-black ship losing its bizarre cloak: for as the wet cement reached my knees and threatened to overwhelm the trunk, the control panel reappeared, at which instant I was able to access the bugs' minds—for Mia's abilities had rubbed off on me in a way we still don't understand—enough to depress the right sequence and cause the egg to open, its greenish fluid flooding the ship's surface as Mia inhaled violently and coughed up yet more liquid—the bugs chattering and cursing indecipherably as the concrete reached for my thighs. And then, somehow, somehow, I was able to scoop her into my arms and climb out of the pit, although, again, the fact that I was able to do so remains a mystery to us even today. Perhaps it was just love and the power it can confer. For I *did* love her, of that much I was certain. And I wasn't about to abandon her to another eternal limbo.

All I know is that at some point the pit had been filled and I'd successfully shut down the mixer, and that we'd stood there for what seemed a long time just watching the cement cure and feeling grateful for our lives. Nor was it a time for celebration considering how much pain and suffering the thing had caused; but rather a time to reflect and meditate and yes, to pray.

Pray that no one ever came and dug the cursed thing out.

Pray that the bugs, whatever they were and wherever they were from, would never send another.

Why did I do it? *Because I was meant to.* Because that's why I had been allowed to live. This was the whole of the affair in one simple statement.

Memory, of course, can be a dodgy thing: why else would my recall of the Benton Boys—and how Old Man Moss had brought their reign of terror to an end—have lain dormant for so long (forty years, to be exact), right up until that moment I saw what I'd at first taken to be a man—but quickly realized was not—ascending the tower crane just beyond our encampment?

The obvious answer is that a lot can happen in forty years. A man could go from being an innocent kid in Benton, Washington (population one-hundred and seventeen) to a scary homeless dude in Seattle—Belltown, to be precise—just as I had. But there's another answer, too, one we don't talk about as much, which is that some things get buried not for any lack of a mental space to put them but for their very unfathomableness and steadfast refusal to make sense. For me, Old Man Moss' handling of the Benton Boys had been just that, something I'd sublimated completely in the years following not because the event—the events—had been forgotten, but because I simply hadn't the means of processing them up until that night; the night I climbed the massive tower crane in downtown Seattle and came face to face with the brute. The night the string of gruesome murders that had plagued the city for months had, at last, come to an end.

"I don't see anything," said Billy the Skid, his boozy breath seeming to billow with each syllable, as he stood beside me and squinted up at the crane. "Who would it be? Construction's been halted for months, even I know that."

"I didn't say 'who,' I said 'what,' as in what is that, right there?" I pointed to where the gray figure could once again be seen (ascending not the ladder inside the scaffolding but the tower itself, like some kind of huge spider). "Do you see it? Like a man, and yet somehow not a man. And look, it's got someone thrown over its shoulder. It's right there, damn you!"

Billy only shook his head. "Whatever you say, boss." He chuckled as he made his way back to his shopping cart. "Someone thrown over his shoulder. I say if you can't handle Thunderbird you ought to leave the drinking to me. Who the hell did 'ya think it was? The Belltown Brute? Ha! And I suppose he ..."

But I wasn't listening, not really. I was still watching the gray man, the gray *thing,* ascend the tower—the hammerhead, I've heard them called—its tail swinging like a cobra (yes, yes, it had a *tail*), its ashen skin seeming to catch the lightning and throw it back, its cone-shaped head turning to face me.

Yes. Yes, it could be. Still ... was it even possible? Well, no, to be frank—it wasn't. But then, everything about the summer of '79 and what had happened to the Benton Boys and Old Man Moss' ancient Jewish magik had been impossible. That didn't change the fact that it had happened—and it *had* happened—hadn't it?

I didn't know for sure, no more than I knew whether the entry point to the crane would be locked or if I had the courage to scale the ladder or if lightning would strike as I climbed killing me just as dead as the Benton Boys. In the end I was certain of only one thing—one thing alone as I gazed up at the tower crane and watched its great jib swing in the wind. And that was that if what I suspected was true, I was at least partially responsible—for the Benton Boys, for the string of murders across Seattle and the so-called "Belltown Brute," all of it.

And that meant I had a responsibility to do something. Indeed, that I was the only person who could.

They'd had names, of course. Rusty, Jack, and Colton—otherwise known as the Benton Boys. But their individual identities had long since been subsumed by the group, the pack—I'm sure if you would have caught any single one of them alone they'd have been just as agreeable as could be. The rub, of course, was that they were never alone—that was something those who challenged them learned quickly. I learned it the day I was to meet Colton at the flagpole after school to settle our differences and he didn't show; which left Aaron and I to hoof it home feeling both victorious and relieved, at least, that is, until we rounded his block —and found them waiting for us. All three of them.

I wish I could say I was shocked that Aaron got the worst of it—it was my fight, after all, not his—but the truth of it was the Benton Boys' race-hatred was well known, and they weren't about to miss a chance to thrash a genuine Jew. Not when his idiot friend had created such a perfect opportunity. And so the racial epitaphs flew, faster even than the Boys' fists—kike, shylock, yid, Christ-killer, a few I'd never even heard before—and poor Aaron bled, and by the time it was done we'd both suffered concussions and Aaron had lost a tooth and Old Man Moss had begun screaming—in Yiddish—from his door, calling the Boys chazers and hitsigers and paskudniks, and informing them the police were already on their way. Which they weren't, actually, because Old Man Moss didn't trust anyone in a uniform.

Regardless, the Benton Boys promptly fled, and after a brief sojourn in the emergency room we were back in Aaron's front yard—just sitting there on the porch with his parents and watching the shadows lengthen across the grass. That's when I first heard his old man utter the word "golem," which he pronounced *goy-lem,* drawing a stern rebuke from Aaron's mother, who said, quickly, "Feh! And bring tsores upon us? Oy vey! *Mishegas.* "

The Old Man only snorted. "It is Mishegas to do nothing." He stroked Aaron's hair absently. "No. An eye for an eye. A tooth for an actual tooth."

"Bubbala ..."

"No. *Meesa masheena.* So it will be."

And nothing more was said—not by the Old Man or by Aaron's mother or by anyone present at all.

By the time I saw Old Man Moss again, Spring was moving rapidly toward Summer and we'd been out of school for nearly two weeks—long enough to have already tired of jumping into the river and/or bicycling out to Shelly Lake; which, in case you were wondering, were the only things to do in Benton, during that summer or any other. I was luckier than most in that I had a lawn mowing business to occupy my time—mostly for friends and family, the Mosses included—which is what I was doing when Aaron tapped me on the shoulder and asked if I could lend he and his father a quick hand.

"Is it out of this heat?" I remember shouting over the lawnmower—which was louder than most—the sweat running in rivers down my face and arms, "Because I'm dying here, and that's no joke."

"It's right here, in the garage," he said breezily, but seemed uneasy as I killed the motor and sponged my brow. "Look ... not a word about this, okay? And, please, don't laugh. Whatever you do. He—he's touchy about his art."

I think I just looked at him. It was fine by me; I'd no idea he was even an artist. "Sure, man. No problem." I must have leaned toward him. "What is it? Some kind of naked pictures?"

He blushed and stepped back. "No, man. Jesus. But it is—strange. Not a word now, okay?"

"Not a word," I promised, and gave him a salute.

It's funny—because the first thing I noticed upon stepping into the garage wasn't the fact that Old Man Moss was holding what appeared to be massive gray arm in his hands. Nor was it the fact that in the middle of the room stood an 8-foot-tall giant—a giant which appeared to have been fashioned from solid clay and resembled not so much a man but a hulking, naked ape. Nor was it even the thing's frightful visage or stoic, lifeless, outsized eyes.

No, it was the fact that the room was illuminated by candles and candelabrums—as opposed to bulbs or work lights or sun seeping through windows (all of which had been covered with what appeared to be black sheets). It was the fact that the garage didn't look like a garage. It looked—for all intents and purposes—like a temple.

"Ah, Thomas, by boy! *Vus machs da!* You are just in time."

It was on the tips of my lips to ask him what for when he handed me the arm, which was surprisingly heavy. "I'll need you and Aaron to hold this while I sculpt. Can you do that?"

The clay was tacky and moist beneath my fingers. I looked at Aaron, who looked back at me as if to say, *Just go with it. Humor him.*

"Sure, Mr. Moss. But—" I followed Aaron's lead as he positioned the arm against the mock brute's shoulder. "What on earth *is* it?"

His face beamed with pride as he worked the leaden clay. "Why, this is Yossele—but you may call him Josef. And he is what the rabbis of Chelm and Prague called a golem—a being created from inanimate matter. This one is devoted to *tzedakah,* or justice."

At last he stepped back and appeared to scrutinize his work. "And justice is precisely what he will bring—once he is finished. Once the *shem* has been placed in his mouth." He took a deep breath and exhaled, tentatively. "Okay, boys ... you can let go. Slowly."

I didn't know what justice had to do with art, but we did so—the clammy clay wanting to stick to our fingers, its moist touch seeming hesitant to break contact. "Aaron, won't you be a good *boychick* and bring me the *shem.* Easy does it, now. Don't drop it."

I watched as Aaron approached one of the workbenches and fetched an intricately-crafted gold box.

"Ah, yes. The *shem,* you see, is what gives the golem its power—thank you, son, *a sheynem dank.* It is what gives it the ability to move and become animated."

I glanced at Aaron, who only looked back at me uncertainly, as his father approached the golem and opened the box, the gold plating of which gleamed like a fire before the candelabrums. "This one consists of only one word—one of the Names of God, which is too sacred to be uttered here." He withdrew a slip of paper and placed it into the golem's mouth. "I shall only say *emet,* which means 'truth' ... and have done with it. And so it is finished. *Tetelestai."* He turned and looked directly at me, I have no idea why. "The debt will be paid in full."

Nobody said anything for a long time, even as the birds tweeted outside and a siren wailed somewhere in the distance. We just stood there and stared at his creation.

At last I said, "So are you going to enter in the Fair, Mr. Moss, or what? How will you even move it?"

At which Old Man Moss only smiled, ruffling my hair, and said, "No—it is only for this moment. That is the nature of Art. *Tsaytvaylik.* Tomorrow it will be gone. Now run along and finish your lawn. I've involved you enough."

And the next day it *was* gone, at least according to Aaron, and both of us, I think, promptly forgot about it. At least until the first of the Benton Boys turned up dead, Sheriff Donner directing the recovery while his ashen-blue body bobbed listlessly against the Benedict A. Saltweather Dam.

It was June.

By July, the body of a second Benton Boy had been discovered—my very own buddy, Colton.

They'd found him in a stone quarry about fifteen miles from town—the Eureka Tile Company, as I recall—his limbs broken and bent back on themselves ("like some discarded Raggedy Ann," wrote the local paper) and his head completely gone—which caused a real sensation amongst the townsfolk as each attempted to solve the riddle and at least one woman reported having seen it: "Just floating down the river, like a pale, blue ball."

But it wasn't until Rusty was killed that things reached a fever pitch, with Sheriff Donner under attack for failing to solve the case and neighbor turning against neighbor in a kind of collective paranoia—for by this point no one could be trusted, not in such a small town, and the killer or killers might be anyone, even your spouse or best friend.

It was against this backdrop that I was able to break from my lawn duties—which had exploded like gangbusters over the summer—long enough to visit the Mosses: which would have been the day before Independence Day, 1979. A Tuesday, as I recall. It's funny I should remember that. Aaron's mother was working in her vegetable garden—just bent over her radishes like an emaciated old crone—when I arrived, and didn't even look up when I asked if Aaron was around. "He's in his room—done sick with the flu. Best put on a mask before you go." She added: "You'll find some in the kitchen."

I think I just looked at her—at her curved spine and thin ankles, her tied up hair which had gone gray as a golem. Then I went into the house and made my way toward Aaron's room, passing his parents' quarters—upon which had been hung a 'Do Not Disturb' sign and a Star of David—on the way. I didn't bother fetching a mask; I'm not sure why—maybe it was because I was already convinced that whatever Aaron had, I had too. Maybe it was because I was already convinced that by participating in the ritual we'd somehow brought a curse upon us—a curse upon Benton—that it had never been just 'art' and that it could never be atoned for, not by Aaron or myself or Old Man Moss or anybody. That we'd blasphemed the Name of the Lord and would now have to pay, just as Jack had paid, just as Colton had paid. Just as

Rusty had paid when they'd found him with his intestines wrapped around his throat and his eyeballs gouged out.

"Shut the door, please. Quickly," said Aaron as I stepped into his room—immediately noticing how dark it was, and that the windows had been completely blacked out (with the same sheets from the garage, I presumed). He added: "The light ... It—it's like it eats my eyes."

Christ—I *know.* But that's what he said: *Like it ate his eyes.*

I stumbled into a stool in the dark—it was right next to his bed—and sat down. Nor were the black sheets thick enough to completely choke the light, so that as I looked at him he began to manifest into something with an approximate shape: something I dare say was not entirely human—a thing thick and rounded and gray as the dead, like a huge misshapen rock, perhaps, or a mass of potter's clay, but with eyes. Then again it was dark enough so that I may only have imagined it—who's to say after forty years?

"Jesus, dude. What's happened to you? And where's your dad? I saw a 'Do Not Disturb' sign on his door. Is he—"

"Like me, only worse," choked Aaron, and then coughed—wetly, stickily. "Listen. I haven't much time. Do you remember the ritual ... and how we inserted the *shem* into the golem's mouth?"

"Of course," I said—and immediately started shaking my head. "Now wait a minute. You don't really think—"

"Shut up, man. Just *shut the fuck up.* This is important. The Benton Boys—what's happened to us—it's not a coincidence, okay? Dad—he created a golem ... do you understand? Not a work of art—not what Ms. Dickerson calls a metaphor. But a genuine, animate golem—right out of the folklore. Now, my mother called Rabbi Weiss when the murders started happening and told him what she

suspected—that my dad had created Josef to avenge the Benton Boys' attack on us. And do you know what he said?"

"Aaron, Jesus, man—"

"He said this type of golem would go on killing, that it wouldn't stop with just the Benton Boys but would continue on to different towns and cities—for months, years, even decades. That it could make itself invisible—at least to anyone who hadn't a hand in creating it—and thus go about killing with complete efficiency; and that not even bullets could stop it, only the hand of its creator or someone who had assisted in that creation—by removing from its mouth the one thing that allowed it to move in the first place ... the Holy Shem, the slip of parchment upon which was written one of the secret Names of God."

He gripped my arm suddenly and I could tell by his cold, clammy embrace that it wouldn't be long; that his flesh had become like clay and his blood had turned thick as mud. "It's you, Thomas, don't you see? You! Only you can stop it now, only you can—"

But I didn't hear anything else he had to say, for I'd scrambled to the door and burst back into the hall. And then I ran, ran as though the world could not contain me, faster and faster and further yet—across forty years and from every type of responsibility—into drugs and alcohol and the cold numbness of the streets. Into a dream of forgetfulness which ended only when I saw the man who was not a man scaling the ghostly tower crane near our ramshackle encampment in Belltown. Until I went to the base of it, and, finding its gate lazed open, mounted the ladder at its center. And began to climb.

I was nearing the top—although still a good fifty feet away—when there was a sound, a series of sounds, actually, *thunk—thunk—thunk,* like a ham bouncing down metal stairs, and something sprinkled my face. That's when I realized that what had fallen (and bounced off the beams) was in fact a human head. By then, of course, it was gone, and I was continuing my ascent: trying not to acknowledge how the city had become so small or that lightning could strike at any instant or that the shaft of the crane was swaying woozily in the wind. Trying and mostly succeeding—at least, that is, until I reached the top, whence I climbed onto the platform next to the operator's cab (which was hanging wide open) and proceeded to vomit, although whether it was from a fear of heights or the smell of decomposition from the cab I couldn't have said.

Nor was I surprised to find that the compartment was stuffed full of bodies and body parts, like a veritable meat locker ... filled with arms and legs and heads and torsos ... or that when I turned away to retch again I saw the golem itself at the end of the crane's long jib—just crouched there in a kind of lotus position, as if he—it—were meditating. As if it—he—were waiting for me.

I can see you, Josef, I thought as the American flag crackled at the back of the crane and the great jib swung languidly in the wind ... *Can you see me?*

And then I began moving forward, slowly, tentatively—the rails of the jib like ice beneath my grip.

You can, can't you? I thought, and knew that it was so. *Tell me, Josef. Why is it you think I was spared—why I've been spared all these years— when your other creators were turned into little more than pillars of salt? Have you ever thought about that?*

Lightning flashed in the distance and turned everything white—turned the golem white—so that its monstrous features fell into stark relief; so that its cone-shaped head shown like a knife.

We are bound together, after all—don't pretend I don't know that. Even as I know you can hear me—just as plain as though I were speaking. And I ask you again—have you thought about it? Because I have.

Thunder rumbled as I drew to within twenty feet of him and paused, wondering just how I would go about it, how I would remove the *shem*. At last I said, "You were created not by God but by a man and the sages before him—now you must return to your dust. Do you understand that? It is not now, nor has it ever been—nor will it ever be—your earth to walk. It is time to go, Josef. It is long past time."

He—it—whatever—just looked at me, its slanted gray eyes inert, uninhabited—lifeless—and yet, *not.* And it occurred to me that creation was itself a kind of blasphemy; a fracturing of some perfect, unfathomable thing into something separate and purely reducible—something alone, something apart. That it was, in a sense, a cruelty. And if that were the case— wasn't it at least possible that the golem—

But then it was *moving*—suddenly, impossibly, and I was stumbling back along the gangway, and before I could do much of anything it had leapt upon me and begun gnashing its teeth—at which instant I jammed my fist into its mouth and groped for the *shem,* and whereupon finding it, yanked it free.

At that it had simply collapsed, its full weight pinning me to the gangway, and its body had broken apart like so much old masonry as its arms and legs snapped in two and its head rolled back from its shoulders—to promptly shatter against the steel mesh floor.

That's when the rains came, washing away the clay and drenching my hair and clothes, which were a beggar's clothes, until finally I rolled upon the gangway and peered down at our encampment—which was visible only because of Billy the Skid's battery-powered light—and realized, abruptly, that I still gripped the *shem*. The Holy Shem.

The Secret Name of God.

I didn't move, didn't breath, for what seemed a long time. In the end, I merely turned my fist and opened it— letting the slip of parchment fall. Watching as it fluttered into the void.

And then I slept.

At length I dreamed, of Benton and summer and freshly-cut grass ... and the first time I'd had matzo; as well as of Aaron and his parents and my parents too, whom I hadn't seen or dreamed of in years.

And when at last I awakened I did so not to the gray ceiling of my tent but a swirl of seagulls and the entire sky.

"Do it," Orley urged, and though I didn't look at him, I could feel those earnest brown eyes looking at me—eyes that always seemed just a little too intense, as if he might burst into tears or kick your ass at any moment.

"We made a pact, kid," said Kevin, his voice low, his intonation world-weary—even though he was the same age as the rest of us—Han Solo to the core, at least for today. "Besides, this was your idea."

I hesitated, the sharpened stick wavering, as the big, green caterpillar inched across the pavement. "I know." I watched as the insect's bulbous sections undulated, rising and falling, glistening in the sun. "It's just that—"

"Here," said Orley.

He took his own stick and used it to roll the caterpillar onto its back, where it curled into a fetal position and promptly froze, looking like a shrimp at the Chuck Wagon buffet, its multitude of little legs ceasing to move, its tiny antennae holding perfectly still.

"Okay, read that passage. The one about daring to approach the gods. You know, where it talks about blood and danger and becoming like gods ourselves. I saw you bookmark it."

I looked at the book, *The Encyclopedia of Death and Dying*—which was lying atop my orange nylon schoolbag precisely where I'd left it—and stood, hefting the volume and cutting to the mark. The sun passed behind a cloud as I read, "Participants in blood sacrifice rituals often experience a sense of awe, danger, or exaltation, because they are daring to approach the gods who create, sustain, and destroy life. Therefore, morale is strengthened by the ritual killing, because the group has itself performed the godlike act of destruction—and is now capable of renewing its own existence."

There was a slight breeze, which seemed to give the proceedings a funereal air, and I continued, "The underlying philosophical assumption is that life must pass through death."

Orley said, "That's it. Okay. So." He looked from me to Kevin—earnestly, intensely—gripping the sharpened stick. "Considering what's ahead of us ..." He paused, letting that sink in. "I think we all know what we have to do." He added: "And why."

We thought about it, the sun beating down, the breeze jostling our hair. The lake. The sword. The visitations in our dreams. We knew.

"So I say we get to it ... before the Valley Boys show up and it's too late. *Way* too late."

I looked at Kevin—who just looked at me with that Zen Master expression of his but seemed to confirm—before again crouching by the caterpillar. And then we all gripped our sticks—and prepared to do something really shitty.

By the time the sun re-emerged the caterpillar had crawled across the sidewalk and into the grass—leaving us more than a little red-faced, not to mention uncertain as to what had just happened. Mostly, I think, we were just relieved.

"I couldn't do it," said Kevin wistfully, "Not with the kid here."

I raised my eyebrows and looked at him, as if to say: Fucking *what,* dude?

He started to smile but caught it.

Orley elbowed me. "Hey, hey, why didn't you?" He looked at me earnestly, calmly—as though he were all ears, all understanding. Then he deadpanned, "It was the gay thing, wasn't it?"

And then they both laughed, falling about on the grass, even as I ignored them, thinking about it.

"I don't know. It just ... it felt like ..." I looked at them in the sun. "Like we would be killing ourselves ... not the caterpillar. Or a part of ourselves. Like, a version of ourselves. The ideal version."

They paused, looking at each other, processing this.

"So the gay thing," said Orley, and held up his hand—which Kevin promptly high-fived.

I must have just stared at them as they bumped fists and swiped palms. "What's that? Foreplay?"

And then they were both crawling toward me, sneering menacingly, and by the time the Valley Boys rumbled up in their chopped and channeled Chevy (as opposed to our learning permits and BMX bikes), everything had devolved into an out-of-control wrestling match; a match which ended only when Todd Benson, the leader of our bullies, shouted, "Are you faggots finished? Because there's a lot of miles between here and the lake. And it's getting late."

"Jesus," he said as we clambered into the backseat, the gear in our schoolbags clanking and thumping. "You think you brought enough?"

"Should have charged them by weight," added Mickelson. He twisted in the front passenger seat and glared at us. "You runts planning on camping there or moving in?"

Just Mickelson. This was going to be easier than we thought.

"Listen," snapped Orley. "Hearing you run your mouth wasn't part of the—"

"Money," said Benson, and reached over his shoulder. "Twenty now, twenty when we get there. As agreed."

We all looked at each other.

At last we dug into our jeans and pulled out our bills—Orley and I, at any rate (I had a five left over from my allowance and he had some ones, tips from his job at the golf course). Kevin, meanwhile, had reached into his backpack and was fishing around for something, straining. It couldn't have been easy; he hadn't taken it off. None of us had.

A moment later he withdrew a purple Crown Royal bag and handed it to Mickelson, whose hand dropped from the weight of it. "Is this a fucking joke?"

"Nope. Seven dollars, counted and rolled."

Mickelson just stared at him—as though he might jab him right then and there.

"Take it, asshole," said Benson. He glanced at Kevin through the rear-view mirror. "It's the money he's been saving for *Star Wars* figures."

Mickelson took the bag and appeared to set it on the floor before turning up the stereo and cocking his arm out the window, still shaking his head. Moments later, looking in the side-view mirror, he said, "There they are. Right on time."

We all glanced at each other—before craning to look through the rear window and seeing Jud Spelvin's rodded out Ford Falcon bearing down upon us, its chromed stacks glinting and its headlights shining, and its cab virtually crammed with pasty-faced seniors, at least one of whom I recognized as Buddy LaCombe—the *third* biggest asshole at

Prosperous High. And, considering twenty was all we'd had and we planned to hit and run, this was a problem.

I looked at Benson through the rearview mirror and saw him smirk at our reaction.

"*Awww,*" he said, and pretended to pout. "Why so sad? You didn't think it would just be us, did you?"

But nobody said anything, just stared straight ahead at the road, the road that would take us to Mirage Lake and the thing we'd left buried under the brush, as Bob Seger and the Silver Bullet Band sang *Fire Lake* and the sun crept toward the stark, blue horizon, and shafts of light pierced the trees—*like spears through a sacrifice,* I thought. Or sunlight through a cathedral.

It's still hard to believe, what happened next. But then, it's *all* hard to believe, especially now, almost 40 years later. Suffice it to say that we were only minutes from the lake when the deer ran out in front of us and caused Benson to hit the brakes— throwing us against the bucket seats (and Orley, who was in the middle, halfway into the forward cab) even as Spelvin's Falcon rammed us from behind, knocking us right back. To this day I wonder if she—*it,* our Lady of the Lake, our Thing from Another World—had something to do with it. If she had reached out from her watery tomb and *guided* the animal into our path—to ensure its intended servants reached their destination. To guarantee its release after so many years trapped beneath the lake.

Regardless, they were all gathered around the bumpers when we made our escape, clambering out the driver's side door (which had been left ajar) and scurrying into the trees— our packs and gear jangling, our shoes scraping the gravel—so that Benson at least became aware of our movement and quickly alerted the rest. This touched off a footrace which wound from the side of the road all the way to Beggar's Dead-fall, which we climbed as they went around—before reversing course and backtracking through the brush, eventually stumbling upon the very same trail we'd taken last time. This we followed (after standing for a period with our hands on our knees and laughing, catching our breath) to the far side of the lake.

Where a massive, overgrown, arrowhead-shaped thing, a blue-black thing, an ancient and broken thing—a thing perhaps only we could see—lay half-buried amongst the trees.

We'd been staring at it for maybe five minutes when Kevin wandered away from us and paused at the water, where he shielded his eyes from the sunset and mumbled, "They're back. The hands, the twelve-string guitar ..."

I followed his gaze, shielding my eyes also, to where the black sword could again be seen in the middle of the lake. As before, it was held aloft by a pair of slim, beautiful hands. "Wrong again—kid. I told you: It's Stormbringer, sister to Mournblade, runesword of Elric, the last emperor of Melniboné."

"No," said Orley, approaching us, "It's neither of those." He shouldered between us and stood with his hands on his hips, like a superhero. "It's Excalibur, obviously. Held aloft by the Lady of the Lake, waiting to be claimed."

The truth of it was, it was all those things and none of those things, but we didn't know that yet, didn't know much of anything—we were only 15. But we knew it was real, whatever it was, and that something associated with it had been visiting us in our dreams. We also knew each other, and so understood that each of us was seeing something totally unique to ourselves: Kevin was learning guitar, his AWOL father's twelve-string, and thus naturally saw an instrument. I was obsessed with the works of Michael Moorcock—Elric, in particular—and had been trying to write something similar. And Orley had been reading about Camelot (and struggling with Middle English) ever since his mother had brought home a copy of *Le Morte d'Arthur* from the Salvation Army. More than any of that, though, we knew what we had to do—although we still didn't know why or how—and it was to that end that we set about our work, breaking off spear-length branches from the nearby trees and whittling them as sharp as we could, fashioning still others into makeshift rowing paddles, and each taking turns blowing up the raft by working the little handpump we'd stolen from White Elephant.

By the time we were ready, the sky was completely red, like Mars, or Vulcan, and we were beginning to feel the press of time—perhaps the surest indication that one has moved closer to adulthood than childhood. But then we were adrift, and all such concerns were forgotten, and though we struggled at first to coordinate our paddles, it became evident soon enough that we would reach the swords, the guitar, *the anomaly,* well before dark—and so steeled ourselves as best we could; mostly by talking about our dreams, both those experienced by night and those conceived of by day—for they were pertinent, all of them, to what lie ahead.

"She showed me a vision in which I was being awarded the Medal of Honor," said Orley at last, working his paddle, staring straight ahead. "Carter himself was the one who affixed it around my neck."

The little raft rocked, dark water slapping, but nobody expressed doubt.

"I was a best-selling author," I said, quietly, solemnly. "Like Stephen King. But really, really good-looking."

"I was a rock star," said Kevin. "Bigger even than Elvis."

We rowed, drawing closer to the thing.

"It is the future you see," said Kevin in his best Yoda voice.

Nobody laughed.

"Maybe," said Orley. "That is, if we free her from the lake. If we—I don't know—return her to her ship or something. Leastwise that's how I interpreted it."

"Me too," I said.

Kevin leaned forward, rocking the boat. "But why the swords and the guitar? And why can't she leave the lake? What the hell *is* she, even?"

We all thought about that as a loon cried somewhere across the water.

"Maybe she's too weak," I said. "Maybe her body is ... mutilated or something—from the crash." I looked to where the black sword seemed to hover just above the surface of the water—as sinister as it was eldritch, precisely as I'd always imagined it. And below that, her—the woman in the water's—hand; her thin, beautiful hand, deaden-blue from the depths.

"Maybe that's just how she establishes contact," I said. "How she gets your attention, and holds it. I honestly wouldn't be surprised if all that just goes away—like a mirage—when we get there."

"Nah. Then why—"

But then, as if to confirm, the hand *did* begin to go away, to lower, taking the sword with it—as if, indeed, it *had* been just a prop, just bait to get us closer.

"*Fuck!*" shouted Orley. He jerked his paddle, doubling his efforts. "Hurry up! Row!"

But it was too late; it was gone. The sword, the deaden-blue hand, all of it.

I'm not sure how long we floated there, just looking at each other. All I know is that by the time we busted out the flashlights the color had bled from the hills and the temperature had dropped significantly; enough so that our decision not to bring coats (there was only so much room in our backpacks, after all) seemed foolhardy and brash.

Regardless, it was Kevin who first saw something, jolting as we trained our lights into the murky water and blurting, in a voice that was one part excitement and at least two parts terror, "Holy shit! I saw her! I saw her! She swam right beneath the raft!"

I remember Orley just freezing and staring at me—earnestly, intensely—before we both dropped to our bellies and shoved our flashlights against the water, angling the beams as far beneath the raft as we could while each taking a side—the hope being that we wouldn't upend the entire boat. Kevin meanwhile actually reached into the drink and felt around, which seemed unwise to me at the time and more than a little out of character, reckless, even. Crazy-brave.

That's when it happened. That's when the girl, but really the xenoform, the multi-dimensional being, the *thing*, just floated up: her face emerging like some porcelain doll and her blue-black hair swirling (like tentacles, I thought, or the snakes in Medusa's hair), her drowned, all-white eyes staring. That's also when she reached up with arms as thin as paper dowels—famine arms, Buchenwald arms—and pulled me into the lake.

What happened next happened very fast—or so I've been told, because it sure didn't seem fast at the time. Indeed, it felt like the longest dozen seconds of my life. All I know is that the girl-thing sank rapidly, briefly, dragging me along with her, before just as suddenly releasing me—discarding me, as it were—and disappearing.

Except she *didn't* disappear, not really, which I found out as soon as I burst back to the surface. Rather, she had leapt from the water and tried to beach herself on the raft—but had overshot it—so that she now hung off its opposite side: flopping and struggling, fighting and twisting, like a fish out of water, or an animal against its leash.

For she was connected, you see, to a kind of umbilical cord, which began at her back, stretched taught across the boat, and vanished into the cold, dark water. Nor was the cord at rest but seemed to be contracting like a great rubber band—pulling her back toward the surface, exerting what must have been a great force. That's when it hit me that I *knew* what the cord was, and that it was neither inorganic material nor biological tissue—if anything, it was both—just as I knew that she had not so much attacked me as merely glommed onto me in desperation.

Because something had happened while we touched beneath the water, something like telepathy, or accelerated osmosis. And I understood suddenly why she had been unable to escape; and why, too, she had called out to us, beckoned us, and suggested we do things like sharpen sticks. More importantly, I understood what she, *it,* was capable of; that the futures she had shown us were not only possible but easily within reach—*if* we but freed her and reunited her with her ship (which was so much more than a ship!). If we but stayed true to our purpose and did our allotted part. And I knew beyond any doubt what I—*we*—had to do.

"Don't let her slip back into the water!" I cried suddenly, kicking toward the raft, grabbing one of the hand-holds. "Keep her inside the boat!"

But the pull of the life-line—for that's what it was and that's what it was tethered to: a *life-pod,* something which had ejected from the ship upon crashing and sunk to the bottom of the lake—was too strong, too resistant, and she began to slip backward across the boat.

That's when Orley stood upon his knees in the raft and brought his makeshift spear down as hard as he could, stabbing the cord precisely at its center—causing blue-black ichor to geyser like blood. Kevin quickly joined him, and I after that, so that the cord was weakened even as the girl-thing struggled and screamed—to the point that she was able to free herself at last and slide back into the water, looking, in the instants before she vanished, not like a girl at all, but a gelatinous mass. A thing without limbs or extremities. A kind of blue-black worm.

Needless to say, the raft did not survive the encounter. And yet we were able to paddle at least partly to shore before it deflated completely— enough so that the remaining distance was easily traversed, primarily by floating on our backs while kicking.

And then we were huddled in the tent like sardines, the fire having been left to die and our over-clothes hung from the branches to dry— nobody making gay jokes, nobody saying anything—as our minds raced and dwelt on the future, as our sharpened sticks stood sentinel, canted in the sand.

I wish I could say that when Benson and his gang showed up we drew on some previously unknown strength and kicked their Rich Kid asses; that we chased them all the way back to their fancy cars and tucked and rolled seats and kicked in their doors and fenders; although we really would do that later, not to them personally but to guys like them, in those dog days immediately after high school— when Orley had yet to join the Army and I'd yet to lose my mother, and L.A. was just a twinkle in Kevin's eye.

Instead they caught us completely by surprise, knocking the tent over and rolling us up in it—like a giant snowball— after which they proceeded to kick and punch us mercilessly—before dragging us out by our feet and gloating over us in the sun: *Like trolls,* I remember thinking. Or Tolkien's fucking orcs.

"Well now look at this," said Benson, and paused to hawk up phlegm. "If it isn't our little faggots—just cozied up like lemmings." He pursed his lips and spat, causing green slime to splatter my cheek. "Our thievin' little douche-flutes, just letting their freak flags fly."

"And sitting on the rest of our gas money," said Mickelson. "I can guarantee it."

"Oh?" Benson raised his brow, as if he hadn't thought of that. "You're kind of the leader, Orley. Is that true?"

Orley just looked at him, his mouth bleeding, his cheek scuffed and bruised. At last he said, "We used it to pay your mother. She said that's what triple-penetration costs."

A couple of them laughed—Mickelson and Spelvin, I think—and Benson shot them a look. At length he said, "Funny—as always." He paused, cocking his head. "You look thirsty. Buckey. Give me your cup."

He held out his hand without looking and Buckey placed in it a large container, one of those 32-ounce super tankards you get at Zip Trip or 7-11, minus its lid. "The stink bugs are terrible this year, as I'm sure you've noticed. Buckey here left this out in the sun too long," He smelled the cup's contents, wrinkling his nose—then motioned to Spelvin and Mickelson, who snatched Orley up by his arms and held him, even as two others grappled his head and began prying his mouth open. "These will probably tickle a little as they go down. A lot of them are still alive …"

Then he tipped the cup and its contents poured out onto Orley's face, into his mouth—the soda spattering his cheeks, the little bugs scrambling helter-skelter over his lips—before he chocked once, suddenly, violently, and began *chewing,* jerking his head free of their hands, smiling like a lunatic.

"Protein!" he exclaimed, and spit something out, a shell, maybe, or a leg. "Thank you, sir! May I have another!"

And then there was a commotion which sent a ripple through their ranks and caused them to stand apart—staring toward the lake, into the sun, where a lone figure stood slight as a wraith, its hair sopping wet, clinging to its face, its skinny arms held straight at its sides.

"Who's that? Is that your mother?" —Spelvin, I think, attempting to sound cocksure but really only sounding frightened and small.

I looked to where the girl-thing stood nude and alone, her hair entwined with seaweed, her one visible eye white as milk. None of us said anything as the Benson Gang approached her and slowly gathered around—triangulating her, isolating her.

"Well, well," said Benson, "This makes sense." He turned to face us, regarding us slyly. "So this is what brought you pervs all the way out here. And here I thought you were just queer."

He looked at the girl again, who couldn't have been more than 15, same as us, and said, mockingly, "Is that seaweed in your hair, or are you just more experienced than you look?" Everyone tittered; a few of them groaned.

"Careful," said Mickelson, "Or she'll sic her boyfriends on us." He shouted over his shoulder: "Isn't that right, douche-flutes?"

But none of us said anything, just continued to stare at the girl, whose milky eye regarded Benson plainly, flatly, as though here were a lifeform hardly worth shooing away; a tsetse fly, maybe, or a gnat.

"You know, it might just be me," said Benson, and moved closer, "but I get the impression she doesn't want to be friends."

He started walking around her slowly, checking her out, looking her up and down. "That how it's going to be, sis? You going to just give us the cold, blue shoulder?"

"Meh, ease off her, Todd," someone said—Jud Hartman, a sometimes decent guy whom I hadn't even realized was with them. "She's obviously suffered some sort of trauma. Probably thought she was drowning, or something."

"Drowning, or something," said Benson, and stepped close to her ear. "What do you say, sis? Were you drowning—or something? Is that why you're just as naked as a jaybird? Or are you just some coked-out whore, turning tricks in the sticks?" He grabbed her by the shoulder suddenly. "Face me when I'm talking to ..."

And then his hand was burning—burning and crisping away—and he was stumbling back over the sand, screaming, hyperventilating, the blood and bones of his arm gleaming, before the sun dipped behind a cloud and all hell broke loose. Before it became clear to us, so very, very clear, that the time for talking was over.

To say that what happened next was, for all intents, impossible to describe, would be to short you, Reader, in a way I am not prepared to do. More so, it would be to skip or gloss over the most salient aspect of what occurred that day; the day in which we learned just how strange and inexplicable the universe really was, and, more importantly, just how dangerous it had become—not just for us but for everything we had ever known, ever would know.

Suffice it to say that when the lightning-like bolts erupted from the girl-thing's eyes, they instantly connected with (and paralyzed) virtually everyone present—Kevin, Orley and myself included. And here is where it gets so strange—and difficult to describe—for what happened next was like, a kind of mass hallucination, one in which all of us, I think, felt we could read the thing's thoughts; not only that, but that we could see where it was from.

And where it was from was hideous beyond measure: a place as barren and blue and seemingly lifeless as the girl's body itself—a place, a planet, a dimension, where everything that had ever lived had long since been devoured and consumed, and where the husks of those drained of their lifeforce had, at last, formed piles as high as mountains.

It was, in short, a kind of Hell, and what we learned in those moments—the moments we stood paralyzed and alone, trapped, each of us, by the lightning-like force—was that this was the fate of all the worlds they, her species, had encountered (via scouts, just as she); and that this was simply what they *did:* They *fed,* and more, that they had learned to create entirely new dimensions, entirely new timelines, exactly toward that end—all to satisfy their ever-growing need.

And we learned one thing more: which was that although Earth was next—*our* Earth, the Earth of this particular dimension, this timeline—a thousand more might yet be created, and that one of these would be the Earth upon which Orley would walk as a war hero and I a bestselling author, and where Kevin would be a rock star, bigger even than Elvis. A place where we wouldn't be losers at all but gods, receiving a blowjob from all the world. The place she had promised us in our dreams—and which would now come. Whether we liked it or not.

For, having chosen us for our very softness and empathy, and loving us—insofar as she was able to do so—for rescuing her, she intended to keep her promise.

One thing is certain, and that is that everyone who was standing when she let loose the bolts was no longer standing when they disappeared—including, to our surprise, the girl-thing herself, who collapsed even as we collapsed, as the Benson Gang collapsed, their bodies shriveled like prunes and their faces sucked in, as though they'd simply imploded when their life-force had been extracted, which, I suppose, they *had.*

Then it was over and we had climbed to our feet, shaking ourselves off, grateful to be alive, but aghast at the destruction and loss of life all around us. For the Benson Gang was dead, each and every one, and their nude bodies had become husks— their clothes having burned away in the incident, I supposed—which rattled in the sand as they were buffeted by the breeze and eventually just dis-incorporated, blowing away like dandelion seeds.

As for the thing, we knew *exactly* what had happened (we'd been in her head, after all, at least that's how we interpreted it, just a few moments before): she'd expended all her energy in the extraction of their life-force and yet wouldn't gain from the transfer until it had been converted by her system, a process which might take hours, even days.

Unless, we knew, we could get her to her ship, which had begun to glow amidst the trees like a white-hot iron and which would restore her to full health if she were just able to join with it—an outcome which seemed increasingly unlikely as we watched her try to stand and come crashing back down, her arms barely capable of breaking her fall and her legs all but useless in their compromised condition. So, too, did we know that any attempt to touch her would result in the same type of injury suffered by Benson. And thus we could only watch as she began to crawl toward her ship across the rocks and sand, pleased that she seemed to be gaining strength with each foot traveled—but knowing, also, that it would not be enough.

"Jesus, look at her face," said Orley at last, and when I followed his gaze I saw that her features had begun to droop and her hair to fall out, so that she was starting to look like Jason Voorhees in *Friday the 13th* (when he bursts from the water at the end of the movie), her brow sagging and her mouth twisting, her head balding, her eyes mismatched.

"She's using all her strength to get to her ship," I said, "and can no longer maintain the ruse. But I don't she's going to make it."

"And yet she might," said Kevin, his freckles standing out harsh and clear in the sun and his red hair a veritable fire. "She might."

At length Orley said, "I feel sorry for them if she does."

I think I just looked at him: at his earnest, intense eyes and his unruly mop of hair, at his shitty, threadbare clothes because his mother was too poor to dress him. "What do you mean?" I said.

"I mean everything—*everyone*. All our parents, all our siblings. Everything we have ever known, just *gone*. Like Benson and his friends."

We watched as she tried to stand, surer-footed this time, stronger, but then came crashing back down.

"That's not it," I said. "You were there. Other timelines will be created, other dimensions, all of them like this one. All of them populated by the same people. It's just that one of them will—"

"Be modified and left alone, I know. But what about the others? What of the millions, the trillions, whatever, that will exist only to be killed, to be harvested, like cattle? What about this world, right here?"

I looked to where the thing was again crawling to its feet—it was no longer proper to call it a she—its fingers and toes shrinking as I watched.

"But they're all the same, don't you see? They're all the same thing, just replicated a thousand-fold. How can ..." I paused, staring at him.

"Are they?" he said.

I continued looking at him, the sun beating upon our heads, the breeze jostling our hair. When I glanced at Kevin I found him already looking at me.

"She's going to make it," he said—calmly, meditatively. "Look."

We peered beyond him and saw that it was so, that the thing was up again and stumbling toward the trees. Stumbling, not crawling, as the arrowhead-shaped ship glowed and the brush we'd piled atop it caught fire, *poofing* like bags full of air opened too quickly, smoking like fireworks about to explode.

"Jesus," I mumbled. "Do you think we're evolved enough to ..."

I glanced at our sticks only several feet away, canted in the sand, their shafts crude but straight— then at the thing, which was nearly to its ship. And the truth of it is I was running before I'd even made a conscious decision to do so, running with the friends I'd had since 4th grade at Broadway Elementary, both of whom beat me to the pikes. Nor did we stop to think about it as we chased the thing down like chieftains and Orley delivered the first blow, lancing its back decisively and pinning it to the earth as I slid mine into what would have been its ribcage and Kevin impaled its neck, all of which caused the thing to struggle furiously even as it tried to scream—this most assuredly—but found it had no mouth; as it melted away from our sticks like butter and reconstituted itself on the go, finally closing to within a few feet of its ship before Orley ran it through its back yet again and smashed it to the ground, stopping it in its tracks—even as Kevin and I stabbed it repeatedly—the sun filtering through the pines as it shuddered and bled, its ship beginning to falter, growing cool amidst the shadows.

And yet we kept stabbing as though infected with blood-lust: exhilarated by each blow, hot for the kill, while nonetheless feeling as though we had lost something with each strike. Something of who we were and might have become. Something which felt good and bad at the same time. Like romantic love, I suppose, which we had yet to experience. Or the bite of cigarette smoke into the esophagus and lungs.

Until at last the ship lie dormant and the Thing from Another World was dead, if it had ever lived at all, at least in the way we understood it. And then we just stood there for a time amongst the shafts of light and brooded in our youth and vigor and passion; there in July of 1980 in the sweltering heat and humidity of the day. There in the forest by the lake, which was shot through with orange and gold, in the brief, burning cathedral of summer.

I'm not sure how long it took us to get home, although we were able to scramble aboard a freight train at Hunter's Rock—we could tell it was bound for Spokane—which cut the overall time considerably. All I remember is that I became fascinated by my friend's faces as we sat between cars and watched the land pass, the late-afternoon sun painting everything redden-gold as the tracks clacked and livestock raised their heads, as we let our minds wander and tried not to think too hard about what had happened, nor our role in it.

Orley for his part was trying to sleep, and though we at first made sport of preventing him from doing so, we eventually relented and let him be. He had a job, after all, unlike either of us. Still, I watched him as the train rocked and he dozed, knowing even then that nothing would ever come easy for him; that he'd been born into the kind of poverty that either perpetuated itself or was overcome by sheer grit and determination. I never told him, later, how much I'd admired his bravery and humor during the whole ordeal, nor how often I'd looked to him as something I might one day like to be: just a skinny guy, perhaps, but one with an indomitable spirit and a spit-in-your-eye confidence; a person as earnest as he was intense and who rose to the occasion and did what had to be done, not to mention one who possessed an incredible head of hair, like one of the Beatles, I remember thinking, or Derick Wildstar.

Kevin meanwhile was watching the landscape pass, his demeanor just as mellow and Zen as could be, as though we hadn't faced the end of the world at all but just enjoyed the great outdoors and built a campfire to bullshit around. Kevin was and remains one of the biggest weavers of bullshit I have ever known—not the least of which is his bullshit about not being very bright—and yet there was a truth to him as he looked out over the fields that could not be denied, for he was also grounded in a way I have never seen, just centered like a rock, accepting life as it was and hacking whatever it dealt him. And what it had dealt him so far was a broken home and poverty not much less than Orley's. And, also not less than Orley, an epic head of hair.

I had to smile a little while looking at that hair: Donny Bonaduce? Why not. With hair like that, Donny could never be far. But Slim Pickens, too. Someone with a big heart and even bigger generosity. And I knew even then what kind of friend he'd be as an adult, which was the kind you could couch-surf with when your wife kicked you out even if you hadn't seen him in thirty years. That friend. The kind that embodied the very word.

I guess it goes without saying that we never became gods or got a blowjob from the entire world, but then, who does, really? At the end of the day you're lucky if you can just make a few friends. Kevin never became a rock star and Orley never received the Medal of Honor, and I never became a best-selling author, though I've published a few books on Amazon and even took my girlfriend to dinner once on the proceeds, and that included the tip.

But we did save the world once, a long, long time ago. And it was not without cost or sacrifice.

And that should count for something. Even if it is, like us, like you, just one of so many things that might have been.

A BOY AND HIS DINOSAUR

We'd been doing so well all day, Shad and I had even helped Grandma prepare Sunday dinner without bickering, when I mentioned that Brown Sugar Meatloaf had always been Mom's favorite—and brought the whole thing crashing down again.

"You just had to do it—didn't you?" said Shad, seething, as Grandma went into full Mr. Bill mode, her voice high and quavering as she began quoting Psalms and disappeared into the kitchen, slamming dishes, banging cupboards. "There will be no more death or mourning or crying or pain, for the older order of things has passed away—Shad! Come get the salad."

"Jerk," said Shad, glaring at me over the candles.

He untucked his napkin and joined her in the kitchen, leaving me alone with the Boston Pops and the meat loaf.

"I didn't mean to ..." I started to say, intending to add: 'to upset anybody'—but quickly trailed off, mostly because it was a fat-headed lie; a lie as big and fat as Mrs. Carmichael's—my history teacher's—calves, which were big as hams. Then I got up and left the table—ducking out the little-used north entrance and double-timing it to the garage—where our poles stood sentinel near the fender of Grandma's mint, black GTO like skinny green reeds.

There will be no more death or mourning or crying or pain ...

I must have bit my lower lip as my fingers hovered near the poles—near mine which was battered and nicked and looked as though it had been used as a whip; near Shad's which was as clean and straight as the day Dad had bought it (and not because he never used it). *For the older order of things has passed away ...* Then I gripped Shad's rod—as well as his tackle box, a fish bonker, and a bucket—and was on my way. Past the kitchen window which I ducked beneath so as not to be seen—and into the California woods. Down to the Mohawk River, the waters of which, this time of year, were as cold and swift—and as unforgiving, Mom used to say, which was funny—as any ocean.

I guess I wasn't surprised to find Dillon already there, sitting on the rock usually reserved for my brother (back when he still fished with us; back before he got his license and began driving the GTO—before he met *Wendy* with her jeans so tight she'd been known to pass out), his pole propped on a stick and the bill of his cap touching his nose, as though he were sleeping.

"You're awfully early," he said, having heard my approach, but didn't look up. "How'd you get out?"

I sat down the tackle box and popped it open, chose a lure. "Brought up Mom."

"Oh, man." He lifted the bill of his cap and looked at me. "I bet she started quoting chapter and verse ..." He laughed without much humor. "Matthew, probably. 'Blessed are those who—'"

"Mourn. For they will be comforted." I shook my head. "Nah. Psalms." I cast my line which plopped into the water next to his. "I don't even know why she bothers. They all say the same thing."

We fished, he sitting in Shad's old spot while I sat in his, both of us using our coats for cushions— which was funny, considering it was mid-November. Nor was that the only thing, because there were mosquitoes buzzing about also— mosquitoes, right there on the doorstep of winter, something neither of us could believe or explain. But then there had been a lot of unexplained things that year; like how a United Airlines 747 could vanish without a trace on its way to Honolulu from LAX or how my brother could grow so tall in the space of several months or how Grandma Grace could refuse even to consider that our parents might still be alive.

At least that's what we were talking about when my orange and white bobber dipped once, decisively, then twice, and I jerked my rod (to sink the hook) before quickly beginning to reel whatever it was—a salmon, I hoped—in.

As it turned out, it was just your garden-variety Rainbow trout, albeit a decent-sized one—about 17 inches—which filled the bottom of the bucket nicely even as it thrashed and flopped about; so much so that we were both looking for our bonkers when the foot-long dragonfly whirred past us—its cellophane wings vibrating, its redden eyes glinting—very nearly scaring us both out of our Converse shoes.

"What the—" shouted Dillon.

"Holy mother," I blurted. It was on the tip of my lips to ask, 'What the hell was that?' when a second dragonfly (as big as, if not bigger than, the first) landed on my shoulder—its wings oscillating, blowing my hair, its compound eye only inches from my own.

"*Aaah!*" I screamed, dropping my pole, slapping my body, dancing like a man on fire, as Dillon sprinted for the trees and the dragonflies buzzed away—back to wherever they came from—until I tripped over a root and fell flat on my face ... a position in which I stayed, too frightened to move, too frightened to breathe, until I was sure there were no more of the things flying around.

Needless to say, by the time I climbed to my feet, Dillon was long gone, having ran straight home to momma without so much as a look back. I wasn't particularly surprised: had I been in his shoes, I would have done the same thing. I don't know about girls, but in Boy-land, in the 1970s, before sensitivity training, it was every kid for himself. All I know is that I couldn't explain what I had just seen—no more than I could explain Shad's sudden growth spurt or Grandma's aversion to any mention of our parents or why Wendy wore such tight pants and so much blue eyeshadow—and quickly gathered my things (or, more properly, my brother's things), reaching, at last, for the bucket—over which I paused, my hand still trembling.

It's funny, because to this day I don't know why I did that—paused to examine the Rainbow trout—when the truth was I had every reason to flee just like Dillon. Maybe it was because the fear and breathlessness of our brush with the dragonflies was still so fresh; and that, because I had become aware of my own breathing, I became aware of the trout's, or rather, its lack thereof. All I know is that I became fixated on its dying and gasping for air in a way I'd never done before, looking into its great, golden eye as though it were a dog, or a cat—even a person—seeing myself there, seeing the whole world, or at least the sky above Comet's Tail, California—population 9,893, at least back in 1978.

Nor could I bring myself to bonk it, even though the tool was right there in my trembling hand. Partly this was because a Bible passage had come to mind—living with Grandma, they could never be far—Proverbs 12:10, "A righteous man regards the life of his animal, but the tender mercies of the wicked are cruel." And I guess I just wasn't feeling cruel that day, because instead of bonking it I snatched up the bucket's handle and moved toward the water, where I crouched, tipping it toward the surface—when something *massive* snorted nearby and a huge shadow fell over me. Something I at first took to be a bear, my heart pounding, my blood racing, but quickly realized, upon seeing its reflection in the river, was no such thing.

What happened next is difficult to describe, especially now, some forty years later. Best as I can describe it is that I was moving instantly: fleeing from what I saw by diving into the cold, brisk water and paddling—desperately—for the opposite shore; only in my mind alone, so that my body remained frozen—its beating heart having stopped pumping, its leaden limbs refusing to follow commands—its eyes denying the very evidence of what lay before them.

For what lay before them, there in the gurgling, eddying, golden water, was, plain and simple, a *dinosaur*—though not, it must be said, one such as Gwangi or the Beast of Hollow

Mountain or anything else I'd seen at the drive-in or on TV. No, this was something as real and smelly (it smelled like cow; a whole truckload of cows, in the sweltering heat, after eating Grandma's homemade chili con queso) and fly-pestered—flies! In November!—as any true-life beast; its white, leathery skin as cracked and yet smooth as the old single-lane road which ran hidden and forgotten along the Mohawk River, its body covered in a film of peach fuzz—tiny feathers, perhaps, or even quills—its eyes twitchy and alert, curious, like an eagle's, but also pink, soft, vulnerable, like a rabbit's. And then I *was* moving—truly moving, not just imagining it—dashing into the frigid water, shaking off its icy shock, kicking as far away from the thing as I could—not stopping until I was fully one quarter across the river, where I seized upon a deaden tree stump and held on tight—terrified of the white dinosaur, but also of the undertow (which Mom had repeatedly warned me about), toe-scissoring crawdads, blood-sucking leeches, flesh-eating piranhas, corpses stuck in the branches and roots—maybe even the gill man. And then I waited, shivering. Waited for the thing which looked like a small tyrannosaur—though still big as a rhinoceros—to go away. Waited for it to slip back through whatever hole in time it had emerged from and to take the dragonflies with it.

But it *didn't* go away, at least not right away ... and not in what felt like an hour. Rather, it paced back and forth along the river almost as though it were lost; sniffing at the ground across which Dillon had fled; craning its powerfully-muscled neck to look over its shoulder (if it had had one), shaking off the flies. Until at last it simply collapsed onto its haunches and laid down on its belly, looking around almost nonchalantly, blinking its soft, pink, rabbit's eyes.

That was the moment, I think. The moment I realized that it wasn't perhaps the danger I'd assumed, and that I had to get out of the river— before I caught pneumonia or even hypothermia. It was also the moment I realized the fish was still in the bucket—just as still and dead as could be—which was laying on its side at the edge of the water.

Caution was the word as I swam closer to shore and stood up in the shallows, quaking from the cold, my teeth clattering, then slowly approached the bucket—which action caused the dinosaur to struggle to its feet and strike a threatening pose, and to growl from deep within its throat, like a wolf.

"Easy, easy," I remember saying, holding out a trembling hand, even while stooping—slowly—to pick up the fish; at which the saurian licked its cracked lips—which weren't really lips at all—and seemed to swallow, then took a step closer, its great, talon-like foot sinking in the silt.

"Easy does it," I said, and held the fish out by its tail.

And then it lunged slightly and, panicking, I tossed the trout and retreated, but not before I saw it snatch the fish from the air smartly—its jaws snapping shut like a trap and its curved teeth clacking—before rearing its head back like a seagull and swallowing the trout down completely.

After which it only looked at me and I looked back, and we might have stayed that way for, well, who knows how long, if music hadn't sounded from somewhere in the trees—yes, music, barely perceptible at first but coming closer, growing louder. Coming up the old road.

Why in the world would anybody put chains on me, yeah? I've paid my dues to make it ...

At first it only cocked its head, once to each side, blinking, processing.

Everybody wants me to be what they want me to be ... I'm not happy when I try to fake it—no, ooh.

I heard a slight rumble and looked to see the GTO coming up the road.

That's why I'm easy ...

And then it just fled—*pow,* like that, dashing across the silt and stones toward the trees, moving like a leopard—or even a cheetah—unbelievably graceful, until it barked once and simply vanished, not into the trees, not behind anything, but just, well, into thin air. Into nothing. Into the twilight, now that the sun had largely gone down. After which I could only look on in disbelief as the GTO grumbled to a stop and Shad approached through the bramble, hollering but sounding relieved, angry and yet not really.

"There you are! I've been looking all over for you!"

But I could only stare after the dinosaur, after 'Ghost,' which I'd decided to name him on the spot. For I knew, even then, that he wasn't really gone. That he'd stepped sideways through time and space, perhaps, like a 747 en route to Honolulu from LAX, but that he couldn't have traveled far; and that, indeed, I could still smell him—just as I could still smell my mother's Aqua-net hairspray; at least on those days when both Shad and Grandma were gone, and the house—which my mom used to say reminded her of a mausoleum—lay quiet as a tomb.

One thing was for sure, I hadn't imagined it—the dinosaur's prints ended precisely where it had disappeared.

"Don't go any further," I warned. "The portal—or whatever it is—is right there." I pointed at the final footprint.

Dillon just stood there, his hands on his hips.

"Okay, so there's prints," he said, looking down at the two-foot-long indentations, the sun having really brought out his freckles. "Who's to say you didn't make them yourself?"

I adjusted the strap of my book bag, which was digging into my shoulder. "Because I'm not a liar, like your mother. Besides, the dragonflies. Did you forget about them?"

Dillon dropped his own bag and knelt beside one of the tracks. "Dragonflies are one thing ..." He touched the roughly-compressed silt, which had a pattern of concentric rings, like a fingerprint. "Dinosaurs are something else." He peered along the prints, following them to the water. "There's not even a tail indentation. Tyrannosaurs drag their tails."

"No, they don't," I said, shirking off my pack. I picked up a stick and crouched next to him, drew a triangle with a line over it. "It was like—a teeter-totter, okay? Only perfectly balanced." I pointed at one end of the line. "This was its head," I slid my finger to the opposite end of the mark. "And this was its spine ... to the tip of its tail." I tapped the triangle.

"This was its legs and torso—the center of gravity. See? Besides, it wasn't fully grown."

"What? It was like—it was like a *bird?*" He burst out laughing, rolling in the silt—which had dried in the sun—holding his stomach. "Like Big Bird?"

I think I just looked at him, as though he were mentally disabled. In his defense, it was only 1978. *Jurassic Park* was a long ways off.

"A little—yeah. Like a wild turkey. What are you doing?"

He'd picked up a rock and stood. "You said the portal is right here. I'm going to test your Hypo Thesis."

"Hypothesis."

"Whatever." He stepped back and began to swing his arm back and forth. "Watch out. We don't know what forces this might unleash."

He was being cute, of course; which made it all the more satisfying—and yet no less shocking—when he tossed the stone underhand over the last of the prints—and it vanished without a trace. Just *poof!* It was Gone.

After which, visibly disturbed, he turned to me.

"Bet you're glad we didn't bet," I said.

And then I stood myself—and prepared to do what I'd decided to do even before lunch: which was to enter the portal—the breach, the tear in the fabric of space-time, whatever—myself.

It's a curious thing, watching your own hand disappear, especially when you lean forward to view what should be a stump and see only your skin infinitely regressing, extending into a kind of invisible fog, vanishing into mist and memory. It's even more curious to walk forward and find yourself in a different place altogether; a place as warm and humid as any sauna and dense with foliage, and not just any foliage but the kind you might expect to find in Hawaii or South America or the jungles of Vietnam—hothouse foliage, tropical foliage, primordial foliage—not far away but right there, by the Mohawk River, in northern California. In 1978.

It's also curious to find yourself talking to someone you can no longer see, but whom you know is right there—only a few feet away. At least I hoped he was still there.

"Dillon? You there, man?"

Nothing. Not so much as a peep.

Until, finally, "I'm right here. Right on the other side of, whatever this is. You can't see me, either?"

I looked at where he should be, where the sycamore and cottonwood trees should be, the white alder, the Mohawk River, and saw only cycads, only ferns, only a hazy volcano in a red-orange sky.

"Nope." I glanced around, looking for dinosaurs, looking for dragonflies the size of eagles. There was nothing. "But it's all right, really. You can come on through."

"I don't know, man ..."

I reached forward without thinking and snatched him by the coat collar, yanked him through.

"Hey ...!" he protested, then stiffened, looking around.

"Holy mother of ..." He trailed off as something caught his attention deeper in the jungle, something which verily gleamed as I followed his gaze; something I'd completely missed when I'd first scanned my surroundings—a mammoth rib cage, just laying amidst the trees. Baking in the sun.

"Oh, man. Is that what I think it is?"

I didn't need to look at him to tell how frightened he was. And yet I moved forward anyway, as young boys often do, not really caring how he felt, pushing through the warm, moist fronds—where a gaggle of dragonflies erupted into flight and made a beeline straight for Dillon, I don't know why. And then he was yelping, yelping and hollering diminishingly (for he was running away), and he must have stumbled through the portal—for there was no sign of him left anywhere—and I was standing alone.

Alone with the remains of Ghost's family (which I knew in a way I cannot explain—not then, and not now), orphaned amidst a village of bones; which gleamed in the sun like a shattered puzzle, curved symmetrically, too perfect to be natural, like the standing, ivory birdcage in the corner of

Grandma Grace's living room. Or the burned out fuselage of a 747—half-buried, perhaps, on a misty island beach—somewhere between LAX and Hawaii.

And then I was following Dillon, through the fronds and back across the transom, where I stopped to take the fish out of my bag and unwrapped it with trembling hands, before placing it halfway into the portal so that only its tail could be seen.

Though the after-school visit had been scheduled for months—since shortly after my parents' disappearance—it wasn't until I opened the door to the counselor's office that the reality of it really hit. *This was it.* Today would decide if I would be allowed to move on to Junior High or if I would be held back a year—and not, I knew, based strictly on poor grades.

"I'm here for my exam," I said, chewing the last of my Snickers, feeling foolish, mainly because I didn't even know what to call it: this test of my sanity; this test of my maturity and character. Are you even human? they seemed to be asking. Do you belong here in our public schools with our beloved *human* children? Or should you be farmed out—to the insane asylum, maybe, or the traveling carnie, with the rest of your kind?

"Mr. Smith," said the counselor, not unpleasantly. "Let's get this started straight away." She pushed a pencil and some paper at me. "It's college ruled, is that okay?"

I nodded.

"There's a sharpener in the room, on the far side of the cabinet." She tossed the hair out of her eyes, which swung, scintillating, like liquid gold. "Shall we?"

I nodded.

She escorted me into a back room, two walls of which had upper halves made of glass, one facing the hallway and the other facing her office. The room had light brown paneling and a single round table with three chairs, one of which she pulled out. Besides the cabinet on the wall and the pencil sharpener, there was only a framed print of some daisies and an enormous IBM clock, which ticked audibly.

The wooden chair creaked as I settled into it.

"I want you to tell me about your parents—okay? About a page should do. Just, whatever comes into your mind."

"That's it?"

"That's it. No questions this time."

And then she exited, closing the door behind her—firmly, completely.

I squirmed in the chair, the seat of which was hard as concrete, then looked into her office—saw the counselor re-seating herself ... hair scintillating.

The big IBM clock ticked, its seconds hand swinging on its fulcrum.

At last I picked up the pencil and placed its tip—which the counselor had sharpened to a fine point—against the paper, feeling the lead break a little as I wrote, WHAT I'VE LEARNED FROM THE DEATH OF MY PARENTS ...

"Mr. Smith? Come on back."

I got up from the hard, wooden chair (the back of which faced the principal's office) and went in.

"Please, have a seat," he said.

He riffled the pages in front of him—lifting his chin on occasion, peering through his readers. A long plaque on his desk read: ROLAND R. BLAIN, SUPERINTENDENT. "You seem to have written us quite a lot," he said, and added, "I understand that wouldn't have been the case a few months ago."

"I've had a long time to think about things," I said.

"Yes, I see that." He took off his reading glasses and slipped a tip of the frames into his mouth. "You sound angry in this. Were you trying to tell us something?"

"Yes sir, I was."

Blain drummed his fingers on the desk. "Well, that explains that."

He put his glasses back on and started scribbling on the page—scratching and pecking, pecking and scratching. "Mr. Smith, do you feel that this was an accurate snapshot of your present emotional state?"

"I do, sir."

"And do you feel that anything was gained from this experience—of writing it down, that is? Anything learned?"

"Yes, sir."

"Which was?"

"That I can grow, sir. That I *have* grown, now that I've accepted the truth."

Blain looked at me over his glasses.

"About my parents, sir."

A final scratch, a final peck.

"Very well." He tossed his reading glasses onto the desk and rocked back in his chair, jauntily, his hands clasped behind his head. "And congratulations. Because you'll be going on to 7th grade."

I must have looked as stunned as I felt.

"Look, son," He glanced out the window as though in deep thought, "Anybody that can go through what you've been through ... and face it down so honestly ..." He looked back at me, appearing altogether different without the reading glasses, younger, more alive. "...has earned his way. Wouldn't you agree?"

I think I blushed.

"Now go on, get out of here. Before I change my mind. Besides, they're waiting for you."

He pointed outside, to where Jenny—the girl I had a crush on—and Dillon were watching, pressed against the glass.

And then it was over and us kids were walking home, Jenny in the middle while Dillon and I pretended to be pinball bumpers, ping-ponging her back and forth, making her laugh, until we reached the intersection at University and Pines and I punched the button to cross north while Jenny punched the button to continue west, and I leaned close and told her I liked her but she didn't say anything, at least not at first—until we were trotting in the opposite direction, when she called, "I like you, too!"

And I felt great, just great, better than I had ever felt before.

Not to mention clever, considering I had just lied my way—lied through my crooked, Snickers-stained teeth—into 7th grade.

It would be hard to describe how elated I felt upon returning to our fishing spot and finding the trout gone, though in truth I couldn't be sure if Ghost had gotten to it or some other predator—at least not until I stepped through (having had some difficulty in locating the portal, I confess) and saw the fresh prints.

And yet of Ghost himself there was no trace, even after I'd called out to him—in the hopes he might recognize my voice— and laid the new fish down (a giant halibut which had cost me my entire allowance); positioning it halfway in and out of the portal so I could monitor it even while studying on the nearby rocks.

Nor did I have to wait long, for I'd barely cracked my history book when I just happened to look up and see the halibut yanked all the way in, at which I stood abruptly and approached—but was beat to the mark by Ghost himself, whose snout emerged out of thin air and was quickly followed by his neck and body—even the entirety of his tail—until we were facing each other next to the Mohawk River: Ghost still swallowing and licking his non-lips, and both of us, I think, chilled by the November wind.

"That's it," I said, rubbing my gloves together, splaying my empty hands. "No more. At least not today."

He cocked his head at this, his pink, rabbit's eyes blinking, before rearing back and barking at the sky—like a sea lion, I thought—just *yark, yark, yark!*

"Nope. All done. You're just going to have to wait until tomorrow—when I'll try to bring more. Can you do that?"

He just looked at me, his little fore-claws opening and closing—a kind of prehistoric hand-wringing, I supposed. And it occurred to me—not for the first time—that, at least in the short-term, I might be his only means of survival; that, indeed, if I didn't feed him he might very well starve.

What did not occur to me, at least until he began sniffing the air between us and slowly moving toward me, is that I myself might be in danger—that, in lieu of more fish or perhaps even a big dragonfly, he might try *kid.* Might try lying little turd-wad who was going to start 7th grade next year. Might try Denial Boy who was still convinced his parents were marooned on a desert isle and would turn up any day.

Which is when, having begun backing away, I tripped over an above-ground root and fell, sprawling, onto my back, at which instant the animal's snout darted for my head and I screamed—only to find, seconds later, that it had not attacked me at all ... but begun licking me; yes, *licking* me, sliding its great, pebbly tongue up and down my face, slathering my cold cheeks in gooey spit, breathing into my nostrils—filling the world with cow. Filling it with heat and musk and stench.

And filling it, too, with something else, something I'd been missing since the last time I'd seen my mother; a thing frowned upon in Grandma's house (where the nape of the rugs always lay left to right and the plastic floor runners always gleamed and the books in their glass-faced cabinets always stood so silent, to be viewed and not read).

Mere touch. Mere contact. Mere things coming into contact with other things. Like what I felt for Jenny or even my favorite T-shirt and wool blanket—the one with the U.S.S. Enterprise on it—like what I felt for my plastic model kits and comic books and beat-up fishing pole (even though I never used it).

Something familiar, something secret. Something, I supposed, like love. Or what a boy could know of it.

I returned many times after that—through the winter and into the spring—always bringing more fish and eventually moving up to chuck steaks and whole chickens (which I bought from the meat market in the strip mall near the school); something, alas, that I soon regretted, especially the chuck steaks, because after eating red meat he began to spurn everything else, and it was getting expensive.

Nor would anything have changed, I think, at least until he outgrew my ability to feed him, if it hadn't been for the escaped convict and the glint of his nicked and worn folding Buck knife—an incident which happened right there behind Larry and Sue Miller's newest 7-11 store just a day after my 13th birthday. Even now, looking back, it's hard to believe what occurred that day, or that it would set in motion a chain of events that would shake not just my world but the town of Comet's Tail—population 9,893—in general; indeed, the entire nation (if the NBC Nightly News was any indication). Mostly, though, it would effect Mrs. Dalton, the Vietnamese wife of my father's best friend, Stuart. Mostly it would make me wonder if I ever wanted to get married, even to Jenny, if it was capable of bringing such pain.

Here's what happened: I'd been playing the stand-up *Space Invaders* game at Larry and Sue's 7-11 (I knew them by name because they were longtime friends of my parents, who had known everyone, it seemed), mostly just to get out of the rain (a storm had hit while I was riding home from Jenny's), when, by virtue of simply looking up, I realized my bike was being stolen—and gave chase.

But I didn't get far, because by the time I'd followed the blur of my bike around to the back of the store its thief was waiting for me—right there, by the drainpipe—and before I knew it he'd grabbed me by the throat and slammed me against the block wall, where he promptly stuck a knife to my neck.

"Okay—now, don't move, dig?" he breathed, releasing his grip, moving the knife to my throat, and I didn't move, not an inch. "Here's how it's going to be. You're going to reach down and empty your pockets—like, *real* slow, okay? And you're going to put whatever is in them right here, in my free hand. Okay? You dig?"

But the truth was I had nothing in my pockets—except my key to Grandma's house and a couple quarters, maybe—

and told him so, my voice quavering, sounding small, and my legs beginning to tremble. "I spent everything on *Space Invad—*"

"Shuttup," he spat, veritably spat, so that his saliva sprinkled my face. "Just *shuttup.* I'll take what you got. Now get on it, let's go, before I swipe this thing straight across your throat."

I could hardly think I was shaking so hard, hardly breathe, but I did as I was told, handing him the key and what turned out to be three quarters— after which I turned out my pockets to show there was nothing left.

At last I stammered: "La-Larry's going to come looking for me, you know. Li—like any minute now." I indicated the back door with a movement of my eyes. "Li—like right through that door."

He didn't waver, didn't bat a Charles Manson eye. "Then I'll *cut* him too, runt. And no, no, he's not; he's too busy counting his money." He pressed the blade still tighter against my throat, hard enough that I felt sure it would break the skin. "You, on the other hand, are someone who could identify me—now, aren't you?" He paused, his dark eyes seeming to glitter, like so much crude oil. "Say now, you're kind of a pretty thing, aren't you?"

I think my heart must have stopped, if only for an instant.

"Look at all that golden hair; why, you should have been a girl." He fondled my shoulder-length hair with his free hand. "You know, it *shines* is what it does. Yep, shines just like the sun—why, it's almost white." He looked me up and down. "That key—is that for your folks' place? Oh, I bet you got a *preetty* mother, just laid out hot and fresh, like a piz—"

In truth, my fist was impacting his nose before I'd even made a conscious decision to do so—impacting it with a squish, not a smack (like on *Star Trek*), so that he dropped the knife and stumbled back as I bolted for the trees—though why I did that instead of running around to the front of the store remains a mystery to me even to this day.

Regardless, I was well beyond the tree line when I first heard him piling after me, shouting something indiscernible, breaking branches—as though he were a wendigo and not a man at all; as though he were some vengeful spirit and not just an escaped con, which is what he turned out to be. And then I was running, running for our fishing spot, which wasn't far, doing it like the punch, without even thinking about it, until I burst into a familiar clearing and found the Mohawk River, and hurried for the portal—

And could not find it. Not anywhere. For, indeed, I had always found it before by following Ghost's prints, and the rain had washed them completely away. The convict, meanwhile, was almost there—hooting and hollering like a chieftain, emerging into the clearing while brandishing his knife, running at me through the muck and the silt.

"Ghost!" I cried. "Ghost! Where are you?"

But there was no response, no familiar *yark, yark, yark,* nothing so much as a mew, and before I knew it the convict had pile-drived me harder than I had ever been hit in my life and I flew, veritably flew, over the rocks—landing with a grunt; gasping for breath, as the criminal straddled me and pinned me against the sand, as he raised the knife and suddenly paused.

For a shadow had fallen over us both—a shadow as familiar to me by that point as my very own—a shadow which said, in a language older than words: *Your day will come—as it does for us all. But that day is not today.*

And then Ghost's jaws closed about the man's head and he was lifted high into the air, screaming at the top of his lungs (though the sound was muffled, which somehow made it worse), grabbing at the animal's head, kicking his feet like a marionette even as Ghost began shaking him like a rag doll and the sounds intensified—before stopping abruptly; just *bam,* like that, because ... Because—

No. I will not speak of it. Suffice it to say that I saw in that instant the most horrific thing I had ever seen; either before or since. And that, having seen it, I found my breath where I thought there was none and scrambled to my feet, after which I ran from the sound of Ghost eating—the tearing and the cracking, the squelching and the crunching—and did not stop, not until I was home and tracking filthy muck across Grandma's perfect white carpet. Not until I was curled up like a fetus beneath the weight of my wool *Star Trek* blanket and whimpering like a beat dog—coughing and sniveling, crying like a little baby.

May became June, which became July, which became August, and I didn't see Ghost ... although I left him something every day, something which was always gone when I returned, at least at first. By September, however, he'd stopped taking what I left him completely—nor would he appear when called—and I began to worry. That would have been about the time I started getting serious with Jenny—holding hands at the indoor skating rink, kissing for the first time in the balcony at *The Muppet Movie*—as well as my first growth spurt, all in the legs, which made me feel gangly and insecure but also made me taller than Jen, which I liked, and which she liked, too.

It was also around the time the murders started happening, and what become known as the Comet's Tail Mangler—at first just in the local paper but soon the national ones as well and finally the NBC Nightly News—started making waves across the country. Nor was that the only national news story to touch me; for my parents' missing flight was back in the spotlight also—primarily because the business tycoon who had resumed the search (after the Coast Guard and Federal Aviation Administration abandoned it) had now given up, too.

For Shad and my grandma, it was case closed—again. For me, it was the beginning of a season of denial that would last clear through September and into the school year; a season in which I became more convinced than ever that my parents were still alive. "Denial can be a powerful thing," my mother had once said (I believe it was in the context of someone's rumored drug and/or alcohol addiction), but for me, in that fear-addled fall of 1979, it became something more; something akin to an obsession or even a psychosis; something which rendered me deaf, dumb, and blind—to the reports of wreckage having been spotted by a private flight out of Honolulu in the wee hours of Christmas morning; to the reports of the victims of the Mangler having been mauled as if by an animal— mauled, and partially eaten. Indeed, I had even begun looking forward to introducing them to Jenny (when they were finally picked up from Gilligan's Island, which is how I imaged their circumstances), had even selected a date: New Years, 1980—the day the call would come. The day the news would be announced that survivors had been found and that they were in good health; the day we would drive to the airport in Grandma's black GTO and watch my parents descend the steps like soldiers returning from Vietnam, their faces tanned from the South Pacific, their necks adorned with leis.

In the end, however, the New Year brought news of a different sort—though news that struck home regardless—for the latest victim of the Mangler turned out to be Stuart Dalton himself: decorated veteran, local hero (for his service in Vietnam), and a close, personal friend of our parents—so close that we were invited to his funeral; where I ended up in line behind his widow for the viewing of the casket, a casket which had been draped with a veil to prevent scrutiny of the body.

Even now, some forty years later, it would be difficult to describe what I felt that day, as Song Li offered her final words and her husband lay hidden beneath the gauze and the reality of what had occurred—what *had* been occurring, ever since the death of the convict—came crashing down; as Song said goodbye to her "darling Stuart" and I said hello to reality (for the first time in months, possibly even since my parents had disappeared), and knew, though the thought of it tore me down the middle, what had to be done. If, that was, I could even find the portal.

If, that was ... I could find my friend.

As it turned out, finding the portal wasn't hard—there were smatterings of blood half in and half out of it, human blood, I knew. Finding Ghost, on the other hand, would be a different matter, one I wasn't sure I was up to—even as I stepped over the transom into his world. And yet that too proved unfounded when I sensed something moving almost immediately, something big, something bipedal, crashing through the cycad fronds like an earth mover, vibrating the ground like a tiny earthquake.

"Ghost? Is that you?"

The fact was, I couldn't be sure, and began backing away—back through the portal to our fishing spot near the Mohawk River, back to what I perceived to be safety—though I should have known by then there was no such thing. Until at last a great, grayish snout emerged and was followed by an equally great neck and trunk, and I knew, as his large feet sunk into the silt before me, that I had found him, even if he'd doubled in size and was no longer pure white (after all, I'd grown too, nor was my hair as light as it used to be). Still, it wasn't until I looked into his dark pink eyes, eyes that had become so dark as to be almost red, that I truly saw the face of my friend—older, yes, and frightening in a way that he hadn't been before, more robust, but, well, still the creature that had saved my life on that rainy day in May of 1979. Still something more than just a dinosaur—at least to me. Still Ghost.

I fumbled for Dad's gun—which I had found in Shad's dresser, as I knew I would—and carefully removed it from my coat pocket, loathing its black, bloated weight, wondering if I would have the strength to pull its trigger (and wondering, too, if it would even be enough, now that Ghost had grown).

Ghost, meanwhile, only cocked his head, his red eyes blinking, his fore-claws opening and closing, his cracked and rutted throat grumbling: *Magrawww ...*

I lifted the pistol and steadied it, wishing he would just turn and go away; that he would just forget me and the portal forever: forget he ever tasted human flesh—forget the world which lie next to his own. It was magical thinking, I knew.

Magrawww ...

I may have trained the weapon on one of his eyes, I don't know, figuring that was the most direct path to his brain. All I know is that he sniffed at the barrel of the gun as I aimed and promptly began licking it—thinking it was a fish, I suppose. Thinking I was feeding him.

"I've missed you, Ghost. I really have," I said, finding the gun heavier than expected, wanting to just lower it and forget the whole thing—to run home to my room (my real room, at Mom and Dad's, not the fake one in Grandma's mausoleum), to run and never stop.

And then he was throwing back his head and roaring—wondering where the fish went, I suppose, wanting to be fed as before—and I *was* lowering the gun (knowing, I think, I could never really do it; that I couldn't even bonk a fish), when there was a rumbling up the road and I turned to see Shad getting out of the GTO—at which instant Ghost crouched like a tiger and leapt: flashing past me like a phantom, bounding for the car.

And then I did do it—fire, that is—not just once but multiple times, hitting Ghost in the head and back, hitting him in the legs, until at last he stumbled and skidded onto his belly in the rocks—all the way into the river—where I like to think he died before ever touching the water. Where I liked to think he died without ever knowing pain.

And then it was over and Shad just held me (for I'd collapsed by the river), gripping me tighter than I'd ever been gripped before—even by Mom—rocking me like a baby; saying "It's okay" and "Let them go" and that he loved me over and over (and that Grandma did to, in her own peculiar way), comforting me as I cried. Until a considerable time had passed and we stood, watching as Ghost drifted further out—gurgling beneath the dark surface, vanishing without a trace—and I found I was able to say goodbye. To Ghost, yes—whom I had loved as only a boy can; but also to my parents, whom I knew I'd never see again. Also to the life I had known—which was as gone as Ghost and his victims. I accepted it and it was good—because it was the only thing to do. There, with my brother, standing side by side, in the fading, funereal light of the day.

EVERY BLADE OF GRASS

We're at our breaking point, myself and Taylor—even the Captain sounds hang-dogged and defeated. "Just a little further," he keeps saying into his mic, as if repeating the lie will somehow make it true, "We're almost there. Feel that moisture in the air? That's the Acidalia Canal and the next Oasis. Just stay sharp. Oh, and Taylor? Quit blowing debris into the fucking pools. Nothing pisses a settler off worse than arriving to a dirty pool."

I laugh aloud at that, knowing Taylor is doing the same. *As if.* We haven't seen a transport or a settler in weeks. Has immigration to the Formerly Red Planet slowed? We don't know.

I look at the houses, so pristine and white, so uniform, their black windows glinting, resolving to ask the next settler I see (and to hell with the no-contact edict). But then something rustles amidst the stalks (so, too, is there a vibration in the air) and I move: having learned, since my arrival at Utopia Planitia, to never linger long in uncut grass; nor to dwell on what happened to the trimmers before me.

"And there she is," comes the Captain again, "As promised. One Oasis with medical rocket, right next to the Acidalia Canal. What do you have to say now, Decker? Something cute, I imagine. Go right ahead."

But the truth is, because of the whir of my light-trimmer's blades, I am not even sure if I've heard him correctly, and so ask him to repeat it, which he does. Then I pause, looking over my shoulder at Taylor (who has caught up to me in spite of his exhaustion), and we just stand there, he with his blower and I with my trimmer, until he shakes his head, slowly, and I key my headset: "So is it the end of the sector, or what? Do you see a bridge?"

His answer is garbled, indecipherable—a favorite trick of the Captain's when he doesn't want to speak. At length we hear: " ...responsible for your asses. I'm going to go in and check for—" And we lose him in a hail of static.

I look at Taylor, our eyes locked, our faces bathed in sweat. "Checking for gnomes, he says. Well? What do you think? Is he telling the truth?"

He looks at me for what seems a long time. "All I know is ... I'm done. I'm just ... done with all this. I'm sorry."

It takes me a minute to process what he's saying. "Jesus, Taylor. You don't mean—"

"Done—if there's a bridge," he says, finally, even as it becomes clear to me he has already thought this out, already looked at it from every angle, committed to it completely. "Total forfeit of bonus, I know. But—I'm taking that medical rocket. I'm going home."

At last I say, "You won't have enough money to migrate, you know that. And they'll never hire you again once you forfeit—you know that too?"

He shakes his head slowly. "It doesn't matter. Besides, I wouldn't be so sure. They've created a monster here—and they know it." He scans the green horizon—balefully, it seems. "It's never going to stop, you know. It's just going to keep growing, faster and faster, until ..."

I slap him a little, wondering if he's succumbing to the Daze. "Until what? Until what, Taylor?"

"Until they'll even hire back a forfeiter," he says, appearing to come out of it, and laughs.

I clasp his shoulder, give it a hearty shake. *"There won't be a bridge.* After twenty sectors? No way. They're greedy—

not stupid." I look to the houses still ahead of us and at the overgrown grass; at the flowerbeds chocked with red-weed and the walkways overrun with Bryum moss. "Either way, we've still got this sector to clear. Unless, of course, you want to forfeit everything?"

"No way, man," he says, and seems to buck up.

And then we are moving, frustrating whatever gnomes have been moving in on us and triggering our nuclear-powered tools, our lips longing for water, our bellies grumbling, our hearts longing— knowing, praying, the Oasis is near.

I cannot decide what is the more horrific sight: the steel bridge leading to the next (and 21st) sector—or Taylor's face as he looks at it, which appears pale as the dead even though it has been deeply darkened by the sun. Worse, the Captain has yet to exit the rocket—which suggests he may have found something (i.e., the kind of trouble only gnomes can bring). So, too, is his bright red Big Trak still running (as if he saw something and had to leap off it quickly). At this point only one thing is certain—none of it bodes well for Taylor's intended departure.

When at last the Captain emerges he is holding an apple in one hand and his knife in the other, shaking his head. "Yuh, it's what I thought. They got the console. Startled 'em real good, but, well, the damage was done." He smiles cockeyed, polishing the apple on his shirt, then plops down in the hatchway and begins cutting the fruit. "It's not all bad, though. I saved the provisions."

I look at Taylor, who also appears skeptical. "They ruined the console but left the provisions? Why would they do that?" he asks.

"Like I said, I scared them off. As for the console, you know they like to strip the wires and use the copper," He bends down suddenly and picks up one of their tiny spears, touches it near the tip. "See that? It's remarkable, really. Holds the Folsom point just as snug as a virgin. What the hell are you getting at, anyway?"

"It just seems weird that—"

"What he's 'getting at' is that he's tired," I say, "And that we got at least one more sector to clear before we can get out of here. So let's bivouac and get going, before they discover our *real* ticket home—the rocket at the end of the quadrant. Yeah?"

Cap just shrugs, eating his apple. "You'll get no argument from me." But something is troubling him, because he keeps eyeing Taylor suspiciously as he cuts the fruit into wedges, looking the man up and down, taking the measure of him. After a while he says, "What I can't figure is, why all this concern over a medical rocket?"

"Forget it," I say. "Let's just eat."

"'Forget it,' he says. 'Let's just eat' ... No, no, I think we should talk about it. See, if someone goes home—that'll break up the crew. And that's something I need to know about." He pauses, the knife glinting in his hand. "How about it, Taylor? You sick? Thinking about going home?"

I glance at my friend—whose face has become red as Cap's apple from heat and frustration.

"If I was, I wouldn't need your perm—"

"Look, forget it," I say, even as the Captain stands, slowly—dropping the apple—so that we are suddenly nose to nose. I add: "No one's breaking up the crew. You'll get your bonus, don't worry. We all will."

"Not if this crew fragments, I won't," he says, coldly, flatly—still holding the knife. "That's the difference between you and me. The difference between all of us. Unless, of course, you think you'd be better—"

"Just forget it," I say, stepping back, standing down. "No one's questioning your authority. And no one's going anywhere. Isn't that right, Taylor?"

"Hmph," says Taylor. "I'm not going to be told whether I'm sick or not by no *white* company's white man—"

"—*isn't that right,* Taylor? We got work to do."

At length he relents. "Yeah, sure, that's right." He steps up to the hatch, which is being blocked by the Cap—then shrugs, splaying his hands. "Y'mind? Nigger's got to eat."

At last the Captain steps aside, mumbling, "Forget it. Sure, why not. Another whole sector. Fine. Take five. Take twenty. Whatever. I'm going to get started on the other side."

And then he's gone, firing up the Big Trak and rattling away, as we just look at each other, wondering if he's getting the Daze, and wondering, too, just how the hell we're going to make it—how we're going to clear another entire sector—as the sun beats down and we head into the afternoon. As the white houses look on, their dark windows glinting, and the temperatures climb, soon to be soaring, and the freshly cut grass begins to regrow at our feet.

I am pilfering a drink from the hose of one of the settlers' homes (something we are expressly forbidden to do) when the yellowjacket attacks: its legs dangling insidiously and its wings vibrating dizzyingly so that I find myself snatching up my trimmer in a panic and swinging it like a bludgeon (instead of just turning it on rationally and targeting the wasp carefully); the result being that while the fist-sized insect is vanquished a nearby window is shattered—which of course brings Taylor running (though fortunately not the Captain).

"Jesus, man! What are you—"

"Whoa, whoa, whoa, watch it," I say, quickly. "There's a wasp on the ground—somewhere. There, by the spigot."

A moment later he pauses to examine it, notably breathless from the run. "Holy shit—look at that." He prods it with the end of his blower, making sure its dead. "Bastard's are getting bigger, you notice that? Ever since they sprayed the M-4."

He stands, shaking his head, still catching his breath. "It's like I said, they've created a monster here. I'm starting to wonder if I even *want* to migrate, to tell the truth. Earth might be wasted but at least there's no bees the size of ..." He trails off, looking at the window. "Well, shit," he says, and scratches his head. "That's bad. Now what?"

I look at it too, thinking, *There's no bees on Earth at all. That's the problem.* "I don't know," I say, exhaling, "but something tells me I just spent my bonus—all of it."

"Jesus, you smell that?"

"Yeah—like rotting grass. Only ..." I look around, not recalling seeing any piles of clippings or other yard debris. "I don't see anything. There's nothing here that would account for it. What are you doing?"

"Following my nose," he says, leaning into the window, sniffing inside the house. "It's coming from in here; from—" He falls silent abruptly, his whole body freezing, tensing up. "Holy Mother of ..."

"What is it? What do you see?"

But he is no longer at the window, having instead placed his hands on his knees and begun vomiting into the bushes, his entire body heaving, trembling like an epileptic, and his blower falling to the ground, where it lolls onto its side and continues to sputter and hum.

We have tied our bandannas over our mouths and begun to explore the house, which has been overrun with crabgrass and vines of Creeping Charlie; with Canada Thistle and Purslane, with sprouts of Shepard's Purse, even as flies the size of silver dollars buzz about the body and the Captain tries to raise us—fruitlessly, of course. For it is his turn to dine on static.

But it is the body that compels me and causes me to keep returning to it (having checked the kitchen and dining area, as well as what appears to be a meditation chamber, and found nothing), batting away the flies, scattering them like dandelion seeds. It's funny, because if it weren't for the red-weed growing from its mouth and the mushroom stools in its eyes and nostrils, not to mention its green flesh, I would simply take it to be a settler who had fallen asleep on his couch—a victim, perhaps (based on his tranquil expression at death) of what we call the Daze.

As it is, I am forced only to accept it as a great mystery, one not apt to be solved by a pair of grass grunts poking around in the dark—whether we find more like it or not—at least that's what I'm thinking as I look out the gigantic window at the deck and see the large white telescope angled on its tripod. As I ignore my radio and hear Taylor shouting somewhere above, somewhere on the second landing, saying, "We got four more up here, brother from another mother! And they're all D.O.A., just like the first."

I do not know what first goads me into looking through the telescope—which is pointed directly at the Earth—perhaps I miss our brown planet more than I dare admit. Regardless, it is not so much a matter of 'why' but 'what'—for what I see through it is a world as green and fertile as any Earth of the past; a world as lush and emerald as the Red Planet herself—now terraformed to resemble the Earth of old—and whose dark side and light side are both visible (thanks to its position to Mars). And yet a world, too, that must ultimately not exist—for it occupies the same part of the sky where the brown Earth must of necessity be. A world, then, I suddenly realize, which is not *like* the Earth—but *is* the Earth. The Earth reborn. Impossibly, breathtakingly.

Beautifully, I think, feeling as though I might touch it, for here is our home as it once was, as it was meant to be: the clean, open fields, the mountains and hills, the seas and rivers—but also the cities and illuminated byways like glowing circuit boards. Also the—

I squint, adjusting the scope's aperture, compensating for glare. I want to see the lights, the intricate web of glitter—like back-lit dew on a leaf—the sparkle of sentience. The proof that Earth is a thinking thing, a dreaming thing, a thing perhaps without precedent.

But there is no proof, no intricate web of glitter, no illuminated byways like glowing circuits. There is only the planet's dark side and a perfect half-sphere of black—only one void against another and two impossible extremes—only the green of endless plant life and the unfathomable chasm of night.

In the end, only an Earth devoid of all human activity—as though we never even existed—and overrun by grass and vegetation. Overrun, I am now convinced, by the company's own super accelerant, M-4.

We hump for the next Oasis, double-timing it to beat the Captain—who we are now convinced has the Daze. (Why else would he not have told us? For surely he has known, receiving as he does updates from Mother, and thus Earth, regularly). The plan, meanwhile, such as it is, is simple: we will blast off in the medical rocket and rendezvous with Mother before hitching a ride back to Moon Plaza and applying for asylum—a long shot, to be sure, but more than we could hope for if the Captain finds out we entered one of the houses illegally. With luck, Crazy Cap will be mowing as he goes and so arrive well after us.

"*If* he's not there already," shouts Taylor as we run through the knee-high grass—referring to the medical rocket, playing Devil's Advocate. "And *if* the gnomes haven't gotten to it. They're getting bold, you know." He adds, looking at me: "Why the hell you packing that, anyway? Ain't *no* grass where we're going ..."

But I don't know why I'm packing 'that,' it—my light-trimmer—only that it feels necessary somehow, feels important, like it's the right thing to do, although I have no idea why.

And then we run, opting to save our breath, praying we get there before Cap, wondering what has become of our loved ones—hoping Moon Plaza will take us in.

The medical rocket is wasted—its consoles smashed, its stores emptied—to the extent that we have collapsed outside its open hatch in total exhaustion and despair. Worse, the air is filled with the roar of machinery—a roar with a bandsaw edge—one we know all too well for it is the sound of Cap's Big Track coming closer every second.

And then he has arrived, riding his tractor like a chariot, goading it forward into the clearing, motoring directly toward us until Taylor jumps up in a panic and sprints for the next bridge—his dark skin shining, his heels kicking up sod—as the Captain veers toward him suddenly and seems to gun the engine.

And then I am running, shouting at him to stop, as Taylor vanishes beneath the blades and the Big Track jounces, once, twice, the Captain laughing and throwing back his head, the iron tracks seeming to catch—until blood begins spewing like grass clippings from the mulch-vents and all I can hear is my friend screaming—gargling—dying beneath the Cap's iron beast.

That's when I realize it is *rotating*, swiveling, committing a zero-point turn so that the Oasis is sprinkled with entrails and the machine is pointed at me; at the center of the clearing—where I am wide open and vulnerable and will be mowed down no different than Taylor if I don't act and act quickly.

Then he accelerates and there is no time for anything—but to run. This I do, unhooking a plutonium sphere as I scuttle and dropping it into his path before diving suddenly to one side and rolling. Nor is it lost upon me that had I not retained the trimmer and fuel bandolier after the house I would surely be meeting the same fate as Taylor.

Instead there is a flash of light and a mighty explosion, and I am blasted no less than twenty feet—even as the Captain and his Big Trak are utterly obliterated.

And then I just watch: as the burning debris twirls down and the Oasis goes up in flames. As the medical rocket keels—and collapses into the fire.

I trim, heading due west, toward the next and perhaps final Oasis. Toward the next and perhaps final return rocket. As for *why* I do—I do not know, for the world of Man recedes further with each step—further, it seems, with each breath, and so, too, with each house left edged and ready for the mower.

All I know for certain is that this is what I do— what I have always done; and that, as a man, I was good at it. That I could channel my energy deftly and efficiently through the instrument so as to perform my duty smartly and surefootedly. And yet, that begs a question: What am I now, if no longer a man?

I'll tell you what I think. And that is that I have succumbed to the Daze, in no less a fashion than did the Captain or even Taylor when he ran for the bridge. Indeed, I cannot say beyond a certainty that any of this has even happened; or if it is rather, all of it, a kind of daydream, something experienced, perhaps exclusively, by those who toil long amongst the grass.

I trim—the blade of my instrument whirring pink and smooth through the stems—but grow weary; the foliage reaching higher the farther I push, my skin and hair and vision turning green, my thoughts turning outward—to the world, to the Formerly Red Planet, to Earth, and everything in them, every rock, every insect, every blade of grass.

T-minus 15 and counting. All set there, Chief?

I look at my reflection in the cockpit's front window—the tired eyes, the premature wrinkles and crow's feet—and beyond: to the blue hole and return mirror—which will remain invisible to the naked eye until I am almost upon it.

Roger that. All systems are go and I am hot to drop.

Roger that, *Diver 7.* Nine and counting: 8 ... 7 ... 6 ...

I brace myself as the launch indicator switches from red to green—like a streetlight in the void—and the helmet's blue visor lowers ... locking into place.

2 ... 1 ...

I grip the Jesus handles.

Launch.

Elton John once sang, "And all this science, I don't understand. It's just my job five days a week." That's how it is when you're a Crash Diver: you don't need to understand blue holes or how they differ from wormholes and black holes or what a mobius mirror does—only that it *must* work, every time—because, at the end of the day, that isn't your job. Your job is to be a guinea pig: to be shot into the vortex at near light speed and experience what effect blue hole-assisted mirror travel has on the human body and psyche. Your job is to penetrate to whatever depth they've set the mirror—and, if you're lucky, to enter that mirror and get bounced back.

It hasn't always been like this. Before there was *Zebra Station*—with its luxurious gravity centrifuge and its row of black and yellow delta divers hanging like bats from the launch jib—there was *Blue One,* a sparsely-manned outpost which had sent the first human souls into the maw of the blue hole, men who had come back white-haired and emaciated, debilitated—mentally and physically—mad.

The Crash Diver Program changed all that. From now on only specially-trained pilots would be sent into the Hole, pilots who had the benefit of the first men's experiences as well as spacecraft designed specifically for the task. A lot was learned in a very short time—one of these things was that men who entered the vortex experienced a series of hallucinations, or Dive Visions, in which they briefly felt they had become someone or something else: a soldier in the Holy Roman Army, say, or a person of the opposite sex. Some even purported to have become animals or alien lifeforms—it was the latter which had apparently driven the men of *Blue One* clinically insane.

Another lesson was the fact that the farther a mirror was projected into the vortex the farther it could "cast" to its attendant portal; meaning the Hole might well hold the key to intergalactic space travel. This more than anything had accounted for the program's generous funding, not to mention its exhaustive launch table, which sometimes saw us drop as many as three times in a week. The chief problem, however, remained—and that was that the deeper one dropped, the more acute the hallucinations; hence, the missions had become increasingly volatile, increasingly dangerous.

Regardless, a decision had been made to make the next drop the deepest yet: all the way through the ergosphere—

right up to the outer event horizon. By which they meant right up to the point of no return, even by mirror refraction.

And I was the one who drew the unlucky straw.

It is raining. That's the first thing I notice, the first thing that tells me I am no longer in the cockpit. The second is that I'm bleeding—bleeding from the leg, which is making it difficult to press the attack. The third is that I'm dying—as is my opponent—dying beneath a blood red sky.

"It is finished," he says, stumbling forward and back—his blood flowing freely, his hair matted in sweat. "Look at you! Your broadsword is shattered. Your armor is compromised. Why is it you continue?"

But I do not know why I continue—only that I was a Crash Diver once and will be so again, and so must face the vision, endure its consequences. Endure them so that future generations may bridge the gulf of galaxies!

At last I say: "Are you better off? We die together, Sir Aglovere. Surely you—"

But I am baffled by my own voice, so familiar and yet strange, and by my own words, which have materialized from nowhere.

And then he is charging, hacking at me wildly, and I am forced back along the hedgerow: until I lose my footing over a protruding root and topple headlong into the mud and bramble—whereupon my opponent falls on what's left of my sword and is promptly run through, his entrails unspooling like loops of linked sausage and his eyes turning to empty glass.

At length he says, "We kill ourselves," and laughs, even as I push him off me.

And then we just lay there, staring at the sky, neither of us saying anything, as our blood pools together and spirals down the slope. As the clouds continue to rumble—pouring rain into our dying eyes.

The diver trembles violently as I shake the vision off.

... repeat, *Zebra One* to Diver 7, are you all right?

I feel my leg through my flight suit, half expecting it to be flayed wide open—but I am unharmed, of course.

Roger that, *Zebra One.* However I am experiencing turbulence I cannot account for—what can you tell me?

There is a long pause which is pregnant with static, after which *Zebra One* responds, choppily, Diver 7 ... *Zebra One.* Be advised ... some kind of anomaly. We are working ... before it effects the mirrors. Please ...

And then they are gone.

I am gone, too. At least, I am no longer in the cockpit. Instead, I awaken from a dream I cannot remember in a place I have never been—no, I can see now that is incorrect. I am *home,* still sequestered in the dingy sleeping quarters at the very back of the Temple—where I have remained now for three days without benefit of food or water, and where I shall stay—unto death, if necessary—until Rue Umbra shows me His face. Until He Who Created Everything bestows upon me the gift of His Holy visage.

"Master Hezekiah ... the Artifact is ready."

"Bring it to me, Jocasta. I will view it here in my chambers."

"Yes, Master."

I rise and swing my legs out of bed, and am startled briefly by my reflection in the bureau mirror. For it seems at first that I am someone—*something*—else; someone/something alien, with a gray, rumpled body and a face that is smooth like glass. Then it is gone and I see only myself: the green scales, the angled brow, the tired eyes of the High Priest of Samara.

At length Jocasta re-enters the room and places the box on the rug at my feet. "It is my hope—*our* hope, Master, the entire congregation's—that you will end your fast soon. May Rue Umbra light your way."

He moves to leave but hesitates, pausing in the doorway. "It is also hoped ... that you will be careful. This so-called Artifact—it is not of this world."

Then he is gone and I am alone with the box, the box containing the meteor which has somehow survived its entry into our atmosphere. The hollow meteor with the strange runes printed on its surface (at least, that is how it has been described to me). The thing whose existence is responsible for my crisis of faith.

Show me, Oh Highest One. Send me a sign. Reveal to me, your faithful servant, the naked face of God.

But Rue Umbra is silent as I open the box and lift out the Artifact, and proceed to examine it by the dim light of the candles. Nor is the object so unfathomable as I'd presumed: for it is clearly something designed to protect the head, similar in many respects to our Centurions' helmets (although charred and blackened from its journey through the atmosphere) and composed of materials I have never seen; some of which glow at the touch of my fingers and cause the Artifact to hum and to vibrate ...

Show me your face, Oh Lord, so that I may believe again!

But in the end there is nothing, only silence, as a glassy shield lowers smoothly and locks into place. As I stare into its curved, indigo-blue surface—which has become a kind of looking glass, a mirror—and see only myself, Hezekiah. Only the High Priest of Samara laid low by his fast.

Something is wrong. This much is clear as I stir from the vision and find the diver shaking—shaking as though it might fly apart any moment. *Zebra One,* meanwhile, is talking at me through my headset:

... get it back. We're trying ... but ... long shot. Repeat: we have ... return mirror. It's just ...

Again, damn you! You're breaking up. What about the mirror?

... has failed. We are trying—

But they are gone—and I am alone. Alone against the ergosphere, whose end must surely be near. Alone—in light of the mirror's failure— against the event horizon, beyond which lies Hell itself.

I pause, feeling it again. As though someone were in the cave with me, as though someone were watching.

I look to the mouth of the cavern, beyond which the snow continues to fall. No, it is nothing—the wind, perhaps, coursing through the opening.

I return to my work, continuing the stroke which will complete our leader (his snout blue with war paint, his shoulders broad and hairy), knowing he will be pleased. For I have captured him in truth—as well as the spirit of his hunt— captured him so that he might live for all time. And yet, as the winds moan and the torches falter, the feeling I am not alone persists, so that I again look to the door of the cave, and this time—someone is there.

The hominid doesn't move, doesn't seem to breathe, as I look at him, and for an instant I think, *Dr. Livingstone, I presume.* Then I laugh a little behind my visor, marveling that I can do so under the circumstances, and take a step forward, eliciting a growl from the creature I would not want to hear twice.

I hold, looking back at the diver—which is suspended nose-down in the middle of the air— before turning again to regard the creature and his art ... only to find them gone, replaced by a very old man in what appears to be a Tudor-style study parlor.

"Livingstone, Einstein, Hezekiah, we've been them all, at one time or another." He begins moving toward me, casually. "You are ... Diver 7. I presume."

I just look at him, saying nothing. Behind him is a blackboard which runs floor to ceiling and wall to wall, and is crowded with equations. Noticing my gaze, he says, "Ah, yes. Well. The hominid has his work, and I have mine."

He stops within a few feet of me, examining my flight suit. "Your helmet. You won't be needing it."

I look at him for what seems a long time. At last I reach up and trigger the visor, which glides up and out of the way, and take a deep breath. The air is fine.

"Where am I?" I ask, glancing about the room, noting its exotic décor: a red, cactus-like plant (without needles) which looks as though it belongs at the bottom of an alien sea; a black and silver obelisk the height of a man; a polished suit of armor standing sentinel in a corner. "And who are you?"

The old man smiles, warmly, compassionately. "I should have thought you'd have guessed. As for where, why, you're stone cold dead in the middle of a blue hole. Where else? The mirrors, alas, have failed—but you knew that already. No, what you really want to know is … what does it all mean? The Hole, the visions, everything. Isn't that right, Diver 7?"

I look at the old man expectantly.

"Beats the hell out of me," he says, and moves toward the blackboard. "A blue hole is where mathematics go to die. No. What I have left is only conjecture, speculation—metaphysics rather than physics, notes as opposed to a complete script." He puts his hands on his hips, examining his formulas, and exhales, warily. "Of the trail of ink there is no end."

At length he begins moving again, pacing beyond the red plant and the black and silver obelisk, past the suit of armor which gleams like gold in the umber firelight. "Say, just say, for the sake of argument, that the Buddhists are right, and that reincarnation is real. And that its purpose is to evolve souls, to grow them—from the first spark of sentience to something approaching divinity. Would you allow that this was a worthy end to our travails?"

I don't say anything, only continue to watch him.

"Say, too, that these incarnations are infinite, or nearly so, occurring not just in this universe but a *multiverse,* so that, in time, we have experienced creation from every window and every door, every viewpoint—in short, we have been everyone and everything. *Mmm?* Shall we say it?"

He stops and turns around, begins pacing back toward me. "And that, as we reach the point of infinite progression, we begin to, slide, if you will, back and forth amongst our lifetimes—putting the lesson together, as it were, making of it a sphere, rather than a line, compressing everything into an infinitely dense mass, an Alpha and Omega, a singularity such as is found in the heart of our blue hole. Would you say then that we had solved the riddle of its phantasmagorias?"

He pauses not three feet away and I just look at him: the tired eyes, the deep wrinkles and crow's feet—at last, I understand.

I lift off my helmet.

"I was you, once," I say. "We were ... We will ..."

He nods, slowly. "Not only us but all men, all sentient beings. Nothing is wasted."

My mind reels. "But ... The Hole. My diver. It took those things to—"

He laughs suddenly. "Oh, that. Why, that's just a happy coincidence. You still don't understand, do you? You never needed the ship, or the vortex. You—we—were ready. Our infinite progression had reached—"

"Madness," I say. "Shadows within shadows."

But he is gone, replaced by Hezekiah. "It's the shadows that exist," he says, and I understand him perfectly in spite of his alien tongue. "The objects that create them; those are the illusions. Put another way: The ghost is real—the machine is not. Now—it is time."

And I am back in the cave, standing so close to the hominid I can smell him, watching him rub chalk on the stone, watching him create entire worlds. Until he looks at me sidelong and hands me the tool—thoughtfully, knowingly—as if he were encouraging me. As if he were saying: *You too can do it. You, too, are the Creator.*

Until I close my fingers on the chalk and everything fades to black.

And that blackness becomes Light.

I am become the White Fountain, the creator of worlds—the Big Bang which will expand outward, creating a new universe. Nor has the previous universe ceased to exist; for it dreams behind us on the other side of the Hole—its galaxies and star systems safely intact, its sentience growing by leaps and bounds.

Meanwhile, even amidst the crash and swirl of creation, I have remained—the godhead of an entirely new paradigm; the observer, and yet, somehow, the observed; the ghost in the rapidly expanding machine. Nor has every vestige of my former self been annihilated; for something has survived the explosion which even now hurtles outward into the maelstrom, spinning, tumbling, drifting ever further. For a billion years, it drifts, until, caught by a mid-size world's gravitational pull, it falls like a shooting star into an alien sea— a sea as red as blood—whereupon, again, it *drifts.*

Until it is retrieved from the water by a pair of eager hands—four-fingered hands—which grip the helmet firmly and place it into the boat, after which it is passed from one being to the other like the physical manifestation of a riddle, and finally put into a box.

Where it will remain—its secrets safe, its numeral '07' unseen—until delivered to the priest.

"What'd you think?" I asked the bouncer—a gargantuan brother named Pinky; I didn't ask—on the way out, even as the jukebox began to play and the room began to return to normal, meaning loud.

"Hmph," he hmphed, staring straight ahead, keeping an eye on the boys in the **MAGA** hats. "I think you're lucky to be getting out of here alive."

"That's live comedy," I said—a little dickishly, now that I remember it. "It's no country for snowflakes. This brother brings it."

Call it a manic response to the thrill of the kill—because that's precisely what I'd done, killed it—though not so manic that I didn't ask him for an escort to my car.

He lingered, seeming pensive, as I got in and started the engine—enough so that I rolled down my window and asked him, "You really didn't like it, did you?"

He shrugged his massive shoulders. "My job is to spot trouble and eliminate it. Not to stir it up. But I do think ... you said you were from New York?"

"I live there, that's right. Going home to visit family. Thought I'd line up some gigs along the way."

The man laughed a little. "That's right. You mentioned that in your routine. 'Haven't left my borough since those Mexicans flew them planes into the towers'—that was good."

I looked at him expectantly, wanting to know what it was he thought.

"Oh. It's just that ... Well, you should get out of New York more. See the country. Be good for your comedy."

I wasn't sure how to take that. "Yeah. Well. Keep an eye on those rednecks. At least until I'm down the road?"

He nodded as I put the car in gear. "There won't be any more trouble. That I can guarantee."

I gave him the Peace sign.

And then I was off—into the Kentucky night which sweated and lay silent across the fields. Into a damp fog which reminded me of New York—and was at the same time completely foreign.

It didn't take long to start comparing the bucolic beauty of the state by day, with its rolling horse farms and verdant, bluegrass pastures, with its indistinctiveness at night. It was like driving anywhere, even upstate New York (except for the complete lack of other vehicles and the plethora of Donald Trump campaign signs, which seemed to stand sentinel in every other field). To tell the truth, I was beginning to nod off when a headlight appeared in my rear-view mirror—just one, a motorcycle, maybe, or a car with a burned-out lamp—and began closing the distance between us. It's funny because I remember thinking distinctly that it was moving too fast—a cop, maybe—which bore out quickly as the little sun grew—resolving itself, at length, into the working headlamp of a dirty 4x4 pickup. A pickup now tailgating me at sixty-five miles-per-hour.

You got anything else to say, Lib-tard? Maybe you've got something to say about my girlfriend. Don't be shy. I'm sure we all want to hear it.

I thought that was your wingman.

Keep talking ...

There was a pronounced jolt as the bumper of the truck hit my car, hard enough that it skewed a little on the damp pavement, and my heart leapt into my throat. Jesus, was it possible? It had been two hours since that exchange, two hours and a junction, there was no way—

Again the bumpers collided, and again there was a jolt.

Tell her you're sorry.

The truck veered into the oncoming lane suddenly, accelerating, and I was forced to do likewise—I didn't want them beside me. Didn't want to know if they had weapons or not. Didn't want—

Who? Your service animal? Or its mother?

I floored it as the truck's battered quarter panel appeared outside my open window, hoping the little Camry's V6 would open up, hoping it had more power than it seemed. It did—and I launched forward, causing the front of the truck to slide back, and the scenery to blur past with dizzying speed. I recall slapping the steering wheel like a pimply kid in his first car. *Eat my dust, suckers! I'll see you in Hell!*

But the old pickup only roared forward like a rocket, instantly drawing alongside. That was the moment, of course. The moment I realized just how much trouble I was in. For what I saw outside my window was not just some car full of idiots. Rather, it was like something from a horror movie— *Duel,* maybe, of fucking *Birth of a Nation.* What I saw outside my window was a truck full of hooded men—like KKK members, only wearing brown instead of white—like scarecrows having sprung to life from the fields. Or executioners.

There were six of them in total, more than had been present in the bar (not that it mattered, they would have rounded up others, I was sure). The important thing is that it *was* them—

the MAGA crew—of that I had little doubt. Three of them were crowded into the cab while three others rode in the payload—all of them wearing crudely-stitched burlap hoods—and each brandishing some form of weapon, whether that meant a pistol or a rifle or a rusty pitchfork. The truck, meanwhile, was right out of central casting—I'd seen others like it in the red states I'd already passed through. You've seen them too: those jacked-up tanks with the huge tires and pig-ear smokestacks (their way of saying "fuck you" to the environmentalists), and the twin flags crackling in their payloads—usually an American and a "Don't Tread on Me," but sometimes a bona fide Confederate Southern cross, which is what this one had, along with one I couldn't clearly see. All I can say for certain is that the men in the back put down their weapons as I watched and appeared to fiddle with something in the payload—I really couldn't say because I had to look away in order to focus on the road.

Meanwhile it didn't exactly surprise me to see that I—we—were going about 90 miles-per-hour—the fastest I'd ever traveled in a moving vehicle, and a speed at which the Camry had become dangerously unstable. I thought then of my decision when I was young to never own a firearm, and laughed a little at my own expense. Only then (and how I'd managed to not think of it until that instant remains a mystery) did it finally occur to me: my bloody phone was right there on the passenger seat!

The truck's engine roared and its flags crackled as I snatched the thing up and dialed 911, putting it on speaker so that I might better focus on the road, not to mention re-grip the wheel firmly in both hands.

A moment later it came: "911, what's the address of your emergency?"

I stammered and babbled before managing, "Old State Route 51—yes—Old State Route 51, between Danville and Tomlinson. I'm being pursued by a truck full of masked men, h-heavily armed. Let me repeat that; they are heavily arm—"

"What is the make and model of the truck?"

I glanced out the window. "I—I don't know. A Ford, maybe. Yes, a Ford, I'm certain of it. It's dark green and has flags flying from the back. One of them's a Confederate. I—"

I noticed movement and focused on the man nearest me—by the window in the truck's passenger seat—saw him training his pistol on, on ...

My tire. My fucking front tire!

I let off the gas immediately and slowed down before veering into the lane behind them, even as the operator asked calmly, "Are you able to see the license number? If so, read it to me—as carefully as you can. Are they Kentucky plates?"

I was distracted by the men in the payload, who appeared to be lifting something heavy, but quickly focused on the plate. "Yes. Kentucky 527 CXS, Franklin County." I squinted in the fog. The lettering didn't look right. "I—I think it's been altered. I'm following as close as I dare, and it looks like—"

"You are behind them?"

"Yes. One of them was—"

"Sir, be advised that units are on the way and that you are not to pursue. Repeat, do not pursue. Pull over immediately and wait for officers to arrive. What is the make and model of your vehicle?"

"I—it's a blue Toyota—a Camry. 2004, I think. I'm—I'm slowing down. But so are they. There's men in the payload. It, it almost ..."

I was about to say that it looked like they were lifting, well, a trough, to be frank, one of those big aluminum vats used to water horses, when the men heave-hoed the thing twice ... and sent its contents hurling toward my windshield. At which point the thick, viscous stuff hit the glass like a hammer—exploding everywhere—and turned the world black.

Black and blood red.

I must have waited there on the shoulder of the road for an hour, at least, during which time I fetched a road flare from the trunk—the closest thing I had to a weapon, sadly—as well as the 5-gallon plastic gas can (which was full, like the Camry's tank, because the car's fuel gauge didn't work), although as to why I grabbed it I can't really say. Maybe I just wanted it close so I could refuel quickly if it became necessary. Maybe I already had some divination of an outcome—whether I was consciously aware of it or not.

What I *was* certain of is that no cops had shown up, nor whirred past through the fog with their lights flashing chaotically, in the entire time I'd been waiting. Likewise, my phone had remained silent—as if my call for help had simply fallen through the cracks, or never happened at all. One thing, for sure, *had* happened: a trough full of blood—animal blood, presumably—had been hurled at my windshield, and it had made one hell of a mess, a mess the worn wipers had been inadequate to clear, thus I'd had to clean the glass manually with wiper fluid and a towel.

I waited another five minutes before tentatively buckling my seatbelt and starting the car, peering down the road intensely, seeking any sign of the truck. It looked clear. Even the fog had lifted somewhat.

At last I edged onto the road, picking up speed gradually, using my blinker, which gave me a little laugh, increasing to 55 miles-per-hour. A portion of my act came unbidden to my mind—I was looking for what could have motivated them to murder, I suppose, beyond merely insulting someone's girlfriend—the Cavalcade of Clichés, I called it. It was the portion of the act where I'd recite, in rapid-fire succession, every bad joke anyone had ever told on a subject: in this case, Southerners. Rednecks.

What's the difference between Virginia and West Virginia? In Virginia, Moosehead is a beer. In West Virginia it's a misdemeanor.

How can you tell if a redneck is married? There are tobacco spit stains on both sides of his truck.

What can a pizza do that a redneck can't? Feed a family of four.

It was all pretty innocuous stuff, hardly anything to go to war over. And yet there had been a moment—just before my confrontation with the heckler—a moment that had struck me as strange, even by Bible Belt standards. It had occurred just after I'd segued into a semi-serious bit on Civil War monuments and social justice—a bit in which I'd gone so far as to defend the Antifa protestors who'd toppled the Silent Sam statue at Chapel Hill. I remembered it clearly because the room had fallen absolutely silent—so silent I heard the big bouncer—Pinky, God bless him—say, and I mean softly, "Move on."

Don't get me wrong. I was used to this sort of response when I challenged audience expectations. Indeed, had I been anywhere else—a college town, say—I would have been pontificating on the evils of political correctness—if for no other reason that when it comes to making an audience more malleable, a little cognitive dissonance can go a long way. But this felt as though I'd committed a real breach, had somehow touched on something I didn't and couldn't understand—and, moreover, had done so perhaps from a position of pure malice. Either way, the trouble had started almost immediately after, and, although I'd rebounded by show's end—some might even say spectacularly— with a flurry of region-specific crowd pleasers, I never got the sense that I'd been forgiven for what I'd said.

I listened in near silence as the radials droned against the surface of the road.

Or, Bright Boy—they were just a bunch of racist pieces of shit. I mean, surely that was possible, in the *fucking South?* Yes—even in 2019?

Forget it, I told myself, as the fog continued to lift and it became clear the truck was gone. It's over.

Whatever it had been.

It would be difficult to describe just how close they'd come to killing us all—how little time I'd had to yank the wheel and hit the brakes in those first awful seconds after they'd shot from the sideroad. All I know for certain is that I ended up facing in the opposite direction—even while they careened into the trees on the other side of the road ... where they quickly reversed, massive tires spinning, and narrowly missed me yet again—for I'd stepped on the gas and chirped out of their way.

And then we were right back where we'd started (only traveling in the opposite direction), piling down Old State Route 51 with our vehicles side by side and the truck's chrome stacks belching black smoke into the night. And I saw in the vespertine darkness what I couldn't have seen before—which was the flag previously blocked to me snapping and crackling in the wind. And I saw, too, that it was identical and yet radically different, for its colors were black, red, and green, and this filled me with a terror I could not define—in part because the combined colors felt alien and yet familiar, and in part because its very existence made of me an illiterate. Made me question if I knew anything beyond my borough in New York at all.

Not that I had time to dwell on it, for when next I glanced at the truck and its occupants I saw that the man in the passenger seat and the men in the payload had, all of them, pointed their firearms at me.

What I did next surprised even myself, for I sideswiped them without even thinking about it, and such was the impact that one of the men toppled from the payload and fell face-first into my window—where the whites of his eyes shown wide through the eyeholes of his hood—before he fell against the rushing pavement with a sickening slap-crunch and was instantly gone behind us. And then they were veering into *me*—although by intention or loss of control I couldn't possibly say—and I very nearly careened from the road—and yet, somehow, did not.

That was the moment, I think. The moment I knew what I was going to do. It was also the moment that the man in the truck's passenger seat shot clean through the door into my leg, spattering the upholstery with blood, and making me feel as if I might black out any second.

It's funny, because the gas can was in my hand and its lid taken off before I'd even consciously decided to grab it, nor did I hesitate before hurling it into the truck's cab and reaching for the road flare—which I quickly managed to uncap while driving and swipe against its striker. Then the Camry's interior filled with orange-white light and I threw the thing—threw it with everything I had, and before I even knew if I'd gotten it into the truck the Ford's cab exploded into something like the sun.

And then we were both skittering out of control, the burning truck toward the left shoulder and I toward the right, and the last thing I thought of before everything went black was how little things had changed in the fifty-two years I'd walked the planet. How little things had changed since Jesse Washington and Mary Turner and Emmett Till and James Chaney. Since Martin Luther King. Since 1981 and Michael Donald.

"Wake up, Yankee."

A voice in the blackness. A rich voice, a radio voice. A voice I had heard before.

"I'm not going to tell you again, New York. Wake up. I got something to tell you."

I opened my eyes, slowly, realizing my entire body had gone numb. The speaker's face swam into focus.

"I guess you're not feeling so smart now—are you?"

It would be hard to say what I noticed first, the fact that half his face was gone and that his brain was partially exposed, or that he was training a pistol on me, or that I knew him—had known him since before starting my act. All I know is that I recognized him immediately and that he was perfectly correct: I *didn't* feel very smart ... didn't feel much of anything now that the Camry and I were sort of one big casserole and the big bouncer was glaring at me from just outside my window.

"You—you *really* didn't like it, did you?" I gurgled—and laughed suddenly, causing a fit of convulsive coughing.

"Smart to the end, I guess," he said, and coughed a little himself, bringing up blood. I looked to where his head had been nearly cleaved in two. "What's gray and black and red all over?"

"Shut up and listen."

"Your brain," I said.

He jammed the muzzle of the gun against my forehead. "What's it feel like? Knowing you're going to where there ain't no God and there ain't no New York, just you and your Yankee friends, burning for what you did?"

I must have just looked at him.

"Knowing you pissed your life away telling jokes—while never once having stood for anything ... never once having sacrificed. What'd y'all think, that no negro served? That no negro ever died in that slaughter you called a war or bonded with his white brothers while defending his homeland?" He *hmphed,* something I found incredibly funny considering half his head was gone. "Maybe they didn't fight, but they were there—scouting, cooking, running supply—there when the battle against federal tyranny was joined, and there when it was lost. And they are here, now, in the bodies of their descendants—working as cops and dispatchers and magistrates; working as bouncers in roadside bars. And they will tolerate no more of the desecration of their ... Of their ..."

And then he was gone, just like that, the pistol tumbling and clattering against the ground, his body slumping unceremoniously out of sight. And it struck me that the 911 operator I had spoken to had almost certainly been one of them—not one of them in the truck, of course, but one of them in spirit—the unlikely sons of the confederacy. Or *something.*

And it struck me too that I would never know: no more than I would know why some people were convinced that Barack Obama or the U.N. or fucking Michael Moore were

coming for their guns or that a global conspiracy of patriarchs
ruled the world or that we were all being routinely poisoned
by chem trails—people built mythologies, it was what they did,
and more, was I any different? Hadn't I been equally
convinced that a group of drunken Trump fans had decided
to chase me down and kill me because they'd taken umbrage
with my act?

*You should get out of New York more. See the country.
Be good for your comedy.*

I laughed a little at that, tasting my own blood.

Get out of New York. Get out of our boroughs.

Oh vey.

Shouldn't we all.

"Meet you at the top!" Kerber hollered—cockily, as always—as he climbed rapidly past us. He gestured toward the cloud ceiling. "We'll leave a light on!"

Sean and Karen looked at each other as his balloon disappeared around the envelope of our own.

"Everything a competition," sighed Sean. There was a deafening roar as he toggled the blast valve. "Had to show us he could beat us on the ascent—even at night."

"Talk about that a little," I said, continuing to roll. "You mentioned that his balloon was different from yours. How so?" I nodded at Eddy, who moved the boom mic closer. "Just look out at the sky, Sean, not the camera."

He scratched at his beard and seemed to marshal his thoughts. "Well, he's running a gas balloon, not a hot-air vulcoon, which is what this is. A gas balloon uses gas instead of hot air for its lift, which is advantageous because you can stay up longer—a lot longer—and because it's so quiet. There's none of this," He toggled the blast valve again and there was a mighty roar as liquid propane vaporized and ignited. "So, on that level, they're extremely sought after. The problem is one of economy. Helium is *expensive.* Like, real expensive. Like five grand to fill a balloon expensive. So people use hydrogen—which, while relatively cheap, is also incredibly flammable. The *Hindenburg* was full of hydrogen, as is The *Excelsior.*"

He was referring, of course, to billionaire Ronald Trimp's promotional blimp—which, winds allowing, we'd be seeing when these balloons and others converged on the Super Bowl in the morning.

Sean looked at the camera awkwardly. "How was that?"

"That was good, Sean. Thanks." I stopped recording and ran the footage back—too far, to the point where the old Indian we'd encountered before takeoff was talking.

"They move," he said, gazing at the snow-smothered hills.

"T-they? The mountains? The mountains move?"

"Uh-huh. They fall from sky ... onto my land."

"Oh?"

He nodded. *"They move."*

I powered the camera down—there wouldn't be much to see until dawn, anyway—still thinking about his words. *They fall from the sky ... onto my land.*

"Wreckage from Jupiter 6?" prompted Eddy, noticing my expression. He was referring, of course, to the unmanned mission to the cloud planet, which had blown up in the earth's atmosphere immediately after its long journey home.

"Yeah. Maybe." I zippered my parka all the way up.

The two-way radio crackled to life. It was Kerber, calling from the other balloon. "West by northwest, you see that?"

It wasn't until Sean had turned on the spotlight and aimed it in that direction that what he was talking about became clear: for a kind of fog bank had rolled in seemingly out of nowhere—and was moving toward us at a shockingly rapid clip.

"Sean ... what is that?" I recall asking nervously.

But he didn't respond, at least not at first, and it took an elbow from Eddy to remind me why we were there in the first place.

I reactivated my camera. "Okay, folks. This is what reality TV's all about. Remember, we're not here."

I zoomed up on Sean's beard and focused as he toggled the mic.

"That's affirmative, *Gas Monkey,* we see it. Not sure we believe it, but we see it."

"The weather report said clear skies," cursed Karen, even as the radio crackled and Kerber came again: "It's nothing to worry about. A little thermal turbulence—*Gas Monkey* suggests letting it pass and carrying on."

I panned past Karen slowly enough to register her concerned expression before focusing on the approaching clouds, which bubbled and roiled and shown mauve-pink, like plumes of dry ice at a rock concert. Then they were upon us, reducing visibility dramatically and smelling faintly of ammonia.

"I'm not so sure," said Sean at last. Though I may have imagined it, it seemed there was a small quaver in his voice. *"Hot-air One* recommends seeing how thick it is before proceeding. Stand by."

"Negative, repeat negative on that. *Gas Monkey* will continue to ascend."

"Jesus Christ," hissed Sean, and released the mic.

I refocused on him, liking the way the purple fog rushed past him in the dark—

And something moved in that dark. Something like a giant scythe, which rose like a whale's pectoral fin breaching water and just as quickly vanished.

"Holy shit, what was that?" blurted Eddy, and jolted, his sudden movement rocking the basket.

Karen had seen it, too.

"Jesus, Sean, there's something out there ..."

"Something out—" He turned and looked into the mists, which bubbled and swirled, and I regained my senses enough to tape him as he did so.

"What'd it look like?" he asked, craning his neck to look up, then quickly cued his mic. *"Gas Monkey* this is *Hot-air One.* What's your altitude?"

"It wasn't them," said Karen.

"I repeat, *Hot-air One* to *Gas Monkey.* What is your present altitude?"

We all waited, shivering in the dark, and as we did so I zoomed up on Sean's face to capture his concern.

"It looked like a wing," Karen blurted suddenly.

He froze for a moment and didn't say anything. At last he looked from her to Eddy and then to me. "Ah. I see." He smiled suddenly and waved a finger. "You got me. Who's idea was it? *Hmmm,* let me guess ..." He looked back to Karen and was about to say something when there was a sound like a slab of meat hitting the concrete and he jolted abruptly and we all just froze, in part, I suppose, because we couldn't figure out what the massive, arrow-shaped thing that had suddenly materialized amongst us was. But then the blood dribbled from his mouth and Karen began screaming and I realized with horror that he'd in fact been impaled— impaled by some kind of spaded appendage, which uncurled in the mists even as I watched and was suddenly stretched taught—so that he was jerked from the basket with a sickening crunch and swung arms and legs akimbo into space.

That was the worst of it, I think, seeing him swung about like a ragdoll like that, and in such an empty void, his body rising and falling as though in slow-motion and his arms and legs flapping almost gracefully—even as the owner of that appendage passed through the beam of the spotlight and revealed itself in full.

In retrospect, I wish I'd continued recording, for what I saw in that instant is difficult to describe, even now. Suffice it to say that it had a body like that of a manta ray—upon who's tail the balloonist had been impaled—or a manta ray combined with a bat, albeit huge, and that it was covered with a kind of camouflage which reminded me of pictures I'd seen of Jupiter—just a roil of purples and pinks and browns. I suppose that was when it first hit me: the possibility that there might be a connection between this *thing* and the Jupiter 6 probe. That the probe might have brought something back, even if it had just been a sprinkling of microbes on its surface.

And then there was an explosion somewhere above us, the concussion of which rocked our balloon, and we all looked up to see *Gas Monkey*—my God, it was like the sun!—on fire; and yet that wasn't all we saw, for as it dropped it became evident that there were more of the bat/manta ray things attached, suckling it as it fell, crawling upon it like flies. Then it passed us like some kind of great meteor—its occupants shrieking and calling out—and was gone below, the heat of it still painting our faces, its awful smell, which was the smell of rotten eggs, filling our nostrils.

And then we were just drifting, all of us crouched low in the basket ... and the only sounds were those of Karen sobbing and my own pounding heart.

I'm not sure how much time passed, maybe five minutes, maybe twenty. All I know is that the sky had begun to lighten and that it was Eddy who spoke first, saying, "Hydrogen. They feed on hydrogen. We're safe."

I must have looked at him, because I remember clearly how pale he looked, how ill.

"Jupiter 6?" I said, although I already knew the answer.

"Why not?" He laughed a little to himself. "Cosmos. Carl Sagan. Hunters and floaters."

"Someone needs to toggle the propane," said Karen, absently, it seemed, as though she were a million miles away.

I looked at her to see a woman clearly in shock. "I'll do it. Okay? You—just relax." I looked at the apparatus for controlling the balloon. "The red lever?"

She nodded and sniffed, like a helpless little girl, and I climbed to my feet. Eddy grabbed my ankle.

"Wait. The cloud. Are we still in it?"

I scanned our surroundings. "Yes."

"Okay, toggle it and get back down. Quickly!"

I toggled it and got back down.

Quickly.

"What is it?" I asked.

"The cloud ... it's ... I think it's a form of camouflage. You know, like how octopuses squirt ink—but in this case it's to confuse their prey, not predators. Right? Okay. So that means as long as that cloud's there, we got trouble."

"But you said they—"

"Feed on hydrogen, that's right," he said. "But they don't *know* we're running on hot air—not yet."

"Which means—"

"Which means they're checking us out, right now."

I looked at the pink and purple clouds. "But wouldn't they have a way to, I don't know, *sense* when hydrogen is present?"

"I'm sure they do. Look, all I know is they just hit the jackpot with Kerber's gas balloon, and it looked a lot like ours, all right?"

"Right," I mumbled, seeing the truth of it. "And that's not our only problem."

"What do you mean?"

"I mean there's a giant meal called the *Excelsior* which could be hovering over the Super Bowl right now. Jesus. How many people does a stadium like that hold? 90,000? A hundred?"

No one said anything.

I climbed up and peeked over the basket's edge.

Sure enough, through a hole in the marmalade clouds, the stadium had come into view, shining like a north star and already crowded with balloons—including the *Excelsior.* I looked at the bullhorn in the corner of the basket, the one Sean had said he used to communicate with people on the ground. At least there was a way to warn the crowd—if and when we got there.

"The burner—it needs to be triggered again," said Karen, distantly. "And our altitude ... what is it?"

I looked at Eddy. The truth of it was, I was sort of hoping he'd take this one. But he only shook his head.

"Right," I sighed at last. "Okay. Is that the altimeter?" I gestured at the readout next to the burner valve.

Karen nodded.

"Okay—hold my beer."

And I counted to three.

What happened next happened very fast—so fast that I was unable to process the enormity of it until Eddy was long gone and so was most the floor, leaving us to dangle precariously as our feet sought the shattered plywood's edges and we hung onto the cold, chromed burner supports for life. For Karen had stood with me as I reached for the red propane valve (to check the altimeter herself, presumably) and thus been spared falling into nothing when one of the creature's knife-like tails penetrated the flooring—harpooning Eddy through his abdomen before jerking him clean through the plywood and dragging him screaming into the void.

But something else happened in that instant too, something which remains the single most terrifying aspect of the ordeal. For as we clung to the burner supports and tried to keep our feet on what was left of the floor, the head of one of the creatures darted from the fog—it was easily the size of a refrigerator laid on end—and just stopped: the tip of its nose all but touching my own and its huge eyes which were full of spirals regarding me with something like curiosity. Then it exhaled, blowing the hat off my head, and arced away into the mists, and as it went I felt a great rushing of wings as though a dozen others had suddenly abandoned their fascination with us and followed.

And then it was just us, Karen and I, gripping the burner supports and trying to keep our feet on what little remained to support them. And I knew that she knew we were safe now—at least from our Jovian hunters—but that we had a responsibility, too. For it was clear to both of us, I think, that the monsters had not merely lost interest but been *lured* away—by the promise of enough hydrogen to fill them all to bursting. By the promise of Ronald Trimp's leviathan blimp, which now loomed large in the slowly clearing mists.

By the time Karen had maneuvered us to a hard landing at the edge of the playing field, the first of the sword-tails were already circling the *Excelsior*—just circling and gliding, as though carefully sniffing the zeppelin out. As for myself, I knew we'd have but seconds before security responded— violently, I was sure—and so was scrambling with the bullhorn before the balloon's envelope had even fully deflated. I only remember that the thing was heavier and louder than I'd expected, and for the latter, at least, I was profoundly grateful.

"Ladies and gentlemen, I'm going to ask you all to get up and proceed to the nearest exits. Please don't panic, just do it now and in an orderly fashion."

But they did panic, almost instantly, probably because someone had already noticed the sword-tails, and the next thing I knew there was a sea of humanity crushing toward the exits even as the security staff ran at me across the field and the first explosion rocked the arena.

"Get on the ground!" I recall someone shouting in the instants before I was piledrived, and then I was literally seeing stars as the heavyset men piled on and at least one of them started kicking me in the ribs.

"Jesus, look up!" Karen shouted, and when I rolled over on my side I saw that she had leapt atop one of the men's backs and was forcibly lifting his head.

To the purple-pink sky and the soaring Jovian hunters. To the massive, dark-skinned zeppelin which was already on fire and continued to explode as additional cells were ignited.

And then I was free, they'd clambered off me at last, and I struggled for breath while still curled up on the Astroturf even as great chunks of burning wreckage began to reign down all around and Karen tried to help me to my feet. And yet even amidst all that it occurred to me: my camera might still be in the ruins of the balloon (for I'd placed it on a shelf below the bulwark right after the *Gas Monkey* had exploded). And the next thing I knew I was searching for and finding it and triggering the record button, pausing only to look at Karen over the viewfinder as she let go of my arms at last and began shaking her head.

"I—I've got a kid, if no longer a husband," she said, the tears streaming down her face. "I can't stay here."

"I know," I remember saying—as gently as I could under the circumstances. "Go. I'll be all right."

And then she smiled almost motherly—and was gone across the wreckage-littered field.

It didn't take long for what remained of the *Excelsior* to come crashing down, its great, bullet-shaped envelope almost completely burned away and its interior girders warping and melting. Nor did the hydrogen-eaters abandon it even then, but continued to draw sustenance from it as their abdominal sacs swelled and their manta ray/bat wings beat furiously and their eyes seemed to spiral like the storms of Jupiter itself.

As for myself, I'd retreated to the relative safety of a roofed area near the dugout, where I continued to record as the now-gorged hunters at last began to rise ... and in very short order disappeared into a cloud of their own making.

And then—finally—it was over, and I could only stare at the ruins of the *Excelsior* as a few survivors stumbled from the smoke and swirling particulate—at which instant I awakened as if from a dream and hurried to assist them.

I was helping an elderly woman get back on her feet when I first heard the gasps and expressions of surprise happening all around us. Nor did it take long to figure out what they were responding to, for when I followed their collective gaze to the blue-gray sky I saw two enormous creatures rising into the clouds—*huge* creatures, as big as mountains, shaking off avalanches of snow with each undulating breath, pulsing upward like man-of-wars in water.

And I remembered the old Indian.

They fall from sky ... onto my land.

And knew nothing would ever be the same.

DEATH GRADER

Statement of Ms. Eleanor "Elle" Westbrook (January 17th, 3:30 PM, interviewed by Detective Ollie Rowe)

Detective Rowe: I want you to relax, Ms. Westbrook—is it okay if I call you Eleanor?

Westbrook: I prefer Elle.

Detective Rowe: Elle. Now I want you to relax ... and tell me about the first time you saw the road grader actually move. Can you do that for me?

Westbrook: Sure. It was the day after Christmas—the 26th, I think. It was a Thursday. I remember it because, well, besides the grader moving for the first time, it was movie night in the community room. *Frozen II.* Which—

Detective Rowe: At Farmington Hall. The orphanage. Is that correct?

Westbrook: Yes, but—we don't call it that. An orphanage, that is. The nuns don't like it.

Detective Rowe: But you were home?

Westbrook: Yes. In my room. I'd had a terrible nightmare and was just waking up, when I heard—

Detective Rowe: Talk about that a little. Your nightmare. Do you remember it?

Westbrook: No. Not really. Just bits and pieces. I remember ...

Detective Rowe: Yes?

Westbrook: I remember ... it had the road grader in it. And it—it killed somebody. It ran over him with its front tires and then ...

Detective Rowe: Yes?

Westbrook: I'd rather not say.

Detective Rowe: But I'm asking you to, Elle. It's okay. It ran over him with its front tires and ...?

Westbrook: And then it dropped that big plow it has.

Detective Rowe: The moldboard. The blade it uses to grade the roads.

Westbrook: (inaudible)

Detective Rowe: I'm going to ask you to speak clearly and not just nod, okay? We're recording.

Westbrook: Yes, sir. That one. The big one. It—it dropped it right on him. And then I heard it strike the ground ... I mean, the pavement under the snow.

Detective Rowe: So it—look, I know how difficult this must be, considering ... So it passed clean through him, is that it?

Westbrook: (inaudible)

Detective Rowe: No nodding. Okay. What then?

Westbrook: He opened up. Like ... like a can of spaghetti.

Detective Rowe: (inaudible) Okay. I can see you're upset by this. Let's switch gears a bit. Did you recognize this—this man? You did say it was a he. Was it somebody you recognized from your real life? Your waking life?

Westbrook: No.

Detective Rowe: I see. And you're sure about that?

Westbrook: Yes. Positive. The grader was looking for someone to kill—when the man stumbled out of that bar on 4th Street, the one where all the homeless people hang out.

Detective Rowe: And where were you, in your dream, that is?

Westbrook: That's what's so funny. Because I distinctly remember watching the grader approach from the sidewalk, which was covered in snow. Just standing there, right outside the bar. And yet when I saw him killed I was inside the cab, looking down through the glass. At one point I was even way up above it—the grader, that is—like, like God. I guess I was sort of everywhere and nowhere, if that makes any sense.

Detective Rowe: Yes. Yes, it does. Okay. That's good. That's very good. Thank you. Let's go back now—to when you first saw it move. Is that all right?

Westbrook: Sure. Like I said, I'd just woken up from the dream when I heard it, just rumbling across the field where they'd been working on the road—

Detective Rowe: The I-890-North Schenectady Corridor.

Westbrook: Sure, I guess. So I went to my window—you know, to see what was going on, and saw it sputtering to a stop near the office trailers and other equipment—which were all covered in snow—just shutting down with a rattle, like it had been running for a long time. That's when I first noticed it, how clean it was—there was no snow on it at all. Like—

Detective Rowe: But it was there when you went to sleep, isn't that correct?

Westbrook: Yes, of course. Covered in snow. It hadn't moved since December, when they had that accident—you know, where the worker was killed.

Detective Rowe: Clarke. The foreman. I seem to recall they had several accidents; including when they rammed into that layer of concrete.

Westbrook: (inaudible)

Detective Rowe: What?

Westbrook: The Meyers. James and Mia. That's where the concrete was at. I used to talk with them sometimes, before the accid—

Detective Rowe: You knew them?

Westbrook: Before the traffic accident. The one with the semi. Last summer.

Detective Rowe: Yes, I seem to recall that too. Something about them accelerating out of control—

Westbrook: I think *they* did it.

Detective Rowe: I'm sorry?

Westbrook: The bugs.

Detective Rowe: The ... *bugs.*

Westbrook: (inaudible): In the concrete. Where the Meyers buried them. At least, until the road grader came along.

Detective Rowe: (inaudible) I want you to hold that, okay? Hold that very thought. There's a psychiatrist coming, Ms. Daniels, a very nice lady, who's going to talk with you about all that—when we're finished, okay?

Westbrook: Okay.

Detective Rowe: Now, and this is important, so I want you to think about it very carefully. Did you at any point see anyone get out of the motor grader?

Westbrook: You already asked me that.

Detective Rowe: Once more—for the record. Please.

Westbrook: No. Like I said.

Detective Rowe: But it *was* dark, isn't that right? Dark, and snowing.

Westbrook: Yes, but not like later. The storm was just getting started.

Detective Rowe: I see. And then you went back to—

Westbrook: No.

Detective Rowe: You didn't go back to sleep? What did you do?

Westbrook: I went down to the community room, to tell Sister Bryant.

Detective Rowe: All right. And ... were they still watching the movie ... (inaudible) *Frozen II?*

Westbrook: No. All the girls had gone to bed. It was just Sister Bryant, who had fallen asleep on the couch.

Detective Rowe: Okay. And did you wake her up, to tell her what you had seen?

Westbrook: (inaudible)

Detective Rowe: I'm sorry?

Westbrook: No. She ... she never liked me. So I thought it was a bad idea.

Detective Rowe: Oh. So there was—bad blood between you?

Westbrook: I wouldn't say that. I was fine with her. She just ... didn't like me. I didn't drive the road grader over her—if that's what you mean. That was them.

Detective Rowe: The, ah ... bugs?

Westbrook: Yeah. The ghosts of them. Their bodies are still in the cement.

Detective Rowe: I see. Okay. And then?

Westbrook: I waited for her to wake up.

Detective Rowe: All right. And?

Westbrook: Which took about an hour—I guess, maybe less—I was watching the news. Then she woke up ... and I told her all about it. About the machine.

Detective Rowe: About the grader. Okay. And what did she say?

Westbrook: She didn't believe me, not even for a second. So I led her to the window and we looked out, and sure enough, the snow had re-covered it—the entire road grader. It had even refilled its tracks.

Detective Rowe: I imagine that didn't go over so well.

Westbrook: No. And I got the switch for it. Which is why I didn't mention it again—to anybody—not even when the reports of people finding body parts in the snow started coming out. Of course I knew what was going on because I saw the grader leave every night—after which I would always dream it had killed someone. And then it would just rattle back and park itself, usually about 11 pm.

Detective Rowe: You were alone.

Westbrook: Yeah. But what's new.

Detective Rowe: And you knew something had to be done. At least that's what you told me earlier.

Westbrook: Sure—if I wasn't imaging everything.

Detective Rowe: And you decided you had to get closer. To inspect it yourself.

Westbrook: Yeah. The day after New Years. The day after they found the Smythe lady all chopped up in quarters.

Statement of Ms. Eleanor "Elle" Westbrook (January 17th, 5:30 PM, interviewed by Doctor Regina Daniels)

Dr. Daniels: So after you trudged through the snow and reached the road grader—and that must have been quite a task on January 2nd, when there was so much accumulation—you say you used a broom to clean off the moldboard—is that correct?

Westbrook: That big blade, yeah. That's when I noticed the blood—just splashed all over it like dried blackberry syrup. But there was something else, too, which was sort of draped over the plow like a garland, all shiny and pink.

Dr. Daniels: (inaudible) What on earth was it?

Westbrook: Oh, It was an intestine, though how it got on top of the plow I have no idea. All I know is I wanted to run away after that—as far away as I could, farther even than Farmington Hall—and would have ... if not for the voices.

Dr. Daniels: The voices. Coming from—where, exactly?

Westbrook: Oh, everywhere. And nowhere. Coming from my head. But also from the road grader—from its cab. Like there were people inside—little people, I thought, I don't know why—all talking at the same time. Like they were arguing.

Dr. Daniels: My goodness. Well. That must have been extremely frightening. What on earth did you do?

Westbrook: I wanted to run, like I said—

Dr. Daniels: Yes, I can see why—

Westbrook: But I didn't, because it seemed to be drawing me in, toward itself—the cab, that is. Like a big magnet. Not only that, but there was a weird light inside—not a bright light, like in a house, but sort of a fog, like those pictures you see of distant galaxies, just sort of a green smear. And the next thing I knew I had opened the hatch and climbed in and the door had slammed shut—which made me jump—and they started talking, just, addressing me directly, as plain and clear as you are now.

Dr. Daniels: Oh, my goodness ... And—and what did they say?

Westbrook: They—they told me that they needed my help. That they were getting too weak to move the grader but that their work wasn't finished and that much infestation remained. That if I helped them they would ... they would spare me. And then they began saying other things, most of which I didn't understand—only the tone, which was hateful. And then I did run, although I had difficulty with the door and banged my hand up real good.

Dr. Daniels: I *see* that.

Westbrook: But it didn't matter because I just had to get away. Because, you see, the whole terrible truth had become clear to me in that instant, clear by a kind of mind transfer, how the grader had cracked the concrete in which the aliens' ship was interred and freed their spirits—despite the Meyers' best effort to contain them—how its owner had been influenced to paint the thing black and write "Black Betty" on its frame (before later using it to run over his co-workers and finally to kill himself), even how they—the aliens, the bugs—had come to be here in the first place! And I couldn't take it— just couldn't take it—and ran through the snow straight back to Farmington, up to my bed, where I stayed all eve and most the next day, refusing to come down—even when they handed out the ice skates for our excursion the next night. Even when they picked the teams for the game at which Sister Bryant was—where Sister Bryant was, oh! Oh! (inaudible)

Dr. Daniels: *Shhh.* It's okay. Everything is okay. Let's just—I think that will be all for today. All right? You must be exhausted.

Westbrook: (inaudible) But it isn't okay. Because the fact is, Sister Bryant is dead. Worse, she's been ... oh, it's too horrible. And although you won't come out and say it ... you think I did it. Don't you?

Dr. Daniels: That's not for me to decide, Elle.

Westbrook: (inaudible) But you have decided— I can see it in your face. And not just for Sister Bryant ... but all of them. I wonder: has it ever occurred to you that I might have saved lives by doing what I did? That I might have even stopped the killing? (inaudible) No? Well, maybe you'll think about that the next time. Goodnight, Ms. Daniels.

Dr. Daniels: Goodnight, Elle. Try to sleep well.

Statement of Ms. Eleanor "Elle" Westbrook (January 18th, 3:30 PM, interviewed by Detective Ollie Rowe)

Detective Rowe: Okay. So. You say you had a plan from the instant you woke up—is that correct?

Westbrook: Yes, sir, since the moment Sister Bryant announced the hockey game—even though I pretended not to notice.

Detective Rowe: That would be the hockey game at Fenrow Park, next to Deep Lake—isn't that correct?

Westbrook: Yes, sir.

Detective Rowe: Which is why you returned to where the road grader was parked at on the eve of January 3rd, 2019, and proceeded to board it. Is that right?

Westbrook: Yes, that's right, at which time they began to speak to me just as before—the bugs, you understand—and told me to place my hands on the controls (the keys were still in it!), and that they would guide me from that point on—like a puppet, I suppose, or a marionette. For what they needed more than anything was my musculature, my bone and tendon, to drive the grader they had previously driven only with their minds. And I told them with my thoughts that I knew where many infestations could be killed all at once (for that's how they view us, as infestations, as a kind of cancer of the Earth; a *disease*) and we moved out, the black grader rattling and rumbling, belching plumes of smoke— its work lights winking on. Nor was it long before—

Detective Rowe: You came to Fenrow Park.

Westbrook: Yes. Because it's close to Farmington Hall. And I saw the lights almost immediately—the lights Sister Bryant had rented to light the game—and her, too, trudging through the snow toward the restrooms, bundled up like an Eskimo. And before I knew it the grader had accelerated toward her even though I tried to fight it and chased her all the way into the building, where it smashed into the masonry like a wrecking ball.

Detective Rowe: But she made it, did she not? Made it into the restrooms.

Westbrook: Oh, yes. Thank God. But then the gears started shifting and we were backing up—way up—not backing up and stopping, mind you, but backing up and launching forward again, circling around, so that we were parallel to the front of the building.

Detective Rowe: But, why? Why would you—why would they do that, Elle?

Westbrook: I didn't know! At least, not until the blade changed its orientation and became vertical—something I didn't even know it could do. Looking back I understand; it was going to shave off the front of the building. But then Sister Bryant stuck her head out (to see if it was clear, I suppose) and the gas pedal sunk to the floor, and we launched at her so fast that I didn't even realize what the bugs intended until the blade struck her neck and—and ...

Detective Rowe: And what, Elle? You must go on ...

Westbrook: And ... I don't want to. You know very well what happened after that.

Detective Rowe: I saw the aftermath, yes. If that's what you mean. But in fact, I don't know what happened; that's the point of all this. Now answer the question, please. What happened after the grader struck Sister Bryant?

Westbrook: (inaudible) I don't want ...

Detective Rowe: *What happened?*

Westbrook: She ... her ...

Detective Rowe: Tell me, you little monster! *What happened to Sister Bryant?*

Westbrook: *She was decapitated, okay?* The blade struck her in the neck and she was split like a cantaloupe and her head flew off and bounced off the blocks of the men's room and she ended up with blood all over her clean white habit and one eye staring up at us from the snow, okay? Are you happy now? Is that what you wanted to hear?

Detective Rowe: I want to hear the truth! I want to hear how a 15 year-old girl became a mass murderer over the course of mere weeks, and how she learned to drive that grader, even to expertly maneuver its—

Westbrook: I told you ... it was *them. The bugs.* They were behind everything, not just the grader but the car, too, that car that killed all those people just a few years ago, the black '66, the original Black Betty—the one owned by James Meyers and before that, a man named Crowley. They *bond* with machines, you understand, moving machines, just like they had a bond with their spacecraft, the one that came to Earth in 1966 and which is buried in the cement where the Meyers' house used to be—the one whose magnetic field might have destroyed the planet if they hadn't—

Detective Rowe: Enough! Admit it: You killed all those people and Sister Bryant too, and then you tried to kill the girls playing hockey, your own neighbors at Farmington, other orphans just like you. That's why you steered the grader toward the frozen lake ...

Westbrook: I *steered* it toward the lake precisely to avoid that, knowing it would break the ice before it ever reached them, knowing it would sink to the very bottom! And knowing, too, that without a machine to possess the bugs would simply dissipate, that they would scatter on the wind, never to endanger anyone again. And that's exactly what happened after the grader fell through, moaning like a keeled ship, groaning like a dinosaur—I know because I felt them, screaming and bickering amongst themselves, furious that they had misplayed their hands, their slimy, green, locust's hands!

Detective Rowe: I've heard enough. Just—just get her out of here.

(inaudible)

Detective Rowe: Just go, take her to the juvenile detention center. Hurry up.

(inaudible)

Detective Rowe: Sure. Send her on in.

(inaudible)

Dr. Daniels: Detective Rowe?

Detective Rowe: Yes, please, come on in. Have a seat.

Dr. Daniels: (inaudible) I take it that didn't go very well.

Detective Rowe: On the contrary, it went almost exactly as expected. Jesus. Just ...

Dr. Daniels: I'd try not to dwell on it. It'll make you crazy yourself. Besides (inaudible), I was told to give you this. Read it. It'll give you something to focus on.

Detective Rowe: It's the report on that chunk of concrete. The one at the demolished Meyers residence. Looks like they cracked it open, finally ... and ...

(inaudible)

Dr. Daniels: What?

Detective Rowe: I don't know ... looks like they found something—unusual. Something big. Something made out of ...

Dr. Daniels: What?

Detective Rowe: That's just it. They don't know.

Dr. Daniels: Isn't that strange?

Detective Rowe: Yeah. Yeah, it is.

Dr. Daniels: You look tired. How long has it been since you slept?

Detective Rowe: I don't even remember. (inaudible) What do you say, nightcap at Mortimer's?

Dr. Daniels: That sounds positively heavenly.

Detective Rowe: It does, doesn't it? Oh, and more thing.

Dr. Daniels: What? What is it?

Detective Rowe: You're closer than me: Turn off that fucking tape recorder.

Dr. Daniels: Oh, that. (inaudible) Don't mind if

Tales of the Flashback

It was funny, that I should think of childhood for the second time that day (the first being when we'd descended the great tree next to the starship while still in our spacesuits, like kids playing astronaut). Still, there it was—just an image, really, a vignette—in this case a scene from a movie I'd seen at the East Fork Drive-in as a little boy (*Escape from the Planet of the Apes,* as I recalled, with Roddy McDowall and Kim Hunter), the one where the returned astronauts take off their helmets—as Maldano and I had just done—revealing themselves to be not men at all but advanced primates. As a metaphor, it was apropos; we hadn't shaved since well before the moon.

I looked at the pure, perfect sky and its few scattered clouds, like white cotton candy. "Okay. So it wasn't a nuclear exchange or a bolide impact, I think we can safely rule those out." I squinted at the sparse blue dome. "No contrails, no homogenitus, no ash. EMP burst, maybe. But not a large igneous province—Yellowstone, say. Not a caldera. That leaves pandemic—something which had to have raced through the population like wildfire. It's funny. All this time dreaming about home, only to end landing via the Doomsday Protocol."

"Yes, well. Like I said," said Maldano. He looked out over the Gulf of Mexico, which sparkled in the sun. "Could have been a malfunction. All that protocol actually means is that Mission Control hasn't been detected. The fact is—we don't know. It could be that Houston's grid has been down, long enough for emergency power to have dwindled. It's just that—what, what is that? There, low on the horizon."

I followed his gaze to where a handful of queer lights could be seen twinkling amongst the clouds. "I'll be damned if I know. They—they don't look like aircraft. More like navigation buoys, but in the air. I honestly can't tell if they're manmade or not. Look, over there, still more of them." I pointed due south. "It's like someone strung Christmas lights in the sky."

I looked at Maldano and found him already looking at me, sweat beading along his brow. Both of us, I think, were unnerved by the silence, or at least the lack of human activity, and by the crashing drone of the sea. I peered along the waterfront beyond him; it was just us and the bearberry bushes.

"Nobody on the road, nobody on the beach," I said at last, quietly.

The tide rolled in and then out again.

"I feel it in the air; the summer's out of reach," added Maldano.

"Empty lake, empty streets—the sun goes down alone."

"I'm driving by your house—"

And together: "Though I know, *you're not hoome.*"

And we moved out, trudging through the sand toward the boardwalk, singing Don Henley's "The Boys of Summer"—trying, as we walked, to ignore the nearby high rises (hotels, mostly), which looked on in perfect silence, stoic, inert, monolithic, like tombstones.

Unfortunately, by the time we reached the first commercial zone (Cornerstone Plaza of Cocoa Beach), we had no better idea of what had occurred than before, only that the entire suburb had become wild and overgrown—more than what seemed possible in the 21 months we'd been gone—its parks and lawns become mere patches of blowing tundra, its structures choked in moss and vine.

I picked an orange from a nearby tree and rubbed it against my spacesuit. "So here we are—in search of the black swan. The unexpected event that led to—all this." I peeled the fruit as I scanned the shopping center, settling on a storefront with a car crashed through its window. "This—what shall we call it? Death by invasive species." I split the orange down the middle and tossed him half of it. "This lost country.

'Untrodden by man, almost unknown to man ... a world tenanted by willows only, and the souls of willows.'"

We raised the portions to our mouths and paused, staring at each other. One of us had to be the Guinee pig, who knew what toxins had bled into the ecosystem, or what poisons had entered the food chain. But which one?

"Algernon Blackwood," I said, attributing the quote—when it became clear he wasn't going to waver. *"The Willows.* 1907."

And then I took a bite—chewing it slowly, as Maldano watched—swallowing, wiping my mouth with a gloved hand. "It's good. Sweet. Go ahead. Try it."

He hesitated before peeling off a wedge and placing it in his mouth, at which he closed his eyes and seemed to melt, hanging back his head, working his jaw in a circular motion, reopening his eyes—pausing suddenly.

"What?" I asked. "What is it?"

He tilted his head, peering into the branches. "Isn't that strange?"

I followed his gaze into the tree but, alas, saw nothing. Which, of course, was precisely the problem; there was nothing—no oranges, no leaves, no uppermost branches, it was as though someone or something had picked the treetop clean.

"Someone has a helluva reach," said Maldano.

I looked around the lot: at the lichen-covered Public Market and the Jersey Mike's Subs with the Prius in its window, at the Vietnamese Nail Salon and the El Buzo Peruvian Restaurant. "We should split up, canvas the area. Make sure—there's nothing else."

"Yeah," said Maldano. "I think you're right."

I headed for the Public Market. "Make a sweep of the strip mall. I'm going to check out that grocery store."

He laughed a little at that—which caused me to pause.

"Orders—Hooper?"

I half-turned, but didn't make eye contact. "Sorry?"

"I mean, in all this? This Big Empty? This 'world tenanted by willows ... and the souls of willows?'"

There was something in his voice. Something subtle, something contentious.

"Call it what you like," I said, and continued toward the market.

I'd barely had time to investigate when I heard him shout, "Hooper! Get out here!"

I looked up from the newspaper I'd picked off the rack—a paper with the headline, DAYS OF DELICATE TERROR: Disappearances, Weird Weather Rock Nation—and tried to triangulate him.

"Outside the Great Clips! Hurry up!"

I folded the paper and took it with me, exiting the building through the jammed-open front doors, and saw him crouched over the asphalt in the corner of the L-shaped shopping center, beneath the Great Clips' cornice. "What is it?" I said. "What did you find?"

He stood and indicated the sidewalk.

I stared at the pavement, which was webbed with roots and lichen, and saw a single shoe lying on its side—a Nike Lebron, which had been stained maroon like the surrounding concrete. More, there was something sticking out of it—two somethings, I realized, broken and brownish-yellow—tibia and fibula bones, obviously, snapped in two midways up their shafts, crawling with maggots and flies.

I used the newspaper to wave away the insects. "Jesus," I said. "What in the hell happened here?"

I scanned the scene, which looked like someone had spilled a 5-gallon bucket of maroon paint (and then flailed around in it), saw an impression the size of a pizza pan in the dried blood. "What the hell is that?"

I glared at Maldano but the bearded astronaut only stared back at me.

I knelt over the impression, or rather the impressions, for there were other, smaller ones next to it—three, to be exact—and studied the configuration.

"This is a—"

"A print, that's right," said Maldano. "Further, I'll characterize it. Or at least what it isn't. It isn't the print of anything that was walking the earth when we left." He added, "It's not that of a bear, for example."

He knelt beside me and indicated the larger impression. "Yuh, see, this would have been left by the lowermost extremity of the metatarsals, the foot bones that connect directly to the tibia and fibula—locked together, for strength." He indicated the smaller ones. "And these, these are the phalanges, or toe bones—see how they're splayed to support the animal's weight? That's because this was a big creature, 7-8 tons, at least. Other than that, they're not so different from our own; here's the proximal phalanx, which is connected to the metatarsal, and the middle phalanx, and the distal phalanx. Or at least that's where they would have been beneath the flesh, which is what left the impress—"

"Stop it," I snapped, and stood abruptly. "Just ... Look. What are you saying?"

"I'm saying this was left by a member of the theropoda clade of the Saurischia order, division Carnosauria." He looked up at me as though it should be obvious. "Whose family was probably—"

I grabbed him by a system umbilical and yanked him to his feet, began shaking him like a ragdoll. "Talk sense, damn you! What are you saying? That whoever that shoe belonged to was attacked by a—by a—"

I paused, trying to get a hold of myself, as his face hovered mere inches from my own. At last I released him and quickly stepped back, breathing heavily, repulsed by my own behavior.

"I—Jesus, I'm sorry. It's just ... it's just that none of this makes any—"

That's when I saw her: like a ghost, or an ashen specter, just staring at me through the glass, through the Great Clips' window, not close to it but much further back, crouched by one of the chairs. That's when I saw her (and she saw me): standing abruptly, stumbling over a broom, regaining her balance in time to bolt for the back door and to disappear into the dark.

"Follow me," I said, rushing to the door, yanking it open. "Hurry!"

Alas, it isn't easy, running in a spacesuit, even if they have been streamlined considerably since Apollo and the shuttle program. The truth of it is that by the time I burst from the building and back into the blinding sun she was already halfway across the lot—and nearing a stand of trees. Indeed, if not for what happened next, I would have surely lost her there; but the bird had other ideas.

The bird. The thing from the sky.

Even now I have a hard time believing it—that such a thing could have ever existed in the first place, much less come to exist again. But the truth of my eyes was undeniable as it swooped in out of nowhere and attacked the girl: its great wings beating furiously as it pecked and stabbed at her with its beak (itself the size of a small kayak) and tore at her with its talons, its eyes flashing malevolently as it attempted to spirit her away but was frustrated repeatedly by her kicking and flailing. And yet it did rise—with her still in its hold—and I sprinted toward them: leaping and grabbing her by the ankles even as the bird lifted us both; absorbing the brunt of the impact when it finally loosened its grip, covering and protecting her as it hovered and pecked and squawked.

Until, finally, the attack had ended—more suddenly even than it had begun—and we were alone (in that moment before Maldano hurried to check on us), at which point I looked at the girl and she looked back—smiling, crying, bleeding profusely—and knew her to be the most beautiful thing on Earth.

As it turned out, she lived at the Discovery Beach Resort, one of the very towers that had looked down on us earlier (and from whose uppermost floor she had watched us touch down). And while I was mystified at first by her choice of residence—there was no electricity to power the elevators, for example—her *modus operandi* quickly became clear: for it was, quite simply, one of the highest and most defensible positions in town (the trek up to the 10th floor alone, especially with her in tow, had more than proven that). What was more, it was high enough from the earth that what had happened below could—if you just listened to the soft jazz sifting from her boombox and tried hard enough—almost be forgotten, at least for a while.

None of which is to say I wasn't shaken as I sat next to her bed and examined the tourniquet on her arm—which we'd fashioned out of a haircutter's drape while still at the Great Clips—and worried over the appearance of the wound, which had developed red streaks around it and was oozing clearish fluid.

"Well now, here comes Doctor Number Two. I shall need your name as well, sir," she said, and smiled, toothily, earnestly.

"Hooper," I said. "Captain Glenn Hooper. Bluespace Aeronautics."

She saluted sharply with her good arm and lowered her voice. "Pleased to meet you, Captain Hooper."

I chuckled in spite of everything. "Just Glenn," I said.

"'Just Glenn'—he says," she quipped. She lifted her chin and arched her back, to gaze out the window behind her. "And I'll tell you the same thing I told him. Ain't no one who's been to Mars is *just* anything."

She yawned and stretched in the thin nightshirt and I looked away. "Well—thank you. But we were just doing our job. I'm sure you had one that was just as important. Didn't you, Miss—?"

"Cunningham. Rachael Cunningham." She rolled her head to look at me. "I was a teacher; an adjunct. Comparative politics. Political methodology. That sort of thing."

Her eyes were cow-brown with emerald highlights.

"That sounds interesting, indeed," I said—calmly, clinically. It seemed especially important to be so; I wasn't sure why. *"And* necessary."

She *hrmphed.* "In the age of Tucker? What did it matter?"

She was referring, of course, to Donald J. Tucker, the 45th President of the United States.

I looked at my moonboots, knowing I should let her rest but not wanting to go. "Whatever happened to him, you think? In this—this Flashback, as you called it."

She faced the ceiling as though in deep thought. "Who knows. He's probably golfing in an underground bunker somewhere. It's funny; I saw a caravan of trucks come through town just the other day, flying his flag—like their own little mobile nation-state."

She lolled her head to look at me and we laughed, softly, quietly.

At length she said, "You must be terribly uncomfortable in that, your spacesuit. You should go check the other units, see if there's anything to wear. I've pretty much cleaned out the women's necessities, but there should be plenty of men's clothing; not to mention razors and shave cream. I'll be fine, really."

I stood reluctantly and moved to go, but paused in the doorway. "That wound, you know, it has me concerned. You'll need to be monitored, closely. Is there a thermometer?"

She shook her head.

"Yeah, well. We'll look for one."

"There's a pharmacy at Cornerstone Plaza, just a few blocks away. You can take my Kawasaki; the key's on the mantle." She laughed. "But go gently—the thing's 46 years old."

I must have grinned. "You don't say? I had a '78. KZ400. It was red."

"So's this one." She seemed to think about it. "Isn't that strange?"

"I guess something's just click into place like that," I said, and regretted it immediately. "Listen. You get some sleep, you hear?"

"I will, if you doctors will leave me alone." She smiled, toothily, earnestly.

"You know it's funny," she added, as I was closing the door. "I used to lay awake at night and wonder if I'd ever have anyone to talk to again. And now I've got two—more than any woman could need."

I stared at her through the crack in the door, unsure how to respond. Then I eased the door gently closed and went to join Maldano on the patio.

We settled into a routine—Maldano taking the morning while I looked in on her in the afternoon—ending our days in deck chairs while drinking whiskey sours and gazing at the Sargasso Sea (and also our starship, which stood sentinel below us like a Minuteman missile). None of which changed the fact that she seemed to be getting worse, not better, or that, in spite of her denials, she appeared to have lost mobility in her hand and fingers—a sure sign of infection, at least with an animal bite. The fact was she needed antibiotics, and soon. The fact was we'd need to return to the shopping plaza at Cocoa Beach.

"Yes, but. With a pair of .22 calibers weapons? How is that a good idea?"

Maldano was skeptical.

I thought about the weapons in question, which were the only ones she had: a Rimfire Pistol and a Model 60 Rifle, both of them well-maintained. "I'm not seeing that we have much of a choice—are you? You heard what she said: the gun stores have been emptied. But you've felt her lymph nodes, her forehead—she's burning up. No. We can't wait on this, Mark. It's going to have to be done. I say first thing in the morning."

He swirled the liquor in his glass, appearing to think about it. "I guess it's hard to say no to the last woman on Earth."

"There's others," I said, and took a drink. "People have survived." I gazed at the queer lights as they shifted and pulsed amongst the clouds and the whiskey burned my chest. "As for how many ..." I looked across at him and his loud Hawaiian shirt. "You're right, of course. She might as well be. Who knows."

"Who knows," he said, and took a drink.

We watched as the gray waves crashed and the tide rolled in and out, as the light itself began to fade.

"Our Lady of the Flashback!" he exclaimed at last, and raised his glass to the sky. "This—this Dinosaur Apocalypse; this Time Storm which has cleansed the world." He swirled the glass, sloshing whiskey. "Our brown-eyed, toothy Galatea; our Aphrodite on a scallop shell. The veritable Eve to these two Adams."

He swung his glass close to mine, as though he wished to toast. "To starting again; and to being home. 'Muses no more what ere ye be, in fancy's pleasures roam; but sing (by truth inspir'd) wi' me, the pleasures of a home." He rattled his glass. "Eh?"

I hesitated before meeting him, I'm not sure why. "John Clare. *The Village Minstrel.* 1821." I tapped his glass (a little harder than I intended). "Scoal."

"Mm," he said, and drained his glass. "She'd like that, I bet. Some poetry. I've been reading to her from the *Bhagavad Gita*—but it's slow going. Found it wedged in amongst all those Eckhart Tolle books in the hall."

I paused, looking at him. "You—you've been *reading* to her?"

"Well, sure. Beats all that small talk and temperature taking you've been smothering her with." He laughed. "Woman does not heal by bread alone, mein Captain. Nor does lamb always trump harvest—regardless of what it says in the Bible. She's smart; I treat her like it. I think she misses teaching. Terribly."

I stared at the lights in the sky, wondering again if they were intelligently directed or some kind of natural phenomenon. "I didn't realize it was a competition," I said, absently.

"Neither did Abel," he jibed, and shoved me in the arm.

I drained my glass as he looked out over the ocean and the silence reasserted itself. "But then, everything is, I suppose," he said, after seeming to think about it. "I mean, isn't that what's going on out there, right now—a competition for survival? For reproduction?" He chuckled, softly, and with little discernible humor. "Sharks versus marlins; monster birds versus women—she said it was a quetzalcoatlus—Tucker fanatics versus, who knows?"

I looked at our starship: at its stainless-steel hull which shown cool and blue in the building's dim shadow. "No. No, I don't think so," I said. "We've ... transcended all that, to some extent. I mean, *look at it,* Mark. Look at what we've accomplished."

He followed my gaze, holding his glass loosely, tenuously, his eyes blurry and red. "It—it looks like a giant hard-on," he said, and tittered. He began looking for the bottle. "Or maybe a middle finger. Like a big 'Fuck You' to God."

I watched as he stumbled through the sliding glass doors into the kitchen. "You should lay off that," I said. "We've got a big day tomorrow."

But by then he was retching into the sink and I was alone, just looking at my empty glass, wondering, a little amused: Did he see himself as Abel? Or did he see himself as Cain?

I thought about Rachael, sleeping in her thin nightshirt, having more than any woman could need; and about myself, and how I saw myself. And then I dozed, dreaming of home—which was curious, since, like Maldano, I had never really had one (hence one of the reasons we were chosen for Mars). A dream which soon gave way to the faint smell of blood and an impulse I could not define; and of gliding through dark water—stealthily, surefootedly—like a predator, or a wraith.

I'm still not sure where it came from, the ramosaurus, as I called it (a kind of allosaurus, but with little ram-like horns on each side of its head), although I'd hazard a guess, based on its later behavior, that it had been watching us for a some time; since well before I'd started the Kawasaki's engine and kicked it into 1st gear—tearing up the street like gangbusters as Maldano hung on for dear life and the carnosaur pursued, chasing us all the way to the shopping center, where we quickly climbed off and rushed in.

"Get back," I shouted at Maldano, "Get back!" —even as the animal's snout darted between the doors and stopped; suddenly, abruptly, jarring the metal framework, cracking the glass into spiderwebs.

"It's okay," gasped Maldano—breathing heavily, holding his chest. "It's okay." He laughed suddenly, euphorically. "Ha! Its head is too big for its own good."

We watched as it struggled and gnashed its teeth—its dark tail whipping back and forth outside, its eyes close to the glass. "It's all those denticles and jaw muscles," I said, finally. "Cost of doing business, I guess."

"Apex predator's burden," said Maldano, and indicated the door to the pharmacy, which was lazed open.

We went in even as the ramosaur withdrew, opening and closing its little claws—shaking itself off.

"Let's hope it doesn't get the idea to use those horns," said Maldano. He handed me a green plastic bag. "We're looking for Amoxicillin and Penicillin. Also Doxycycline, Metronidazole, Clindamycin. If you see Dicloxacillin, grab that too. And painkillers. Ibuprofen and Tylenol."

He went to the glass partition which separated the pharmacy from the rest of the store and peered out.

"What are you doing?" I asked.

"Making sure there's no light pouring in anywhere, no opening. Nothing that *thing* can get in through. So far, so good." He took out his flashlight and pressed its lens against the pane. "And also that there's nothing in here with us. I don't trust this glass."

I pulled the blinds to let in more light—in time to see the ramosaur's tail disappear behind the Holiday Inn next door, followed by its head peeking around the corner—cautiously, stealthily. "Our friend doesn't give up easily ..."

I turned to look at Maldano, saw him still peering into the darkened store. "We're going to have to ditch the bike and slip out the back," I said. "How's it looking?"

He began to back away from the glass, slowly, blindly, as though he were in a daze. "I—I can't do it. I'm sorry."

I watched as he drew the pistol from his belt and chambered a round, then pointed it, waveringly, at the partition.

"What the hell are you talking about?" I took a step toward him. "Maldano. What are you talking about?"

"We—we have to go. *Now*. I—*I* have to go. Out the front doors. Out—"

"What is it, Mark? What do you see?" I shoved past him and put my own light to the window, squinting as my eyes adjusted, thinking I saw something move.

And I did. I *did* see something move, several somethings, a hundred—a *thousand,* maybe more. For the store was crawling with centipedes, *huge* ones, and ones still larger than those, ones ranging from 3 feet to 8 feet and some several feet across, ranging in color from lime green to faded salmon, from drab brown to sickly ochre, all of them winding and weaving, gliding on scurrying legs, flopping and scrambling over themselves, glistening like moist, wet clay.

"We have to go!" he shouted, dropping his gun, and bolted for the door.

"Wait! Maldano! It isn't safe!"

I moved to follow him but froze, adjusting the rifle sling, looking at the shelves and shelves of medicines. Rachael. She was counting on us. Rachael in her thin white nightshirt—in her room full of soft jazz and incense; in her tower by the sea. Rachael who was not simply a woman but something akin to *home* itself.

I rushed to the shelves and began searching for Penicillin, for Doxycycline and Metronidazole, for painkillers of any kind. Searched for them and found some, even as the motorcycle sputtered to life.

"Hurry up!" shouted Maldano. "We have to go! Now!"

But I couldn't, of course; I had to gather the medicines. I had to save Galatia, our Aphrodite on a scallop shell. Had to think of home and a final place to rest. "It's not safe, damn you!" I cried, sweeping pill bottles with my arm, filling the plastic bag. "That thing, it's still out there!"

I gazed out the window at the Holiday Inn, saw the creature creeping forward with its body slung low, intently, single-mindedly, like a wolf or a great cat. I jerked to look at Maldano and saw that he too was aware of it; that he had apprehended the animal and was trying to figure out the motorcycle's gears—that he was kicking down into 1st, which was correct, and releasing the clutch. And then he leapt forward, suddenly, and travelled about 50 feet—before the engine stalled and he was immobile again.

I dropped the bag and unslung the rifle, smashed the window with its butt. Then I aimed and ground the scope, sighting the dinosaur between its eyes.

I must have gone into what they call *hyperfocus,* because it gets foggy after that. All I know for certain is that I understood in that moment what was required to move forward; that Eve would need her Adam and that I would need to choose survival, for this above everything was what the world now demanded. And I knew, also, that while a .22 caliber round was unlikely to stop the creature, a fresh kill would surely give it pause, enough, perhaps, for me to escape through the back with the medicines—even if it meant running straight through the centipedes.

I lowered my sights to Maldano, who tried to kickstart the bike and failed, then raised to try again.

It would have to be fresh. It would have to be alive.

And then I fired—once, twice. A third time. Knowing the battery was directly beneath the seat. Knowing it was shielded only by a thin layer of plastic.

Knowing it had exploded only when the cover blew off and white smoke started to billow—after which, shaken and confused, Maldano turned to look at me—pitifully, mournfully; resigned—and the animal pounced, pinning him to the pavement like a moth on cork, clamping its jaws about his head and chest, pulling him asunder as though he were full of blood red centipedes.

I am running, running along the back of the strip mall, gripping the medicine bag in one hand and the Model 60 rifle in the other, trying to get home. I run the entire two blocks to the Discovery Beach Resort—my heart thumping in my chest, my eyes stinging with something like tears—until I gain the door and go in—pausing only briefly to catch my shuddering breath; beginning the 10-story climb as though I were scaling Babel itself.

When I get to the unit it is dark, the generator sitting silently out on the deck (the door to which is open), the curtains rustling in the breeze. But there is no time to waste, none to delay, and I quickly gain the bedroom—at which I realize the bed is empty and she is no longer there, the sheets left in a jumbled mess, the draperies blowing as if to accentuate the solitude.

I look for her for hours, all throughout the building, kicking in doors which were previously unexplored, searching the utility rooms and common areas and dining accommodations, doubting my very grip on reality; until at last I burst through a door and find myself on the boardwalk, back on the beach, feeling cold, all of a sudden, and shivering, feeling as though my flesh were thin as paper. Feeling, for a reason I cannot explain, that I must return—to the starship, of course, the only home I have ever known, but also to myself, who would never have slain his own friend, his own brother—no matter the madhouse the world has become, or the perceived stakes of any given situation. Until I find myself stumbling from the boardwalk onto the beach— and across the sand like a drunkard—collapsing at last at the base of our starship, raising a hand, which trembles, to its steel.

That's when I remember them, the queer lights in the sky. That's when I slide to the sand as though having no bones—gazing at them disoriented, knowing them to be alive. Suspecting, in my heart, that we have somehow been judged, and that by doing what I've done they have judged me again. Fearing, in my mind, that Rachael has never existed, or, if she has, has done so only at their pleasure, their humor. Their terrible intent. At which I begin to crawl upon the sand like a snake, gripping handfuls of granules and coughing and gasping as though dying, seeking the edge of the world and the nightmare; groping for a way back into reality itself.

After which I stand, teeteringly, and stumble on, banished and shunned, naked and alone, bearing the mark of Cain.

In the movies they call it a "smash cut"—when the scene shifts so suddenly and abruptly that the viewer is knocked off balance, if only for an instant. That's what it was like when Puck attacked the nanotyrannosaurs—which we hadn't even known were there—smashing the silence into a thousand pieces as the animals burst into the clearing thrashing and gnashing their teeth and one of the predators broke off in pursuit of the man with the knife—the man who, only an instant before, had been holding the weapon to Lisa's neck.

Not that I knew it was Puck yet. That wouldn't come until after the mini-tyrannosaur had bitten off the man's head and shoulders (and swallowed them whole) and returned to the fray; after which I snatched my pistol up from the ground and tried to find an opening—mortified that I might accidently shoot my own dog—and, finding it, squeezed the trigger.

Krack!

I fired twice more.

Krack! Krack!

And then the nanotyrannosaurs were down (but not before one of them had shaken Puck like a ragdoll and launched him into a nearby tree) and we were running toward him. Toward my dog who had gone missing during the Flashback and whom we had long since presumed dead. Toward the broken bundle of fur that had somehow found us and saved our lives.

"Puck!" I cried, trying to rouse him. "Come on, Boy. Wake up."

"Omigod. Omigod, Nick. Is he—?"

I crouched over him and felt his belly—which was bloated and distended, like that of a starving person—with my gloved hand.

"No. No—he's breathing. But shallow. Like he's in a coma." I looked around the clearing, at the dead tyrannosaurs and the dead man missing his head and shoulders, and at the *deadfall,* which was scattered everywhere, like rubbish. "It's going to take time. But look, there's firewood. And that brook can't be far—not at the rate we've been moving. I say we camp here."

Lisa fidgeted about nervously. "Here? How is that a good idea?"

"I don't know what else," I said. "We can't move him. He could have a broken neck, or internal bleeding—I mean, who knows. Besides, Nano-Ts are territorial. Which means the apex predators of this entire area are likely right here, just as dead as that man with the knife." I squinted at the animal that had killed him. "I hope it choked on it."

I was referring, of course, to my golden dog whistle, which the man had taken from me and put around his own neck when it became evident that we had nothing else of value.

"My God, Nick, but we're in the middle of nowhere. What if they hunt in packs and not pairs? That would mean there's still—"

"I'm not leaving him like this, okay?" I shot her a glance and she recoiled noticeably. Then, seeing how the harshness in my voice had disturbed her, I took a deep breath—and tried again. "Just, help me with the camp, okay? I can sit with him while you sleep. All right? I'll stay up and keep watch. If he doesn't wake by morning—I'll take care of it myself."

She looked at me as though she were about to cry. "I didn't say we should leave him, Nick. I— It's just that ..." Her eyes welled up suddenly and she batted away the tears. "Oh, fuck it all."

And she wandered off—to gather sticks for the fire, ostensibly, but really to avoid saying the only thing left to be said. Which was that in a world where the vanished outnumbered the living by something like 3 to 1—the "Big Empty," the old man at the filling station had called it—a world without civilization or creature comfort or compassion, which had regressed to the Stone Age and beyond—yea, even to primordia itself—in *that* world, what could it possibly matter?

I paused as the wind picked up and rattled the leaves. Well, what could it? What was it worth amongst so much human suffering, so much grief and loss? One animal's life. One mixed-breed dog.

I looked at Puck who lay motionless but breathing in the lengthening shadow of the tree.

Just a dog.

And then I did something I had sworn to never again do; something I had promised Lisa I would resist—did it knowing full well what consequence might come in a world populated by ghosts; by disappeared souls; by a few scattered survivors living every minute and every hour—every waking moment—in something like Hell.

I slipped off one of my gloves and laid a trembling hand on Puck's head.

After which, noting the itching sensation in my palms and fingertips, I let the golden eyes open—crustily, sleepily—one after the other, like blinking boils. And I began to *see*.

They'd appeared shortly before the Flashback—that strange system of storms which had caused so many millions to disappear and that had brought the terrible lizards; that cataclysm which had re-mapped Time itself—opening one by one over a period of weeks, itching and burning like white phosphorous. I suppose in time we would have sought medical help (although it is difficult to credit, even now, after witnessing the Flashback and its impossibilities firsthand, what could have resulted from that); but, as it turned out, Time was something we had not owned and never would—for it was owned exclusively by them: the masters of the lights in the sky. The architects of the storm.

None of which mattered during the Great Collapse, for by then we'd become like everyone else, struggling merely to survive, and the strange eyes—as inexplicable as they were—

had, with the help of a pair of thick gloves, been almost forgotten. Nor, in truth, was this particularly difficult; the eyes, once covered, tended to close their lids and scab over.

All of which was just as well—because I hadn't been able to see through them anyway. At least, not until I touched the dying girl in Seattle—an incident I shall not speak of except to say, that—for a period of time—I saw all her yesterdays and all her hardships; all her life condensed up to that very moment, and more, I saw, for the briefest of instants, what had come *after*—which had been a thing of such raw beauty and terror it had nearly driven me mad. Indeed, I *would* have been mad had Lisa not been there to pull me away—nor, for that matter, had the ghosts of the Flashback—millions upon millions of them, pressing down on me from every corner and from every nook and cranny of the world—not driven me to distraction.

Suffice it to say that had been the last time—the last time I had allowed them any free reign: to see, to feel, to live vicariously through the lived experiences of others. After that, the gloves had stayed on. Stayed on as we trekked from Seattle through Tacoma and across the Olympic Peninsula to Aberdeen, where we had hoped to find Lisa's parents, but found only a house with a collapsed roof and a protoceratops nest in its kitchen. So, too, had we lost Puck, who had chased a turkey-like creature into the ruins of a T.J. Maxx in Olympia and never come out, even though a search revealed no other egress but the shattered front doors—which left us no choice but to assume he had vanished in some aftershock of the Flashback.

And now here we were, somewhere between Hoquiam and Ocean City, travelling through the forest instead of following the road because the road was rife with bandits and outliers (one of whom must have spied us through the trees before getting the jump on us shortly after the brook), and no closer to hope than we had been before—indeed, further from it than ever, and with three less bullets in the gun. Worse, another would have to be used to put Puck down in the event he didn't wake up; something which seemed increasingly likely as the eyes in my hand perceived only a mottled fog and Lisa could be heard approaching us through the scrub.

"You're a fool, Nick Callahan. A fool. But I suppose you already knew that."

I allowed my hand to drop before plunking down in the fir needles and just staring into space. "There was nothing. I saw nothing. It—it was like he didn't even exist."

She sat down next to me and exhaled, tiredly.

"He's an animal—what did you expect?" She picked up my glove and offered it to me, but I didn't take it. "You said it yourself; it's like they see memories. The eyes. I don't imagine a dog has a particularly long one. Do you?"

I sighed. All I knew for certain was that I felt numb and more than a little tired. "I don't know. I don't know what I expected. Or what I was looking for. An incident, maybe. Some kind of clue."

She laid her head on my shoulder and stared at nothing, same as me. "What kind? A clue to what?"

"That's just it—I don't know. A clue to what might wake him up, I guess. Something I could say. Something that was important to him."

"His butt was important to him," she said. "A source of endless fascination."

I had to smile.

That's when it happened. That's when he yelped, ever so slightly, and his paw twitched.

I looked at Lisa and she looked back. And then my hand was on him and we were running—Puck and I—down cobblestone lanes lined with streetlamps and through pools of foggy light; through tides of rusted Maple leaves, which leapt and swirled as we passed.

"What is it?" I heard Lisa say, her voice growing smaller, more distant. "What do you see?"

I turned to look at Puck as we ran and saw his tongue loll and his eyes shift—as though he wanted to look behind himself—behind us—but didn't dare.

"Fear," I said. "Confusion." An image entered my mind of a dug passage beneath the rear wall of the T.J. Maxx; of the turkey-like thing crawling through it with Puck hot on its heels. "He escaped from beneath the wall and now he's lost somewhere in the fog. And he's terrified ... but of what I don't know. It's almost like—wait a minute. Wait a minute." I looked behind him—having heard something huffing and snorting—and saw a fully-grown therapod dinosaur (colored orange and black, like a Gila monster) bounding after us in the dark, gaining rapidly. "There's something coming—some kind of predator. An allosaur, I think. Whatever it is, it's closing, and I mean fast."

"Oh, my God. Nick. Can't you do anything? H-hello? Nick?"

"Lisa!"

But she was already gone, lost amidst the vision and the ghostly white noise of the dead; constrained to some other time and place—erased from my present condition completely.

Understand this. While there are several dog breeds known to climb trees—the New Guinea Singing Dog; the Louisiana Catahoula; the Treeing Walker Coonhound, and the Jack Russell Terrier (I know this because I have since read up on it), the Miniature American Shepherd, which is what Puck mostly resembled, is, most emphatically, *not* known for such behavior. So, you can imagine my fear and consternation when Puck veered for the nearest Maple tree and attacked it like it was a set of monkey bars—even as the allosaurus collided with it directly beneath him and proceeded to do the same, or tried to. Even now I'm in awe of the pluck and determination he showed that day—to seemingly defy gravity in such an impossible way and to dash up the tree's trunk like that, and then to hold onto the lowest branch in such an unshakable manner—it was truly a sight to behold. Especially when the allosaur began to leap and lunge and to snap at him and he briefly lost a paw-hold; before his hindlimbs kicked in and propelled him the rest of the way—into the tree's bowl and a relative amount of safety; into a position from which he could run along one of the branches onto the roof of the nearest house ... but didn't, as he needed to give the allosaur a piece of his mind.

Which he did, barking and yapping and snarling, even as I watched from below like Johnny Smith in *The Dead Zone*—I even had the collar of my peacoat turned up—standing next to the allosaur but in virtually no danger; inhabiting the scene while somehow remaining apart. Like a ghost.

That's when the other allosaurs showed up—at least one of them passing right through me—and began to triangulate the tree, at which Puck *did* run along one of the branches to the house—but hesitated before jumping from the eave; it was, after all, a long way down, even for a man. And that is where he remained—as the predators moved from the tree to the house and effectively surrounded it—after which there was little he could do but to sit on his haunches and try to wait them out.

Which, eventually, he did, although by this time the moon—which was visible through a part in the clouds—was directly overhead, and even I, a ghost, had the sense that several hours had passed. That's when he retraced his steps to the tree, and, after many false starts, skidded partially down its trunk before leaping the rest of the way to the ground.

"Good dog," I said, and attempted to pet him, "Smart dog ..."

But my hand just passed through him and he didn't notice me at all, just sniffed about the ground as he walked in tight circles and finally trotted away. Back up the lane toward the little strip mall and the T.J. Maxx; back through the gloom which was slowly starting to lift.

It was then that the scene changed and I was standing outside the store, standing where I had stood not 24 hours ago, blowing on that dog whistle; where I'd finally admitted to myself that he was either out of range or had been taken by the Flashback. Puck was there, just sitting on his haunches. I knelt in front of him and studied his face. Studied the patch of black fur around one eye and the eyes themselves, as deep and brown as any person's. Saw the doubt and desperation and the confusion and the *complexity*. And I saw something else, something I can only call, for lack of a better term, his humanity.

The wind gusted and trash skittered across the empty lot.

And yet there was something more—something deeper— wasn't there? Something just beyond my perception. And this was something—which was *not* human. A thing which, now that I've had time to understand it, was as pure and ephemeral as light itself.

In short, a thing utterly without guile or self. Perfect. Irreducible. Uncreated.

And then Puck barked, causing me to jump, and the moment was past, and I came out of it to the sound of a campfire crackling and Lisa shaking and cursing me awake, after which she said, with a clear tremor in her voice, "There's more of them out there. More Nano-Ts. *We have to go, Nick. Now.*"

I looked at the corpses of the first Nano-Ts, which were being picked over by compies, the small but deadly predators which always accompanied a kill, then deeper into the dark, where I detected no movement. "How do you know? I don't hear anything ... just the compies."

"I did hear them," she said, and picked up a stick. "Two of them, at least, calling from different directions. They're triangulating us. We have to go, Nick. We have to go right now." She looked at Puck, her face half-painted in firelight. "I'm sorry."

I looked at him too—at the patch of black and his closed eyes, at his paws which had been bloodied by the tree's rough branches. "I—I can't. I'm sorry. Because ... there's something in there. Something I need to see. The eyes—Puck—there's something they want to show me. Something I need to understand."

I approached her suddenly and gripped her arm. "Something that might save us all—*but I need more time!*"

That's when we heard it—both of us—the unmistakable bark of a nanotyrannosaur, which was quickly answered by another, closer. Right at the tree line.

She cursed and jerked away. "Tell them!"

I looked at Puck and then back at her, then back to Puck ... when I noticed the revolver laying in the grass. "Ocean City—it's not that far." I rushed forward and snatched up the gun. "There's still two bullets. Take it."

She froze, looking at my extended arm, then into my eyes, which she searched. "You bastard ..." She welled up suddenly and intensely. "You *fucking bastard.*"

I shook the gun. *"Goddammit, Lisa.* Take it."

She reached up slowly and took it.

"I will meet you in Ocean City. I'm ... I'm just going to try this one last time—okay? If it doesn't work ... I'll leave him. I promise."

"No—you won't." She smiled like a crazy person. "Because they're going to come in here and *rip you to shreds ...*"

"You don't know that. The fire will keep them away. The smell of their dead buddies ..."

She swiped at her cheeks and sniffed loudly. Then she moved toward the opposite tree line, the one facing the road—and paused. She turned around. "You're a fool, Nick Callahan. A fool. But I suppose you already know that."

"Get out of here," I said.

And she went.

I rushed over to Puck and dropped to my knees.

"Okay, buddy. You need to show me what you got, and show me fast, all right?" I placed my hand on his head and squeezed slightly. "You remember Dad. He used to take you fishing—like, every Sunday. Remember that? Well, he used to say that to understand a man you had to walk a mile in his shoes. That, to open a man's heart, you had to know

167

something about his journey; about what made him tick. So ... I'm walking in your shoes. I'm walking in them right now. And what I need to know is ... what will wake you up, okay? I need you to show me. Show me, Puck. Be a good dog one last time. Come on, buddy. Let it go."

And then I closed my lids and let my hand take over—let the golden eyes re-open and peer through Time itself. Let them read Puck's yesterday as the compies chittered and the Nano-Ts barked, coordinating their attack; as Lisa made her way to Ocean City and the lost souls of the Flashback began to cry and howl their laments.

The trail had gone cold. I could see it in his eyes as he trotted to a halt at the edge of Highway 109 and sniffed at the air, his white coat blowing.

Come on, boy, I thought, beginning to worry. I was standing by a green and white road sign which read: OCEAN CITY—22 MILES. *You can do it. Don't give up on us.*

He sat on his haunches and looked around, panting. At the abandoned motor home Lisa and I had dozed in only a few hours before; at the cracked and potholed highway which had been overrun with prehistoric lichen.

Come on, buddy. Go sniff up that RV—it'll put you back on the trail. Just get up and get moving. Because that man with the knife is probably watching us—Lisa and I—right now. So are the Nano-Ts, like they are in the present. And we're never going to make it without you.

Then, like a miracle, he was up again—his tail wagging furiously, his ears twitching puckishly—investigating the Coachman, tearing off toward Ocean City. Barking and yelping, which rode the wind like an echo.

I opened my eyes—*my eyes,* not the alien things in my hands—and saw the branches shaking deep in the dark. They were on the move again—the Nano-Ts—closer even than before. They were getting ready to strike; to do what they did best, which was to rend and kill. I shut my lids and refocused, feeling as though Time had fast forwarded, as though it had leapt ahead.

Show me, I thought. *Show me now, or forever hold your peace. Show me or see us all join the choir of the damned!*

And that's when it happened: that's when I saw it, the moment that had changed—still would change—everything. That moment Puck had skidded to a stop after surpassing our location and begun to cock his head, and to tilt it quizzically; to look from the road to the tree line and sniff at the briny air—to bolt into the woods like a maniac and, apprehending the situation quickly and accurately, to attack the Nano-Ts.

For that was the moment the man with the knife had tested the dog whistle. The instant in which he had placed it to his lips and blown once, hard and long, and that he had grinned his rotten-toothed grin and said, "Now kick that gun over here, nice and easy. Come on, now. Nobody wants to see Missy here all cut up like Sharon Tate."

Indeed, it was the moment that had led to our rescue and to Puck being in a coma; and to him being in limbo, like the victims of the Flashback and its great and terrible Vanishing, trapped in Time, caught between worlds. A place I knew I could never have left him, not if it had cost me everything I had.

Which it may have, I thought, as I came up out of the trance and looked at the dead beast that had killed the knifeman—for I knew what I had to do—and also through the firs, beyond which Lisa had disappeared. *It may have.*

Then I was up; I was on my feet—snatching the man's knife from the forest floor, falling on the carcass like a jackal—scattering the compies in a flurry.

Drawing the blade across its belly so that its innards exploded out like writhing red snakes.

"Hold on, Puck," I shouted, as I waded into its guts. "You're going to like this! Going to jump right to attention, I guarantee it ..."

I slashed and slashed—clearing away the bowels, cutting away viscera—even as the compies returned, leaping and scurrying. "Hold on, buddy! We got this—"

And they descended on me, or rather ascended me, scurrying up my legs and back, piling up on my shoulders, attacking my face as I located the stomach and cut it open and began feeling around. *"Ahh—ahhh ....!"*

I collapsed amidst the guts and gruel, batting at my face, at their little beaks and talons, even as the firs shook and I realized I could *smell* them—the Nano-Ts—hovering in the black between trees, getting ready to pounce.

I pulled one of the compies off and wrung its neck before climbing back up and reaching into the T's stomach again, after which I felt something unusual, something round and smooth, and withdrew it quickly—only to realize it was one of the knifeman's eyeballs.

"Jesus!" I cursed, and dropped it—even as the compies swarmed over me like mutated sewer rats, like blood-sucking bats, causing me to fall into the viscera again and to roll up like a fetus, to cry out in anguish—knowing, at last, that it was truly over; that there would be no escape for us this time, neither Puck or I, and wondering what Lisa would do now that she was all by herself—and how she would survive—wondering if she would always hate me for the decisions I'd made and for my bullheadedness, and for a thousand other—

"Goddamnit, Nick, find the fucking whistle—I got this!"

I swiped the blood from my eyes and looked at her—saw her stomping and stabbing compies as though she were a mad woman, as though she were fighting in the trenches of France. She knew. She had figured it out herself. Woman's intuition, perhaps, who knew?

And then I was up and reaching into the thing's stomach, desperately feeling around, praying that the stuff that felt like macaroni and cheese wasn't the knifeman's brains—and yet knowing it was—finding the golden whistle suddenly and unexpectedly and placing it in my mouth.

Where I blew on it as hard as I could, sending a frequency only Puck could hear pulsating through the air.

After which, like gray ghosts, the Nano-Ts began to emerge—slowly, cautiously, not pouncing suddenly as I'd expected, but surrounding us in a loose but ever-tightening circle. Corralling us.

"I'm sorry," I said, as the Alpha bull approached the corpses one at a time and sniffed them carefully, thoroughly. "You should have gone to Ocean City."

She looked at me in the dark, the fire having long gone out. "And live ... I suppose," she said. She smiled wanly. "For what?"

And then something moved and we turned to look at it, and it was Puck, standing on all fours and just as awake as could be.

Puck. Who growled at the dinosaurs threateningly even as he crept forward like a puma and finally paused between us—facing off with the bear-sized predators resolutely, glowering at them without fear or hesitation.

The wind blew, and the trees swayed. The Alpha bull sniffed at the air. My heart thudded in my chest even as it looked at the corpses and then back to Puck. Then it did it again.

And then it swung its great head away and turned, its massive bulk pivoting smoothly, gracefully, and glided back into the trees, after which the others began to peel away and follow—until they were gone, all of them, and we were alone.

Just us and Puck, who was still covered in the predators' blood. Just us and a shepherd mutt—ostensibly an American Miniature—who had been on one helluva journey, but was home now.

A mutt who licked our faces as we surrounded him and looked at us with such seasoned calm and selflessness that I was both spellbound and awed, as though I were in the presence of something at once human and more than human—something which was the epitome of love and faithfulness—something perfect, something divine. Something which came up the same thing no matter which way you turned it.

"Dog" is a palindrome.

Okay, easy does it. Just nock your arrow—easy, easy, it's going to click—now put it in the rest ...

I looked at the allosaur as it fed, there in the slim shadow of the Mirage's entry arch, in the shimmering heat of Lost Vegas, and drew back the string—finding my anchor (which was just under my right ear), aligning the peephole with my sights.

Easy, easy ...

I stabilized the grip between my thumb and forefinger, sighting the area between the arms, the claws of which were covered in gore.

Great Spirit, thank you for sharing with me your glorious nature and abundant wildlife—

There was a *thwish* as a I released the arrow.

Grant me always wisdom and respect in its pursuit—

Which struck the taupe-colored animal with a dull thump, causing it to rear up like a stallion, baying and squealing, barking at the sky.

And keep me ever humble in the harvest—

I nocked and released two more bolts, embedding them into its chest, into its great, beating heart.

So that I may be worthy of my place on this earth. Amen.

And it fell, the fast-acting microraptor venom locking its jaw, paralyzing its limbs, so that it squirmed briefly upon its belly before solidifying like stone (as though it had gazed upon Medusa herself) and lay still, at which Kesabe leapt from the palm bushes and bound toward it, barking and wagging his tail, and I followed, grateful for the meat yet distressed by the loss of the arrows—which I knew would never be recovered—and overall preoccupied enough that I didn't even notice the girl standing just beyond the kill—until she yelped once, taking me in, and bolted out of sight down S. Las Vegas Blvd; after which I heard a small engine sputter to life and begin to rev.

"Sic, Kesabe!" I barked, for she was the first person we'd seen since San Diego—but the Dutch Shepherd was already on it, leaping over the allosaur's tail and sprinting after her even as I shouldered the compound bow and fetched Blucifer, whom I mounted quickly, gracelessly, before cracking the reins and giving chase.

And then there we were, she on her motor scooter (which sputtered and whined and left a trail of oily blue smoke) while we pursued, weaving between empty cars, maneuvering around stalled buses, racing down the Strip past Harrah's and Caesar's and the rows of transplanted palm trees—all the way to Planet Hollywood and a wide set of stairs (which she attempted to navigate but failed); all the way until Kesabe fell upon her like a threshing machine and I at last trotted to a halt, calling him off.

Fortunately, she hadn't been hurt, at least not seriously: she had a few nicks from Kesabe's teeth—a given—along with some minor cuts and bruises, but that was it. She was, however, pinned beneath her scooter; a circumstance she could do virtually nothing about—considering Kesabe's close proximity.

"Bastard!" she cursed—her voice full of venom—and spat at me. "What do you want?"

I recoiled as though slapped in the face, as though her small voice were instead the loudest thing in the world (which, at that time and place, now that I think about it, it *was*). And then the silence reasserted itself, as total and sublime as anything since Death Valley—only worse, for I now had something to compare it to—and because I was a man, and alone, with no rules to govern me, and because I'd heard nothing but death birds since the Cleveland National Forest, I decided I would not just slake my curiosity and let her go (who she was, where she was from, what did she know) but that in fact I would keep her, as a bound prisoner if necessary. In part this was to protect her, for she wouldn't last long with no weapons and no guile, but mainly it was for myself. Because, having heard her voice once, I intended to keep hearing it.

I *needed* to keep hearing it.

By the time I'd established a camp in the covered breezeway of the Luxor obelisk—"Cleopatra's Needle" it was called, at least according to a bronze placard on its wall—and bound her hands and feet, the sun had set and a slight rain had started to fall; something I fully welcomed after so much time in the desert. As to whether the girl welcomed it also, who could say. For even though I set her near the opening (as well as the fire) and provided her my own bedroll to sit on, she only continued to glare—probably due to us eating in front of her; for I had decided, though you might think it cruel, that I would starve her into speaking, if necessary. Which, of course, she finally did—speak, that is—although only after a considerable time, saying, hoarsely, yet clearly, assertively, "Is this some kind of torture? I mean, don't you have to feed prisoners before killing them? Isn't that what the Geneva Convention says?"

I looked at her through the flames, saying nothing, even as Kesabe snarled.

At length I carved a piece of meat from the spit and dropped it on a paper plate, which I carried around to her—but didn't hand over. Instead, I knelt and sliced off a single bite-sized morsel—then held it close to her nose.

"Trade," I said, matter-of-factly. "One bite per something about you. It can be your name. Where you're from. How you've survived ... Just talk."

She started to protest but hesitated, searching my eyes, trying to judge intent. At last she said, "So what's with the war paint?"

I stood and began to walk away.

"Wait a minute—wait a minute—jeez, so we don't go there—fine. My name is ... it's Essie, all right? Essie McIntyre. I'm from Spokane."

I paused, looking over my shoulder. "Where?"

"Spokane. It—it's a city. In Washington."

"... D.C.?"

"State. Washington *State.*"

I returned and crouched near her again. "Okay. So ... how'd you get to be here?"

She didn't say anything—only opened her mouth wide.

"It—it's got an aftertaste ... just so you know." I fed her the piece of allosaur.

She chewed it up eagerly, voraciously—before pausing, making a face.

"It's the game," I said. "You have to get used to it."

"It's not that. It's just ..." She swallowed slowly, tentatively. "I had alligator once, in New Orleans—this, this reminds me of that. Only heavier, oilier. With an acrid aftertaste."

"That's the predator in it ... at least that's what they say." I cut her off another piece. "Would—would you like some more?"

"Yes, I think so, please. It's not terrible."

I fed her the piece from the end of my knife.

"What, what was the question?" She finished chewing and swallowed. "Oh, yes. How did I come to be here. Well, that's just it—" She paused suddenly and tilted her head. "Can I ask you something?"

I must have looked confused.

"Just one," she said, and tried to smile. "What is your name?"

There was a pregnant pause as I thought about it. It seemed only fair. "Satanta," I said, and cut her another piece. "Satanta—the Last."

"Satanta, the Last," she repeated, and shrugged. "Okay. Thanks. Guess I figured you weren't a Brad." She opened her mouth wide, waiting for the next morsel, but relented when I shook my head. "Right. So—how I came to be here. Well, see, that's the conundrum, isn't it? Because the fact is— *I don't know.*"

I squinted, unsure how to take that. "What do you mean?"

"Again, I'm sure I don't know. Only that ... I was at a stoplight—in Spokane—watching a stormfront roll in, when the news starting talking about, well, power outages, mostly, but also that people were going missing—I mean, not just one or two, say, over the course of weeks or even days, but, *dozens* of people, maybe hundreds, all at once, as though they'd never even existed. And I was just sort of wrapping my head around that, or trying to, when I noticed there were ... lights in the clouds. Shapes. Things that were above me at that point and seeming almost to ... to be looking down at me. To be targeting me. Me—on my little motor scooter— somewhere in the Spokane Valley." She laughed. "And the next thing I knew I was here," She indicated the Strip. "Scooter and all—just sort of dumped over on my side at Circus, Circus, and feeling ... almost as though I'd been tasked with something. As though there was something I was supposed to do. Though what it was I couldn't remember— and still can't, no matter how hard I try."

I'm afraid I just looked at her. What was there to say, exactly? That what she had described was impossible? That even though most the world's population had vanished and the dinosaurs had returned—an impossibility itself, but something we had accepted—her blacking out in one place and waking up in another was ridiculous?

"You should eat," I said, offering her more meat. "No more questions."

She pulled the flesh off the fork with her teeth and chewed, her eyes never leaving mine. "I have some," she said, talking around her food, "Questions, that is. Like, what the hell brought *you* here? And where do you get off on kidnapping me?"

I paused, knife in hand, as the fire crackled and popped.

"I—I came to sift ashes," I said—quietly, obliquely—but did not elaborate.

"You came ... to sift ashes," she said, and nodded once, twice. "Okay. I'll play. Why not. And these ashes are here, in Las Vegas?"

"In the suburbs, yes. On Canosa Avenue. It—it's all so foggy. I haven't been back for a very long time. But I'll know the way once I find the gas station."

"The gas station."

I nodded. "The one on the corner. The RGB. If it's still there."

"I see. And—and what do you plan to do with me?"

I looked at her in the firelight—at her auburn hair, which blazed in the fire's glow, and her green eyes, which caught the light and glimmered. "It is my wish that I should continue hearing your voice," I said.

She peered at me intensely, glimmeringly, as though she'd won some sort of victory. "Is that so?" Then she laughed, brusquely, boorishly, and held up her bound wrists. "Well, then. I guess you better start cutting, Chief. Wouldn't you say?"

"You're a real asshole, Satanta. Just so we're clear."

I turned around and looked up, shielding my eyes from the sun, and saw her glaring at me from Blucifer's saddle (to which I'd bound her with zip ties), before jerking the rein, tugging them after me.

"And here I thought you were different—if only for a minute," she continued. *"Boy,* was I wrong!"

"And I thought you were—how did you say it? On a speech strike," I said.

"I am," she snapped. "I just needed to say that one thing. Again."

We *clip-clopped* up S. Las Vegas Blvd, past the fairgrounds and a gaudy strip mall called the Bonanza, saying nothing, during which I found myself gazing at the sky lights— our ubiquitous friends since the Flashback—and noting how angry they seemed today, how inflamed; and noting, too, that Kesabe had not circled back in some time (for it was his tradition to run far ahead), a fact which was beginning to trouble me.

That's when I heard the strange sound: a kind of forlorn mewing, like the note of a horn being drug out too long, coming from just around the corner, just beyond the liquor store—and paused, holding up my hand.

"What? What's going on?"

I waved her into silence, dropping the rein, then hustled to the edge of the building—where, after peeking around the corner, I saw a juvenile sauropod of the Diplodocus family (meaning it was the size of a typical school bus) collapsed in the middle of the street—its right front leg stuck in a manhole.

"What is it? What do you see?"

I looked from the sauropod to the corner of a nearby building, where something had moved, then across the street to an overgrown alley. *Yes,* I thought. *There. And there. Between the tattoo parlor and the marijuana dispensary ...*

"Allosaurs," I said, gravely. "An entire pack of them. In desert camouflage. They—they've got something trapped."

"Omigod. It—it's not your dog, is it?"

I returned and picked up the rein, began leading Blucifer forward, into the intersection. "No."

"Wait ... what are you—"

"We're going through," I said.

"But what if those things—"

"They don't care about us; they want the bigger game. *For now.* Just hold on."

The horse's hooves went *clip-clop, clip-clop* as we passed, the bluish-gray sauropod coming into full view ...

A moment later she said, "It—it's stuck. In the manhole. Do you see that?"

I eyed the predators warily, continuing to lead. "There's nothing we can do about it."

"But she'll be helpless against—"

"That is the way of it," I insisted. "The way of the—"

"Look, would you stop with the Indian clap-trap? I'm not even sure—"

There was a *thwomp* as the allosaur by the building leapt into the road—not by us but about fifty feet away, near the sauropod.

"Jesus, can't you do *anything?* What about your bow?"

"And risk bringing them down on us?" I intensified our pace, sprinting toward the Stratosphere. "No!"

And then they were coming—the allosaurs from across the street—passing so close we could smell the meat on their breath; closing in on the frightened herbivore ... until we passed the scene completely and sought refuge in a nearby gas station (its storefront had long since collapsed) and gathered there trembling as the sauropod cried out—for it wouldn't be long now until they fell upon her.

"Jesus," said Essie, listening. "What a world."

"Yes," I said, remembering. "My father used to say it had a demonic sublime; every tree and every rock, every animal, including man, down to the lowest insect." I listened as the sauropod moaned, seeming already to give up, to resign its fate. "And yet."

"What do you mean?"

"What?"

"You said, 'and yet.' What did you mean?"

I unshouldered the compound bow—rubbing my aching deltoid, stretching my arm. "Nothing. It's just that ... maybe it doesn't have to be this way."

When she didn't respond I looked at her—found her already looking at me: calmly, meditatively, her eyes seeming to glimmer. "I'm sure I don't know what you mean."

"I mean ... that I could end it. Her confusion and terror. That I—could prevent her from suffering." I looked at the bow and the dark, poisoned bolts attached to it. "That it's in my hands to do so."

"A mercy killing, then. Is that what you mean?"

"Yes," I said.

She seemed to think about it. "Well, you know, you'd have to expose yourself first—in order to take the shot. And there's always the risk they might turn on you. Is that—is that a risk you're willing to take? And if so ... why? How would it benefit you—or us?"

I stared at her, confused by the change. "Look, just a minute ago you were—"

"Just a minute ago I was participating," she said, sounding cold, analytical. "Now I'm observing. And I'll ask you again ... why? What could it possibly change?"

I gripped my bow and thought about that, wondering what had come over her, and why her eyes seemed to dance, to shine—as though they'd been illuminated from within.

At last I said, "Jesus. Maybe because we're still human?"

And then I was moving: stepping over the overgrown rubble, hurrying around the nearby buildings; dropping to one knee near the allosaurs where I sighted the mewing diplodocus and released two arrows, one after the other, into the soft tissue of her eye orbit, killing her instantly—after which the predators fell upon her like wolves, snarling and clawing, opening her like a bag of sausage, tearing out her throat ... as I walked back to the station and was greeted by Kesabe, barking and licking my hand. As I looked at Essie and found her returned to normal, seeming almost not to know what had happened.

As she indicated the orange Union 76 sign and said, in her usual tone of voice, "So would this happen to be it? Your gas station?"

After which I looked around in a daze—recognizing the soda fountain (now an antique) with the American bald eagle on top; recognizing the wooden Indian which stood by the door—and knowing, at last, that I had found my way home.

"It—it's not what I expected," said Essie over my shoulder, as Blucifer whinnied and Kesabe pissed on the nearest tree; as the overgrown rancher sat—its nearly flat roof baking in the sun ... its slat fence partially collapsed.

"It's not a teepee; if that's what you mean," I said, and dismounted.

"I didn't expect a *teepee,*" said Essie, as I helped her down. "It's just that—it's so *white.* Like Wally and the Beav are gonna come running out any minute."

"My father didn't believe in reservations," I said, leading Blucifer to a bush, abandoning the reins. "He thought they were museums full of defeated people; just so many relics, withering in the sun. He wouldn't even take us there to visit our grandparents; they had to come to us."

"That must have sucked."

"No, actually—it really didn't," I gripped the doorknob and paused, wondering if I was really up to it; if I was fully prepared for what I might find. "It taught us—my brother and I—to see ourselves as individuals, not a collective—and a defeated one at that. Maybe that's why neither of us wound up pickled in Thunderbird."

I twisted the knob and eased the door open, watching sunlight spill across the floor, then stepped in slowly, cautiously. "He didn't buy the idea that land could be any sort of birthright, said living things had always competed for resources and always would, and that, change being the only constant, to deny that was to deny the fundamental nature of reality."

I paused in front of a framed picture of my mother, touching it gently, tracing a finger through the dust. "He always said, 'Should I apologize for winning your mother from a white man?'"

I laughed a little, and so did Essie.

"'No, of course not,' he'd say. 'Because that's what nature does, it *conflicts.* It competes.'"

I stared at the picture, hoping it had been painless for them and that they had just vanished like so many others. Hoping they had gone together.

"Well, that explains that," said Essie. She had leaned in and was examining my face.

I must have looked confused.

"Your war paint," she said. "It's red and white."

And I had to laugh; because she was exactly right, even though I had never thought about it—had never even considered it, at least not consciously—after which, feeling cavalier, I said, "My real name is Steve, by the way. At least, that's what my mother used to call me."

She paused, looking at me with something like pity. "Steve."

"Yeah. It—it means victor—"

"I'm gonna stick with Satanta. If you don't mind."

"Sure," I said, and shrugged. "I prefer it. More apocalyptic."

And then we moved on, picking our way through the overgrown house (liberating a stack of photo albums along the way as well as my mother's Polaroid camera), after which we came to my old bedroom—the roof of which had collapsed so that the palm trees were visible outside—and sat on the bed.

"You had a beautiful life," said Essie at length— perusing the photos, turning the pages. "You were very lucky."

"I know," I said.

"Not everyone is."

"I know that, too."

I peeled the plastic coating from one of the sheets and removed a picture, staring at it in the late afternoon sun, in the burnt ocher wash of what photographers called the Golden Hour. "That was us—my entire family—at Disneyland; in Anaheim—must have been about '78 or '79. I can tell by the hair."

She leaned close to examine it, her own hair tickling my cheek. "Hard to believe that's you. *Mercy.* You had prettier locks than I did. So did your brother."

I rubbed the Polaroid between my thumb and forefinger, slowly, absently. "All dust," I said quietly. "Everything in the picture, both the red and the white." I laid back on the bed, feeling suddenly tired.

"Nonsense," she said—and, to my astonishment, laid down next me. "You seem alive enough to me."

And then she began to doze—or so it seemed to me—and it was just myself and the queer lights: which glowed all of a color and showed nothing of their usual chaotic rhythms, but only looked down on us softly, ambiently, like Christmas lights hung from the very firmaments; serene.

If not for her having taken off her over-shirt during the night, we would never have found her—for it was only after giving it to Kesabe and having him sniff it that the Dutch Shepherd was able to track her: a trail which had led straight to the gas station and the allosaurs from the day before—not to mention Essie herself; who stood trembling yet defiant amongst the ruins and seemed almost to be goading the animals on, daring them to attack.

"Essie! Good God, Essie!" I shouted, fighting the reins, as Blucifer—panicked by the predators— leapt and circled and whinnied, kicking up dust. "What have you done?"

"Oh, don't you see? We had no right! No right at all!"

I dismounted quickly—having wrested Blucifer into submission only briefly, for he snorted and charged away even as I found my footing—un-shouldering my bow as fast as I could, nocking a bolt. "Back up into the store, dammit; do it, now! *Why, for God's sake?*"

But she only held her ground—even as the sky strobed and flashed and the clouds roiled with thunder—her feet planted firmly; her arms held wide. "But don't you see it? *Oh, how can you not see it?* Look into my eyes, Satanta. Look into my eyes and tell me you don't understand ..."

I sighted the animal nearest her and released an arrow, *Thwish!* —which struck the beast in its eye and dropped it, instantly, even as Kesabe barked and snarled and the others seemed to zero in on me.

"Look at me, Satanta. Slay ... *me*. Because *they* are in me, now, fully manifest. They—who have caused all the suffering. They, the very architects of the Flashback. And I want them to *feel* it. Oh, can't you understand? I want them feel what it is they have wrought!"

I caught a fleeting glimpse of her before the remaining allosaurs attacked: saw the eyes like a fire in the sky and the sallow skin shot through with green—until the animals charged and I loosed another bolt, dropping one as it ran, and yet leaving two, both of which would have fallen on me if Kesabe hadn't leapt into the fray like a pointy-eared threshing machine, barking and biting, scratching and snarling, peeling the predator away, as the other bit for my neck and I dodged, leaping onto its back; then stabbed it with an arrow again and again, hanging on as it leapt and bucked, groping for its eyes (which I would have gouged out had it not fallen), thanking the Great Spirit as it shuddered and died.

And yet I'd barely had time to climb off it when I heard Essie scream—not from the store's rubble but high above it, in the sky—where a pterodactyl wheeled like a kite in the sun even while gripping her like a ragdoll and beaking her as if with a sword—that is until it too was attacked by another, bigger bird—at which I snatched up my bow and nocked my last arrow, aiming into the flail of talons and wings, and shot the first bird clean through its skull.

And then it was over, or nearly so, as the thing fluttered down and dropped her; at which I ran to her and cradled her in my arms even as the bird next to us thrashed and died.

"They felt it," she gasped, "I know they did. They felt it through me."

"*Shhh,*" I said, "Save your strength. We have to get you—"

"They thought they could just see through my eyes—that they could observe us that way, study us ..." She coughed violently—shudderingly—hacking up blood. "But what they didn't know was that they'd *feel* through me too. Feel it all, Satanta ..." She groped for my hand and found it, began to squeeze. "The pain ... the terror. But also the compassion. The mercy. Like the kind you showed the herbivore. The kind—" She seized up suddenly as though her insides were being torn apart. "The kind you showed me. That—that we showed each other. And for the briefest of moments ... they understood. Go—go north, okay? You'll find people there, good people. I know—because *they* know. Our watchers. Our destroyers. I have been in their minds. Go north. But first ... first help your ..."

And she died.

I closed her eyes. And that's when it hit me how quiet it was, and that I could no longer hear Kesabe barking—that indeed, I could no longer hear him at all.

My grandfather once said, in response to my father, "We all live on reservations, some of us just don't know it yet." And though I didn't understand that then, I was pretty sure—as I stood over my friends' graves and watched the house go up in flames—that I did now; for he'd been talking about our limitations and the fact of our own mortality (trying to tell me, I think, as I got ready to leave for Los Angeles more than 30 years ago, that if I were going there to escape I was in for a disappointment). All I know for certain is that as I stood there over the crude markers—one for Essie and one for Kesabe—I felt smaller and less significant than ever before (and I'd felt pretty small and insignificant since the Flashback), to the point that I questioned going on at all, north or otherwise. But then Blucifer showed up with a familiar snort and whinny—where he'd gone I didn't know, nor did I ask—after which, feeding him what remained of the oats in my pocket, I decided we would head back to the coast and follow it north, for maybe there *were* people there, 'good people,' as Essie had said, and if that were true, then, truly, anything was possible.

Even so I hesitated—even after mounting and slinging the bow across my back (for I hoped to find arrows before leaving the city entirely), thinking on Essie, whom I had come to love even though I'd known her only for a short time, and on my friend, Kesabe (whom I'd named 'Kemosabe' but had shortened to 'Kesabe') ... a dog who had just been a dog but thought he was a wolf; and who—as evidenced by his final act—sometimes was, sometimes was.

Like you, maybe? I wondered, and laughed. *Satanta the Last—come Steve?* And yet wasn't it at least partially true? For the Flashback made of you only what you already were—however veiled that may have been in the world before.

And then I snapped the reins and we went, Blucifer and I—back toward the coast and the passage north. Back to the winding trail, which, like all winding trails, went everywhere and nowhere at once.

Because our days were so exhausting, I was usually out the instant I hit the pillow, entering a deep and perfect sleep the dreams of which I could not recall; on other days, the work continued—the only difference being that in the dreams I flew over the island like a hawk (rather than search it house by house, or, just as often, beach café by tiki bar); and was able to spot a bread crumb even while soaring high enough to see most of Alice Town (though not so far as Bailey Town). And always, always, I returned to the Bimini Big Game Resort and Marina, with its ruined, capsized boats and broken, shattered docks (now undulating against the seawall); its multiple floors and long, red roof—which, only weeks before, had been the only thing standing between Búi and I (and Amanda, too) and the tsunami. Nor did I merely revisit it in my dreams, for it was where I started and ended each day's search regardless of how much of the island we'd cleared (we'd reached Resorts World Bimini—the approximate halfway point between Alice Town and Bailey Town). It was where I was at, looking at Búi's many half-filled water glasses, when I heard Amanda's voice crackle suddenly, startlingly, over the walkie: "Sebastian, I'm a few houses past Resorts World—on the state-side of the key. And, ah, you're going to want to see this." She quickly added: "It's not a body, nothing like that. It's nothing to do with Búi. Just—get over here."

I stared out across what was left of the marina; at the crystal clear water and the reddening sky—in which a solitary pterodactyl whirled—and the golden clouds, like heaps of fleece pillows. Her tone of voice had given me pause. "Sure. I—I was re-checking the Big Game. The Bar and Grill. I'll ... I'll head up right now."

And I went, hurrying to where the Jeep was parked in front of the Sue and Joy General Store and laying the flare gun on its passenger seat—before turning the ignition and heading up Bimini Bay Way, staring between houses as I drove and peering into their tall windows (although for what I wasn't sure; we'd already checked them for Búi and their original owners had long since vanished in the Flashback). It was easy to do; driving so carelessly—there weren't any other drivers or pedestrians to think about; only the Compies scattering before you like flightless gulls or the occasional newspaper or plastic bag. That's how it had been since the Event; and, as a consequence, you tended to get to where you were going quickly and effortlessly, before the melancholy of the place could really sink in (it was the seeing of it all at once that did it; the sheer totality of all that emptiness blurring past), something I was immensely grateful for as I turned left on Queen's Street and jounced onto the beach—and saw Amanda's Prius parked next to the overturned truck and custom boat trailer; next to which lay, well, whatever it was. Because it looked like a kind of miniature submarine, only shaped and painted like a shark, replete with rows of sharp teeth. It even had a dorsal fin.

"What the hell is it?" I asked, getting out, then hurried to help her as she shouldered her rifle and gripped the thing by a fin.

"Seriously?" she asked. The sand loosened and slid from its hull as we pulled the object upright. "It's a Seabreacher." She stood back and dusted her hands. "Sort of a jet ski, only enclosed. It—people use it to dive under the water ... then breach the surface, like a dolphin."

I stood and looked at it—at the Seabreacher. "Okay. Great. And this helps us—"

"Don't be obtuse." She moved forward and tried the hatch handle, which turned—then opened the cockpit, slowly. "Seats two. Might even be able to slip in a third. Knew a guy before the Flashback, said he could pilot his all the way to Miami. That's what I meant by, 'Don't be obtuse.' It means we're not stuck here."

I must have looked—unenthused.

"That's a good thing," she said. "In case you were wondering."

"A good thing," I said, and looked back the way I'd come.

"Yes, *a good thing.*"

I focused on the small church further back along the beach—Gateway Outreach Ministry—which we'd already checked. Except for the sacristy, which had been locked (this had been before we found the rifle). Wasn't it at least possible she'd taken refuge inside it?

"Sebastian ..."

The answer, of course, was no. She'd have responded when we called out (and we'd called out a *lot)*. But what if she were sick, or wounded— unconscious, even? What if she'd been unable to hear us, or to respond even if she did? What if she'd been too debilitated to reach the door? Was it really magical thinking to suppose—

Amanda exhaled, defeated. "Sebastian ... what can I do?"

I turned to look at her as she shrunk down in the sand, looking more tired than any twentysomething had a right to— more haggard, her eyes vacant and puffy, her cheeks sallow. "I mean, how long do you think they'll last? One small, overgrown grocery store ... and a mini food-mart? (by 'overgrown' she'd meant the ubiquitous moss and vine— presumably prehistoric—which had come, along with the Compies and the pterodactyls, immediately after the Flashback) Six months? Couple of years—if we're lucky?"

I scanned the nearby homes. "Longer than that. Plus there's the bars and restaurants—not to mention all the houses." I looked at the darkening horizon. "It'll be light for a while. We should keep searching."

I felt her eyes follow me as I walked toward the Jeep.

"Sometimes I don't know what you want from me," she said.

I paused before climbing in. "I want you to help me find my wife," I said.

After which, realizing how cruel that had been, how unfair (for she'd been helping me tirelessly), I added, "You should get some rest. It's—it's going to be dark. I'll push on from here; okay? Don't wait up."

And I put the Jeep in gear.

The first thing I noticed when I got home to the duplex—it must have been around midnight—was that Amanda's unit was dark while mine was illuminated; something quickly explained when I swung open the door and saw the burning candles, not to mention the tinfoil-covered plate and half bottle of wine; or, for that matter, the greeting card-sized envelope—from which I withdrew a letter that read, simply, Happy 50th, S.B. *We'll find her.*

I guess I must have smiled.

"S.B." —*Sebastian Adams.* She had a memory like a steel trap.

I lifted the tinfoil and peeked at the dish—a fusilli pasta topped with white marinara sauce—but wasn't any hungrier than the last time she'd cooked; and merely re-covered it. I looked around the table. That wine, though.

I snatched it up and fetched a glass (funny she hadn't left me one) and then went out onto the deck—startling a Compy in the process, which leapt from the round table next to my chair and strutted—its little head bobbing, its tail jouncing— across the planks; into the cycad bushes.

"Boo," I said.

Then I settled in: propping my feet on the stool and looking out at the Atlantic, purposefully ignoring the little framed picture of Búi; disregarding the spilled peanuts and disturbed water glasses, some of which had been knocked over and some of which remained standing, but all of which contained or had contained small amounts of water, because now *I* was doing it (wasn't it funny, how couples could rub off on each other?).

"Tomorrow we'll do Resorts World," I said, still not looking at the picture. "If that's okay with you. I mean, it's like I've always said: You're the boss. No, no, that's how I want it. You should know that by now."

I took a drink straight from the bottle, which Amanda had left open, and exhaled. Then I tipped it again and drained the entire contents. "Well, honey, you wanted purple yams, remember? But it looks like your *dinky dau* sense of direction finally got the best of you. So you lost your way and mistook north for south; and now you're probably on the other side of Bailey Town—alone, confused, and terrified, I'm sure."

I looked at the sky—just a vast, black pit, mostly, like the ocean—but didn't see any lights, nor the prism-like jewels that had hung there since the Flashback—the time-storm; whatever—I suppose because of the clouds.

"Or ... have you disappeared to somewhere else; like everyone else on this island? Another time, another place, another epoch ..." I lolled my head against the backrest, woozily. "What the hell is this Flashback, anyway? I'll tell you what I think; I'm afraid Time itself has somehow been changed so that half the planet never existed. I'm afraid the first wave took the others and the second wave brought the dinosaurs and a third wave, well, a third wave took you. Because, honey, I've searched ... and searched ... and you just don't seem to be here. Not fucking anywhere."

A moment came and went; a moment in which I might have shattered, a moment in which I was capable of anything. But, as I said: It came ... and it went.

And then I *did* look at her picture; at her round, youthful face (although we were both precisely the same age), and her large, straight teeth. At the big brown eyes I'd often joked would eventually outgrow their sockets (to just dangle from their stalks, I'd said), and her ability to smile for the camera even after a terrifying ride in Miami (with a drunken boat captain) had almost ended our vacation—and our lives. At the girl from Bình Du'o'ng Province, South Vietnam, whom I'd married 7 years prior and experienced the initial Flashback with—as well as the meteor-caused tsunami which had happened immediately after—but who had then vanished without a trace on a trip to get purple yams. And chia seeds.

I laughed a little at that in the warm, bitter darkness, wondering if she'd ever found them.

"I bet you did," I said, my faculties beginning to fade, the wine beginning to kick my ass, before reaching out and laying the picture face-down on the table.

And then I slept, and eventually dreamed; of the island as seen from the heavens and of floating through a kind of limbo, a kind of purgatory. Of passing over Alice Town and Bailey Town and on to the open sea, which was infinite. Of being joined by another so close that our wings brushed, and flying—not like Icarus, not like Daedalus—but purposefully, fearlessly, without regret, into the ancient, seething, fire-pit cauldron of the sun.

Of what went through my mind when I saw the turkey-sized predators congregating at the end of the jetty (or rather the start, for we were heading back toward shore from the ferry terminal), I have no memory; other than to say I'd felt suddenly good, suddenly content, while striding along beside Amanda over the lapping surf (and laughing at some joke), and that, when I saw the predators, all of that just went away, just drained from the world, like the sun going behind a cloud.

Because it *had* been a good day; the first since Búi had disappeared. Nor could I put my finger on why, exactly: maybe it was simply because the weather had been so agreeable; or because the company had been so good. Maybe it was because we'd cleared an entire block of houses as well as the ferry by late afternoon and I'd been reminded of just how many places—safe places—she could still be. Or maybe it was because I'd forgotten, however briefly, that the world was a necropolis: a windswept graveyard, and that we—Amanda and I—were likely the last living souls.

Until we were coming back along the jetty from the ferry, that is. Until the slim, lithe predators with their long, dark tails and blue-gray coastal-patterns; their white, unblinking eyes, their little, undulating mohawks comprised of blood-red feathers, saw us.

"Are those—what did you call them? Comp—compsognathuses?" asked Amanda. "They don't look the same, for some reason."

I peered at the animals—just animals—through the shimmering heat: the three of them having become four, the four of them about to become five (as yet another emerged from behind an abandoned SUV) ... no, *six.*

"No," I said, absently. "I don't think so. They're too big."

I watched as the things seemed to focus on us, one of them shaking off while another used a foreclaw to scratch itself behind the ear. "Plus, they've got longer arms. And those toe claws; they're extendable—you can see it from here. More like a deinonychus (I had a dinosaur encyclopedia back at the duplex), or a—"

"Or a what?" She stared at the animals as though she were seeing a ghost. "Or a velociraptor, like in *Jurassic Park?*" She started to back up. "Because if that's what you were going to say, *don't.* Besides, they're too small."

"Movies exaggerate," I said—also backing up. "Just easy does it. They're as scared of us as we are of them."

But now there were more, about twelve at least (with still more streaming in), one of which darted forward abruptly ... and then hesitated, craning its neck to look at the others and shrieking—angrily, it seemed—just like a bird.

"Yeah," said Amanda. "That's bullshit. Look at them. There's strength in numbers."

Alas, I *was* looking at them, at their eerily intense focus (like cats starring at a pair of robins) and their coiled shanks; at their tails which were moving back and forth like knives.

I felt my vest for the other flares and touched the heel of my knife. "They're going to try and rush us; we're going to have to run for it. Are you up to it? I'm thinking all the way to the ferry ... how about it?"

"It'll bring them on, I guarantee it ..." She unslung her rifle and looked over her shoulder. "I don't think we can make it. I mean—wait ... what about that island shuttle?"

I watched as the others filed after the first and they regrouped—just a gaggle of heads and tails—then glanced at it myself. "Forget it. It's got a canvas roof— remember?"

"With steel ribs, though."

"Yeah, but—we'd be *stuck.* There's no key."

And then they were coming, not in a gaggle but in a staggered formation, bounding forward but in turns, running and pausing, as we turned and flat-out bolted—sprinting for the ferry as the sun shone hot and merciless and without compassion; veering for the island shuttle once we realized we'd never make it, piling through its driver's door and slamming it behind us as the raptors fell upon the vehicle like a threshing machine and began climbing and tearing at its canopy.

"Wait, don't—"

My ears rung as she started firing, blindly, into the animals, at least two of the slugs hitting the beams and ricocheting—one of them close enough to nick my ear.

"There's too many of them," I shouted, even as a dark snout stabbed between the beams and banged to a halt, gnashing its teeth. "Just stay low, they can't get through."

After which I eased the rifle from her hands and we hunkered near the floor; the raptors screaming and tearing the roof apart even as ragged pieces of it fell and they began reaching between its beams with their human-like forelimbs— swiping at us with their curved talons, blindly; reaching and groping and searching—like zombies.

Neither of us behaved bravely or kept our wits about ourselves. It was the screams that were the worst; which tore through the air like knives—like fighter jets passing so close you could see the rivets. Which split your mind so that you were too disoriented to think, to do much of anything. I'm afraid they got the better of us both as we cowered near the floor and covered our ears; as Amanda reached for me and pulled me close and I wrapped her up in my arms and squeezed her tight.

"Just hold me," she said, as the entire vehicle rocked and shook around us. "And don't let go."

And so I held her and didn't let go; cradling her head in my hands as the raptors screamed and continued their assault—as the entire truck was lifted on one side only to crash back down, as she said almost softly, "We—we have a responsibility. I never told you. A purpose. Because ... we're the last, and someone ... someone has to continue. Do you understand what I'm saying?"

I squeezed her tighter even as the glass and canvas rained down. *"Shhh,* save your strength. They'll give up and go away ... we just have to wait. Just—hang in there."

More broken glass; more shredded canvas. I squeezed my eyes shut; I was no longer certain they wouldn't get in.

"I want you to promise me, Sebastian. Promise me you'll meet me there—no matter what. Because if not us, then who?"

The raptors cried out in unison—like a perverse choir; it was almost as though they were celebrating, like this was their victory song.

I pulled back enough to look at her; at her dark blue eyes, so much like my own, and her youthful face—which was beautiful by any measure—understanding with perfect clarity what she'd meant; and realizing, too, to my great and utter astonishment, that I agreed; that we owed the world that, every bit as much as I owed Búi. That it was our duty, in a sense ... to ensure the bloodline survived; to propagate the species. And I realized something else, now that we were so close we could smell each other's sweat and I could feel the back of her hair against my hand and her body pressed against my own—like a rock; now that I had a raging hard-on in the face of what seemed certain death, God help me. And that was that I *wanted to live.* Irregardless of if we found Búi or not; I wanted to live—to continue the journey—to spit in the eye of whatever had selected me for extinction, whatever had selected Búi for extinction, selected the *whole world.*

Whatever had just crossed us out like a grammatical error: 'Remove this,' and scrubbed us from the sands of Time.

That's when we noticed it; at precisely the same instant, I'm sure. That the sound and the chaos had stopped. That the raptors, the screamers, the bloody *things,* had called off their attack. That the world had gone quiet again and we could hear the water lapping against the jetty's pilings.

We disengaged from each other and got up—looked out the driver's side window.

The majority of the horde was gone. We were still trapped; there remained about six animals—yes, six, exactly— but the larger pack, the larger pod, herd, murder, whatever, was gone.

I picked up the flare gun (which I'd found in the wreckage of a yacht after the tsunami, when Búi was still here), and unsheathed my knife. Amanda did the same, chambering a round in the Marlin rifle and taking out her own knife.

We never discussed it; never weighed the pros and cons of what we were about to do, never questioned what we were both feeling, which was that we wanted to live, and to not be afraid. We never asked the other if it was the right thing or the wrong thing—if it was worth the risk, say, when the other raptors could come screaming back at any moment. We already knew it was the right thing, because it was the only thing. Instead I just gripped the door handle and looked at her, and when she was ready—she nodded.

And then I threw open the door and we piled out.

There were six of them, as I said—all of whom rushed us the instant our feet touched the ground. All of whom snarled and charged us like wolverines as we raised our weapons and fired—the flare gun cracking and hissing, blanching the scarlet haze (for the sun had painted everything red and gold), its projectile punching through one of the raptors' chests and lighting it up so that its ribs were backlit briefly and I could see, if only for an instant, its burning, beating heart.

Yet still they came, another one leaping at me even as I dropped the gun—which clattered against the planks—as I dropped it and grabbed the thing by its neck—then brought the knife down with my other hand and stabbed it between the eyes.

"Run!" I shouted, even as Amanda shot another—her second—and then bolted toward the shore, drawing the others so that I was able to snatch up the flare gun and quickly reload it; so that I was able to pursue them and to shoot one in the back—while Amanda turned and took out the last of them (shooting it in the head so that the back of its skull exploded like a spaghetti dinner thrown against the wall; so that it collapsed, writhing, about 10 feet in front of her—whereupon she quickly approached it and shot it again, just to be sure).

And then she looked at me (as the dead and dying animals lay all around us) and I looked back: our chests heaving; our faces covered in sweat, our worn clothes bloody and disheveled, and I knew that *she* knew—which was that today *we* were the predators, the thing needing to be feared— the killers. And that neither of us needed to worry; not about food or other predators or mysterious lights in the sky or anything. Because we were the masters of our fate, we and no one else, not even God. And we were the master of the world's fate, too.

At which she ran to me and we collided and I held her fast, there on the long jetty in the Atlantic Ocean (in the Bermuda Triangle), there beneath a day moon and the blood-red sky, in an instant in which it was good, so very good, not to be afraid, not to be alone. And as to what may or may not have happened in those breaths, those pulse points between that moment and the next—the next day, the next search, the next milestone; as to that, I offer only a quote from Gandhi: "Speak only if it improves upon the silence."

It's possible I'd never felt so alive as when we took the Seabreacher out the next day. All I know for certain is that diving into the gurgling darkness at 50 miles per hour (and then breaching again, like a dolphin) turned out to be a lot of fun; so much so that we spent the better part of the morning doing just that: diving and breaching, plunging and rising, racing up and down the island (and around its horn, to Pigeon Cay) like damn fools; like college kids on a spring break, which I suppose Amanda was.

That is, until we broke surface and saw the meteor, which was arching across the sky like some orange and black torpedo—like some great, cyclopean flare—painting a trail of smoke and fire as though driven by God Himself; shedding chunks and pieces of itself, like an avalanche. Nor did we slow and try to see where it impacted but rather steered for the shore straight away, beaching the Seabreacher in the shallows near the Big Game Resort and Marina and popping its jetfighter-like hatch, clambering out of it swiftly as the meteor vanished beneath the eastern horizon and the sky exploded: first yellow, or rather a kind of golden amber, then orange, then pink, and finally, after several moments, blue again—although not before the shockwave hit us and blasted us off our feet—straight onto our backs.

"That ... that hit about the same distance away as the first one," I said—after we'd caught our breath and determined neither of us were seriously hurt. *"Holy shit."* I stood and dusted myself off, then peered at the glowing horizon. "Different location, but same basic distance." I must have looked white as a ghost. "Jesus—another P wave. Another primary. And that means—"

"Another *actual wave,"* said Amanda. "Another tsunami—headed this way."

She glared at me and I glared back, both of us knowing full well what that meant. We had about two hours. Two hours before it hit and all hell broke loose. At the max.

She looked at the Seabreacher, which gleamed in the sun, then into its cockpit. "We're going to need that fuel can; the one from the truck. And supplies: food, water, a way to start a fire—"

"Now wait just ... I can't—"

"Do you want to live or not?" she snapped— before placing her hands near the Seabreacher's caudal fin and pushing, trying to turn the boat around. "Because I do. And there's only a quarter tank left in this beast—which isn't enough."

I knelt beside her and helped; shoving as hard as I could, sinking and sliding in the sand—until we'd succeeded in turning the thing around.

"Okay," I said, leaning on the metal, our faces close. "I'll go to the duplex and get the gas—if you want to hit Sue and Joy's and see what you can find. Definitely some bottled water. And a lighter—several of them, if you can. Some toilet paper wouldn't hurt. We'll meet back here in, say—twenty minutes. No later. Okay?"

She looked at me uncertainly, compassionately. "You want to get your picture—don't you? I saw it next your chair. When I—when I left your birthday dinner."

I stared at her for a moment before lowering my gaze, focusing on the sand. "To prove she existed," I said, almost whispering. "To show that—that she was here. She deserves that." I looked out over the ocean. "So do I."

"Well—*go get it, then,* Sebastian. Go get it and get the gas can and get your ass back here. Because I can't do this alone."

And we went—on foot (our vehicles were still parked where we'd found the Seabreacher; on the opposite side of the island): Amanda splitting off for the General Store while I continued on to our duplex, which wasn't far. The hardened twentysomething going one way while I went another— haunted, guilt-ridden, alone.

Understand this: while it certainly *was* a T. rex—or something very much like it—it was not, by any stretch, a monster. It was not, for example, Godzilla (or any other behemoth as depicted in popular movies and books; including, I dare say, *Jurassic Park*). No, this was just an animal, big as an elephant, it's true (but no bigger), and yet, ultimately, no more outlandish than a spotted leopard or a crocodile (at least not since the Flashback); meaning it played well enough with its environment that I hadn't even noticed it—until it was too late.

Too late to get a shot in, anyway—not too late to run; which I did, dropping the gas can and bolting (even as the rex paused to sniff some spoor) before coming to a massive tree (a Caribbean pine, as I recall) and—after jamming the flare gun into my waistband—starting to scale it.

Alas, I'd barely attained the middle limbs when the T. rex arrived—its jaws snapping shut only inches from my shoes and its bellows echoing, furiously. Yet there was little it could do; I'd already climbed beyond its reach (and was climbing higher still). And so we tried to wait each other out, the tyrannosaur and I, as fragments of the meteor began lancing the earth and the doomsday tsunami drew inexorably closer. As the clock ticked mercilessly and Amanda surely fretted and Búi seemed almost to whisper in my ear: *Where have you gone to, my husband, my love, and why have you abandoned me? Is it not obvious—so very, very obvious— where I am? Why, oh why, can't you see?*

At which, inexplicably, I *did* see—something.

A roof.

Just a roof.

Indeed, there wasn't even anything special about it—this roof, other than it was attached to a house I had not seen from the ground—and so had not searched.

I rubbed my eyes and looked at it a second time.

How could we have missed that? Right here, in a wooded section of Alice Town? Right here—not even a block from the Big Game Club Resort and Marina?

I gazed out over the treetops, toward the ocean—and saw it. Saw the wave. Or at least a band of white along the horizon that *looked* like a wave. Was it possible? Búi—I mean? Had she gotten lost—or even injured—and just wandered into the first house she'd come to?

And did I have the time to find out?

And then something just snapped and I was taking out the flare gun and aiming it into the rex's mouth and squeezing the trigger—even as Amanda appeared at the corner of my vision and trained her rifle—after which the rex's maw lit up like a firework and blood jetted from its head (for that's where Amanda had shot it) and the tyrant lizard just collapsed—not threshing about like in the movies, not unfurling its foam latex or CGI tail, but simply slumping forward into the grass like a beached whale until the tip of its snout touched the tree and it was gone. After which I quickly climbed down.

"See?" she said, and chambered a new round. "We make a helluva team." She frowned a little as though she'd just thought of something. "Where's the gas?"

I nodded to where I'd dropped it—about 50 feet away.

"Thank God," she said. She slung the rifle over her shoulder and moved toward it—then paused. "What's wrong?"

I think I just stared at the ground. "I—I spotted something ... up there in the tree. Something we missed. It ... it's in that woodland—right next to the duplex." I lifted my eyes to look at her. "An entire house."

She only gazed at me, saying nothing.

"So, what," she said, finally, "You're just going to mosey back up there and check it out—with the wave practically on top of us? Is that it?"

I nodded, slowly. "Yeah. That's about it." I reached out to touch her but she slapped my hand away. "I'm sorry," I said.

She glared at me as though she might strike me. "Oh, you will be, Sebastian. You will be. Just as soon as that wave arrives." She started to storm off but stopped on a dime. "And for what? Another empty house? Another room full of ghosts? Because there is *nothing here*, Sebastian. *We're it.*" Again she started to go, and again she stopped. "What—you think you're the only one who's lost someone? The only one who's lost a wife, or a child, or their parents? Well, I've lost people too—everyone I've ever known. I did! Amanda Everett." Her eyes welled up suddenly and profusely and she swiped at them. "Just because I'm younger than you doesn't make it any easier. And yet we've been given this *chance,*

Sebastian. This one chance to face it together; to reboot the world. To literally save it. *To make babies,* for God's sake. And you just want to—you want to—"

And she came at me and we collided, briefly, before embracing—not forcibly (even violently), as had been the case on the jetty, but gently, softly. And then I handed her the flare gun.

"Take it—please," I said. "It—it needs to be with you. And the boat."

She hesitated, staring at the thing, before offering me the rifle, which I declined. Then she took it—the flare gun—decisively, resolutely, and stuffed it beneath her waistband.

"I'm going to wait for you as long as I possibly can, okay? Understand? Five minutes before I leave—I'm gonna to shoot a flare; that'll be your signal to drop anything you're doing and to run, not walk, back to this location." She stared at me with conviction. "Okay?"

"Look, you don't have to—"

"Ah, but I do," she said, and held out her palm. "No less than you have to go check out that house. The flares, please."

I dug them out of my jacket and handed them to her—there were only three. "You shouldn't wait too long. I mean, who knows how big this one will be, or how fast it's moving. But okay. One flare equals five minutes." I stepped back to look at her—to take all of her in. "It—it wasn't just because—"

"Shuttup. Just ... just go do what you got to do. All right?"

She moved to leave but paused.

"Five minutes," she repeated, and then really did go.

What was I feeling as I ascended the stairs to the upper (and last) bedroom of the house? It's impossible to describe; other than to say 'despair' is too weak an expression. No, this was hopelessness and anguish as I could not have imagined—not in my loneliest dreams and nightmares—made worse, no doubt, by my fantasizing along the way; by my sheer, undiluted optimism that each step had somehow brought me closer to my Omega Point, closer to Búi.

But the steps had not been kind—nor had they been quick. And by the time I opened that final door to the final room I had largely succumbed to the inevitable; by which I mean I hardly gave the space a glance—seeing only a jumble of blankets on a four-poster bed and a rickety nightstand crowded with half-emptied bottles of water—before quickly turning to leave.

At which, before I'd even gained the stairs, I froze. Dead in my tracks.

The bottles of water. The plastic containers labelled Aquafina and Dasani—all of them half-full.

My heart thumped against my chest.

"Honey?" I said, in the near perfect silence, "Are you there?"

And then I waited; feeling that even an apparition; even a ghost, a chimera, would be welcome. But there was nothing. Not so much as a creak in the floor. Not so much as a rustling curtain.

But then there *was* something. Just the smallest of voices—indeed, a sound so faint I might have imagined it. Just a small, feint voice which said, simply: "Honey? Is that you?"

And—*Dear God*—I scrambled; rushing back into the room without a moment's hesitation; finding her head exposed outside the tangle of pillows and blankets.

"Honey! Honey!" I knelt beside her at the head of the bed—between her and the open, curtainless window—placing my hands upon her: one on her stomach and one on her head. "Are you all right? Jesus, how have you ..." I looked around the room and saw several empty cans—Dinty Moore Stew and Jack Mackerel, mostly, one of which was entertaining a rat. "Can you move? Can you move, honey? 'Cuz we gotta get you out of here. And I mean, like, *now.*"

I suppose that's when I noticed it; that her eyes were jaundiced and her skin had turned a sickly yellow. And I knew, also, even before I asked her (and she explained it), precisely what had happened: for she had been bitten by something poisonous—a breed of Compy, she said—and had stumbled her way into the house, where she'd been lying, delirious and partially paralyzed, for some three and a half weeks now. Nor was she going anywhere, because the paralysis had presented itself as a kind of full-body muscle spasm, which meant even the slightest movement could cause her excruciating pain.

"But where—where are we now?" she managed—and was interrupted by a coughing jag. "I mean, I remember getting lost; and I remember being bitten, and I remember being stuck in a house for a long, long time. But what I don't remember is how I got *here* ... with you."

I moved to respond but paused, listening. For there was a sound now. A kind of low rumble—which rattled the panes.

I clasped her hand in mine and stroked her forehead, tidied the strands of hair. "We're home, honey. We're back home now. In our stupid little apartment. And—well, it's been a wonderful day, just really nice. We went to Greenbluff—do you remember? To pick cherries. And you picked so many you could hardly carry your buckets, so I had to do it for you—as well as carry my own; but that was all right because I started singing "Beast of Burden" by the Rolling Stones—you know, how I do: badly—and it made you laugh; which to me has always been the best sound in the world. And then we went and got pizza and ate it in the car, and after that, went to my Dad's—to celebrate his 89th birthday. And it was wonderful, just wonderful, with all of us there and the dogs chewing on our shoes and the sky sheltering everything like a big, blue dome; and later, like a dark umbrella."

I heard a *crack!* and a *whoosh* and a *fizzle* and looked out the window; saw the flare rising high like a rocket bound for the Moon: just rising and rising and levelling off—even hovering, briefly, like a UFO—before beginning its glorious fall, its sparkling and brilliant demise, its deep and fatal dive into the Big, Vast Nothing.

She rolled her head on the large, dirty pillow. "Is it—is it the Fourth of July? Are we watching fireworks?"

"Yes, sweetheart, we are." I moved out of her line of sight. *"Look at it, sweetie.* See how it sparks and shines."

"It's so beautiful," she said. "But what—what on earth is that other thing? That sound? It's like—it's like thunder, almost. Or an earthquake."

I moved around to the other side of the bed and got in—nuzzling up against her, holding her so we were perfect spoons. "It's the fireworks, honey, echoing off the buildings. It's nothing to be afraid of. Just a sound. Remember—remember when we went to the Air Show that year, and the sound of the jets scared you so bad that you started hyperventilating? And do you remember what I said to you, that you should just count to 10—and breathe?"

She nodded, her black hair tickling my nose, as the rumbling became a thunder, and then a *roar.*

"Try that now, okay, sweetie? Just count to ten and breathe, all right? Go ahead."

And she started counting, her voice clear and child-like, her accent as strong as ever. "One (inhalation) ... two (inhalation) ... three ... four ..."

"Remember to breathe, honey; do it after every number. I'm right here. *We're all here.* Your children and your parents and my Dad and all your friends. We're in this together—every one of us. And I love you. More than you will ever know. Goodnight, honey."

"Eight ... nine ... ten." There was a moment of silence, or so it seemed. "I love you too, sweetheart."

And then came the waters, surging, crashing, churning, roaring.

And we just breathed.

Deeply.

And yet we did not die—not really. Rather, it felt as though I slept, dreaming ... of the island as seen from the heavens and of floating through a kind of limbo, a kind of purgatory. Of passing over Alice Town and Bailey Town and finally out to sea: where a grain of rice turned out to be the Seabreacher. Of watching that Seabreacher skip and jounce over (and through) the waves like a dolphin—heading toward Miami—

and knowing, somehow (for I could see the future now as though it were laid out before me, like a tapestry), that it contained not just Amanda but the dreams and aspirations of all mankind; and that I'd had a part in that.

And, lastly, of being joined by another—so close that our wings brushed—and flying, not like Icarus, not like Daedalus, but purposefully, fearlessly, without regret, into the ancient, seething, fire-pit cauldron of the sun.

THE WINE DARK EARTH

I look at the shadow of the *Sarpedon's* conning tower, rippling through the waves like a boxy, black sail, its periscopes and radar like spikes on a war helm. Because it hurts my mind to stare at the illuminated cloud above—the Flashback Borealis, as they call it—which hangs over Seattle like a shroud, for very long, I have again diverted my eyes; this time to the water—the dark, roiling, whitecapped water—which, reflecting the cloud's ephemeral light, has become the color of wine, the color of blood.

Atop the sail are three shadowy figures: a tall, thin man in a pea coat and captain's hat (Captain O'Neil), a shorter form with long, windswept hair (Beth), and yet another—bearing what is called in Korea the 2-block haircut—a figure so short that only her head is visible.

A figure, I suppose, which is me. Pang In-Su. Survivor of the Bainbridge boat fire. Teen member of the Delta Dawn excursion force, which will go ashore soon. American-raised Korean deafmute whom, because of her big ears (never let it be said that God doesn't have a sense of humor), they call "The Mouse."

The Captain offers me his binoculars, which I take—they are heavier than I expected—and I look through them: at the towering office buildings and mirrored condos, black against the red haze, and the multicolored lights, which flicker, specter like, amidst the stoic, wine-dark clouds. *Amazing,* I sign. *That they can see so close.* I focus on an American flag—which is blowing from the mast of a sleek, blue-white tower with an angled roof. *It's almost like you're there. Right up against the buildings.* I look at Beth, incredulously. *How?*

She moves to sign but pauses, as though realizing she doesn't know, then exchanges words with the Captain—which I am unable to read.

He says it's because they contain prisms, she signs—even as the hair whips frenziedly about her face, stabs at her eyes. *Little crystals, which serve to bend and refract light.*

I hesitate, shaking my head. *I don't know anything about that. About prisms.*

I watch as she communicates with the Captain—verbally—but look away as he begins to explain, down through the plexiglass shield in front of us, to where the great, domed snout of the sub is parting Elliott Bay like a torpedo.

At last, she signs, *A prism is a faceted block of glass that splits light into its constituent colors. When light enters a prism it is refracted so that all the colors of the spectrum are dispersed—spread out—and you can see them.*

I look at the cloud, like a scaled-down interstellar nebula only right here in Earth's atmosphere, and the many-colored lights, which pulse and flash. *And what then? Do they ever recombine? I mean, do they ever become one again?*

Beth only smiles, as though seeing something in me I could not possibly see myself, and lolls her head toward the Captain, at which I can read: "She asks if the colors are ever reunited." And she winks at him.

She translates as he speaks: *They can be, yes. By using a second, parallel prism, an inverted one, which recombines the colors of the spectrum.*

I think about this but can only shake my head. *But—I don't get it. How is the light refracted in the first—*

There is a commotion and I look down to see Engineering Officer Puckett, who has stuck his head up through the hatch, and watch as they talk back and forth. It's hard not to notice how thread-worn he looks, how pale. I worry over how exhausted he must be: keeping everything functioning, everything up and running, and with only a skeleton crew to help him. Keeping us all *afloat,* literally—with ten men instead of one-hundred. More, he seems upset—although about what, given the darkness of the tube and my insufficient skill at reading lips, is hard to say.

Beth signs (as if noticing my confusion): *He's upset that he can't go ashore with the rest of us; that he's been chosen to remain on the ship. But the Captain says the same rule applies to him as it does to himself: That he is essential personnel and cannot be risked. That it's for everyone's safety; and that we all agreed to it.*

I watch as the fur lining of her hood, which is bunched up at the back of her head, undulates in the wind. I sign, *Am I still going?*

Yes, she says. *We'll still need you to get us past the retina scan—into the storage facility. But he's not too happy about it.*

I sign, feverishly. *Who else?*

Just Will, myself, CS Beasley; Petty Officer Slater ... He doesn't want to risk any more than is necessary.

I breathe a sigh of relief, feeling suddenly strange, suddenly buoyant. Because I *like* Will. I *trust* Will.

What I am less confident about is getting us into the storage area of what was once my uncle's company; i.e., Patriot Foods and Life Preserves (suppliers of ready-to-eat, freeze-dried meals to survivalists and preppers worldwide; people whom, though he'd made a fortune off them, he didn't seem to actually *like*). Or that an eye-scan made when I was 12-years-old—so he could watch my delight when, visiting the factory months later, the door to the vault suddenly unlocked (without my hand ever touching it) and swung open like a magic portal—might remain in the system; or that I might have changed so little that it will recognize me fully five years on, or that we will find a truck that still runs— and the keys will be in it—or, failing that, that Benny (CS Beasley) will be able to "hotwire" one (because he grew up in East L.A. and knows how to do those things); or any of it. Any of the things that we've planned and wargamed and rehearsed—but still are not remotely prepared to do. Not in this world, at least; the world left us by the Flashback. Not in Primordia; this Savage and Primeval Garden.

I watch the Captain as he unhooks his mic and studies the shore—then says something into it; which Beth translates. *We'll dock at Pier 59, on the south side of the aquarium.*

I look at the shore: at the gray and white aquarium building and the Ferris Wheel on the adjacent pier, which is hung with moss and vine; at the green and white Washington State Ferry—derelict; a ghostship, floating idly next to that.

Beth speaks as she signs: "We should get ready."

The Captain nods.

And then we follow Puckett: down through the hatch and into the cold, dark tube. Into the bowels of the ship.

Hold, indicates Will, with an upraised fist, and we hold: bunched together beneath the overhang of the aquarium's entrance like children, like boys playing war, our 45s and shotguns and M14s (for Beth and me) poised; our guts (or at least mine) tied up in knots.

He waves two fingers, which means *Column Formation,* and we form up; Beth and I near the back, so that we can still see the sub (as well as Captain O'Neil—lending cover from the sail), followed by Petty Officer Slater, preceded by Will and Benny.

Then we wait: as rain begins to spot the pavement and the city lays dormant, comatose—choked with moss and cycads, bereft. Then we watch to see if our arrival has been in any way remarked upon—and if so, by what—as the nearby fountain splashes (silently) and I wonder how it could possibly still be working.

But there is nothing. No cudgel-wielding survivors shambling, zombie-like, toward our position, their eyes full of stark despair. No saw-boned animals—prehistoric or otherwise—stalking us, warily, across the shattered pavement. Just the necropolis; the Big Empty; the stoic, faceless towers standing sentinel for no one. Just five hungry people—all of them expendable.

Go, hurry, indicates Will, and we move out, humping (as Benny likes to put it) around busted down barriers and rubble and construction equipment (they had just finished demolishing the viaduct when the Flashback hit), clamoring toward Pike Street Hillclimb. Watching for people—for life.

Watching for Murder Birds—that's what I call them—raptors with hungry, distended stomachs and the Flashback in their eyes.

Seconds later we're there, we've reached the bottom of the steps—the wide, broken, moss-covered steps—where, again, Will instructs us to hold and we hold, standing in the rain, standing in the open. Exposed—even as a pack of rangy, feral dogs begins sniffing about our trail.

Caution, he signals.

He looks at Beth and me and indicates his eyes; then the rain-dappled foliage to our left and right. *Watch our flanks,* he's saying—then points to Ensign Slater, his lips moving rapidly, "And *you* ... watch the women."

And then we proceed: climbing the cement steps toward the market and my uncle's two-story warehouse (which is on Pike Street, right next to the original Starbucks). Covering the distance like soldiers; like a seasoned platoon, all the way to street level and yet another set of stairs—into the Main Arcade, where something stirs, abruptly, violently, causing fishbones and rotten produce to cascade onto the floor. Where we train our weapons on everything and nothing— because it is nothing, really. The wind, perhaps, which moves through the arcade like a shoal.

"Okay, listen up," says Will, as I focus on his lips, one of which has a small scar, which isn't unattractive. "Here's the plan. We're going to move forward in what is called the *rolling-T formation;* all right? By which I mean: Benny and I up front, spread apart but abreast, each covering the side opposite ourselves; Beth and Pang in the middle, ready to shoot between us, and Slater in the rear—covering everything." He makes eye contact with virtually everyone, not just me and Beth. "Then it's through the North Arcade and onto the target; which will be directly across the street." He adds, softly: "And go *quietly;* all right? That might not have been just wind."

I look at Beth to find her already looking at me; attentive as ever, terrified. *I got it,* I sign, my stomach doing loopty-loops, and try to smile. *Thank you, Beth.*

And then we're moving—following Benny and Will, who cover the shops and day stalls, past Pike Place Bakery and Zabb Thai and Chicken Valley; past Catanzaro's and Pure Food Fish Market—all the way to Swanberg's, a gift store—where we pause, abruptly, probably because someone has heard something.

What is it? I sign, gripping the M14's handguard (which has become slick with sweat); locking eyes with Beth.

Will thinks he heard something; something in one of the shops. Something big—heavy. He says to check our flanks.

I just stare at her, bewildered. *But I don't want to check my flank,* I think. *Because if I do, I might see something; something I won't be able to unsee. Something I'll have to react to. And I'm not ready for that.*

But then, of course, I do—check my flank, that is. Then I look into the dusty, broken window of Swanberg's and, seeing only handcrafts and crystals and strings of fine beads, begin to exhale—deeply; wondering what it was I was so afraid of (for it is only the dogs, I am certain; the stringy, pitiable creatures we saw in the street; the slim, spare scavengers whom, having now inherited the earth, have simply followed us up from the pier). Then I just stare at the crystals; the prisms—the lovely, pure, many-faceted gems—which manage to glimmer even though there is so very little light.

At which, strangely, something seems almost to blink—to shutter and reopen. At which something *does* blink; just as surely as I am standing there. Something blue; ovoid, which glitters like a gem. Something which is encompassed by dark, tapered brow ridges and cruelly-curved hornlets; and bright-yellow markings—like a witch-doctor or a cannibal. Something I glimpse only briefly, fleetingly, in semi-profile—before it flits back into darkness and is gone.

We are no longer proceeding through the market slowly, cautiously, but are in fact fast-walking—*double-timing,* as Benny would say—out of the enclosed portion of the piazza and down a corridor full of craft stalls—into a space which stretches, or seems to; into a state of mind: like when Jimmy Stewart looks down the stairwell in *Vertigo.* Nor does anyone still believe it was the wind that disturbed the produce; or that, as in my own case, the dogs somehow followed us onto the concourse (in perfect silence, apparently, like ninjas). No; the feeling now is that, as evidenced by what I saw (or think I saw), we have been met by something new; something unknown; and that we are, beyond a doubt, *no longer alone.*

Not, of course, that we ever actually *were* alone—not really. How could we be, when the weight of everything, *everyone,* gone before us presses down like thunderheads—like the countless tons of water displaced by *Sarpedon?* How, when everything once coveted by the Vanished—the shirts and hats and watches, the rings and bracelets and sunglasses—still lay about us everywhere, like the piles of personal effects at Auschwitz? When, even on the sub, the ghosts outnumber the living—and by a comfortable margin?

How, indeed, when the atmospheric pressure has become such that we are finally as of the dead, only walking. That we are all just lost—each and every one of us, and worse, that we are beholden. To the Flashback and our own worst natures. To the black and yellow predators who may even now be near—such as on the other side of this wall—stalking us like psychopaths; herding us like cattle. Tensing before they—

And then, like a miracle, *we're out;* we are out of the market and into the open, into the rain—where I can breathe; where *we* can breathe; and my thoughts vanish like ephemera, like smoke, at least for the moment. Then we're crossing Pike Street and into a narrow alley—the alley between Starbucks and Patriot Foods; which is scarcely three feet wide—en route to the loading dock and the "proverbial bank," as Will put it. En route, at a clip, to the luckiest break of our lives.

And yet it is so much more than that; rather, it is a series of lucky breaks: from the box-truck backed up to the loading dock just as snug as could be; to the solar panels working precisely as predicted (as evidenced by the dim light over the man door); to my easy passing of the retina scan; it is, in the end, a kind of revelation, a kind of magic. As though God Himself has looked down through the lights and the wine-dark clouds; and, seeing our hope and fear and desperation—our *truth*—extended to us the Horn of Amalthea.

That's when I feel it; that's when the ceiling shakes and I turn to see a fireball crashing deep inside the warehouse (not the foyer, which is where Beth and I are waiting as the men return from their sweep). That's when everyone freezes and Will snatches up his radio and seems to belt, "Go ahead."

I look at Beth but she quickly shakes her head: *Not now,* she indicates, watching Will, listening intently—as her face lights up and the floor jolts yet again.

Then Will is lowering the radio, addressing the group, as Beth begins to sign, frantically, *So there's good news and bad news. The bad news is: those aren't just giant hailstones—which I reckon you've already noticed. They're meteors. Golf ball-sized bolides. Worse; there's more of them—and I mean a lot more; coming right now—which means the submarine is gonna have to dive, and quick. Which means it's just possible we are in a world of shit.*

He focuses exclusively on Beth and me—I'm not sure why. *The good news is, that truck parked at the loading dock is already stocked; I mean, it's packed to the gills—they must have been ready to ship out when the Flashback hit, and the keys are in it. So, if you'll be so kind as to just climb on board, we've got a sub to catch.*

And then he winks at us; to inject a little humor, to put us at ease, because that's the kind of guy he is; the kind of guy who would risk (and finally capsize) his own boat—and Beth's, too—to pull you from yours—which is burning. Who would do it not knowing there's a submarine coming which will rescue you all; which will lift you from the cold, dark water into its dry, cool hold—its beating, nuclear heart; its close-knit *family*. Who would just simply do it—even were there a storm of meteors, as there is now: punching holes in the ceiling, letting in the rain.

Benny, I want you and Slater in the rear—okay? To sort of—

Benny interjects and I read his lips: "... in the rear with the gear. Ain't no skin off our teeth, Boss."

"With the door open," adds Will, his scarred lip curling up a little—like a swashbuckler; or a pirate. "To act as tail gunners—in case any of those things, whatever they are, decide to pursue. You can do it."

"But the cases of food—"

"The food will be fine; you saw the shelves. It'll be just like a B-17; with communication through the central passage. Beth and Mouse will ride with me—up in the cab, where there isn't enough room for you, anyway. Anything moves—I want you to light it up. Okay?"

But then my concentration flags and I lose the rest—not that it matters: the look on everyone's faces tells me everything I need to know. Then everyone just nods and shoulders their long guns—grimly, resolutely. Stilled for whatever may come; undeterred.

And we move out.

I am looking in the side-view mirror when I see them: just a blur of black and yellow, like wasps—rounding the corner from Stewart Street onto First, pursuing us down the avenue. Nor am I oblivious to the vibrations in the air—as though reality itself were being pricked by a pin—or the whiff of sulfur and graphite in the cab, meaning Benny and Slater have engaged, have already opened fire—on *them,* the allosauruses (I can see now clearly); the *wolves of the Jurassic.*

Nor do they fall—not even one—but continue the chase: weaving between the stalled vehicles (and falling meteors) like dolphins, like black and yellow orcas, bounding over them like cheetahs as Will navigates the same obstacles and tries to pick up speed, tries to outrun them.

Which he comes close to doing—before one of the animals veers close and picks Slater off like a lamb, like a sacrificial calf (I can see it through the passageway); biting him in the leg before yanking him from the truck—pinning him to the road as his blood splashes like red wine and mingles with the rain.

And then we're slowing—were grinding to a crawl, as Will turns onto Seneca Street and the truck leans precariously, threatening to tip, and the predators swoop past on both sides, like hawks. Then we're speeding toward the waterfront and the sub as the animals regroup and relaunch their pursuit and the meteors fall all around us—exploding like grenades.

Indeed, then we are almost home—having turned onto Alaskan Way and even passed University Street—when the impossible happens and a juvenile allosaurus leaps *into* the truck—even as Benny retreats, firing. Then it all falls apart as the wet animal pins him to the floor and he drops his shotgun and Will—before we can even react—draws his sidearm and tries to target the beast. *Whilst driving.*

That's when it happens—that's when time just sort of stops, or at least slows down, practically on a dime. That's when everything starts moving in slow-motion, like in a movie. When, watching as the beast tries to advance but is prevented from doing so by Benny—who's got it in a headlock and is punching it repeatedly, even as he himself bleeds out—I realize he isn't just trying to survive but is trying to protect us; to protect Beth and Will and myself. And, too, that I've raised my own rifle and begun to squeeze the trigger—even though I know it's too late and that we are swerving out of control. That the whole truck is tipping, falling, impacting against the street—not just once but three times. Four times, at least. *Five.*

That we are in fact rolling: tumultuously, shatteringly, riotously—over and over and over again.

It takes a moment to realize, but, we've survived, somehow, in spite of having been ejected and scattered like sides of beef, like floppy-limbed test dummies, so that Beth and I lay in the fountain while Will lay in the avenue—as broken and bloodied as we are. As for Benny; well. *I can't.* I just can't.

Nor, for that matter, have the great predators left us but have in fact regrouped and reconnoitered—scanning the area like cameras, like Martian Death Machines, identifying everyone's exact whereabouts.

At which I help Beth up and look at Will; see that he has crawled to a long gun amidst the wreckage and is even now gesturing with it, barking something I can't read, indicating we should go. At which he stands and begins to stumble off, distracting the allos away from us, away from the ruined truck and impossible fountain, still flowing, drawing them across the street into the construction area.

That's when Beth collapses—just crumples like paper into the icy water—and I look on in horror as her blood spreads like ink, like a wine-dark cloud. So, too, is it the moment the sky erupts in color—as though the alien lights themselves have been agitated by her pain—colors which blend and bleed in and out of each other like spotlights intersecting, like time and space coalescing, until they show a sudden, perfect white—like an A-bomb going off or the sun itself exploding—and everything is cancelled, just glared out completely—if only for an instant, if only for a breath, an eye blink.

Alas; it's also when I look back at Will to see him pinned against the cyclone fencing and firing again and again—taking out as many allos as he can, going down fighting. It's when I turn to Beth and see her smiling; see her staring into that strange cloud even as her body seizes and starts to tremble and her legs twitch; as I kneel beside her in the water and sign—because I know she hasn't very long: *What is it? What are you seeing?* —as the white light flashes yet again.

At which she just smiles—only weaker, fainter, and signs, *The second prism.* Then adds, *Where is Will?*

And I turn in time to see him crumpling beneath the onslaught of the allosaurs—disappearing from view—before refocusing on Beth with the intention of telling her he's fine—but find her shrinking noticeably, almost as though she's been vacuum-sealed, and her eyes rolling around white. And then she's gone.

I stand, the silence begetting silence, at least until a meteor hits not ten feet away and I am pelted with debris, which burns like white phosphorous, scalds like hot pokers. Then I am being pushed and yanked along by Captain O'Neil and Enge Puckett— being rescued, I suppose—as we return to the sub and it begins to drift, to move away from the pier and the aquarium—back out to sea. As everyone gestures from the hatch for us to come but the captain and I stand transfixed, gazing at the overturned box truck and the cases of food everywhere; looking at the body in the fountain and the animals feeding at the fence line—not with sadness, which we are so far beyond, nor anger, but meditatively, blankly.

Looking, finally, at the red-black clouds and the dead city, the eerie lights, the wine-dark earth. Looking and wondering what's next for us; if anything. And wondering, too, if it's true—what Benny said about Vashon Island; which was that there's a doomsday compound there with enough food to last a decade (if, that is, one can outfox the security systems—which he said were lethal), and, of course, if it wasn't just an urban legend, which he said was likely.

Just wondering and meditating—until a meteor hits the nearby water and the captain says it's time to go; it's time to submerge. After which, reluctantly, we follow Enge Puckett—down through the hatch and into the cold, dark tube. Into the bowels of the ship.

THE BIG EMPTY

Photographers call it the golden hour, that period of time right before sunset when the sky glows orange and the shadows lose their edges, and the world becomes, for the space of about 20 minutes, something elevated and painterly—ephemeral, even sublime. Add to that the ocean breaking over the rocks and the black and white 19th century lighthouse, and, well, you have some idea of how seeing Granite Point that first time affected us (when we were taking it all in by Jeep, whose top we'd removed in spite of the pterodactyls swarming the beach). So, too, were there the strange lights in the sky, which peered down, relentlessly, disapprovingly, as though we had no right to even celebrate (by going on what Amelia had called our "post-apocalyptic honeymoon"), nor to end our crushing isolation.

Beyond that, though, beyond the fact that it was the golden hour and the waves were crashing and that one side of the lighthouse gleamed like polished brass (or that we were still euphoric over having encountered each other less than 24 hours before), beyond all that was our shared epiphany; which was that the lantern, far from being illuminated from without, was, now that we'd had a chance to observe it up close, shining from within. That it had somehow been kept on—either by electricity or gas or the burning of oil or kerosene—and that it would have had to have been carefully maintained. Which meant that someone, somehow, someone just like us, perhaps, had managed to survive.

"It's beautiful," said Amelia—and swallowed, batting away the tears. "My God, Francis. Look at it. I never thought—"

"That you'd see a light again, I know." I peered at the house attached to the tower's base and the old truck parked in its drive—which looked to be in surprisingly good shape. "Nor did I." I looked at her sidelong and gave her a little wink. "But then, I didn't expect *you,* either."

She didn't notice, only continued staring at the lantern house, as if she were in a daze. "It shifts ... the light. First white, then blue, then purple. And then a color—sort of like bottle green, only iridescent. Like a mallard's neck. And yet shot through with ..."

She looked at me as if for help.

"Beats me," I said. "I'm color blind. Red-green color deficiency. Either way, I suggest we make contact—if we're going to. It'll be too dangerous after dark."

She seemed to come out of it, whatever *it* was. "Is that a good idea? I mean, with just our knives?"

"No," I said, studying the darkened house. "But— whoever they are—they're using *something* for power." I lifted my gaze to the rotating lamp. "Enough to turn and illuminate that thing. And I'd like to know what it is." I looked at her across the cab, which was bathed in golden light. "Wouldn't you?"

And we just stared at each other: there by the lighthouse at Granite Point on the Oregon coast, after the time-storm— the Flashback, as someone had called it at the beginning—the dinosaur apocalypse. After everyone had vanished and the entire world had become a landscape of cycads and ruins, a place inhabited by winds and the souls of winds, a lost country.

"Jesus. Just—Jesus," said Amelia, staring at the decomposing body. "How long do you think it's been here?"

I examined it where it was sprawled on the back porch, facing the ocean, its skin blackened and clinging to the bones—like it had been vacuum sealed—its wispy hair fluttering. "Hard to say. Few weeks. Maybe a month." I batted away the flies. "Long enough for the organs to liquify."

"How—how do you know?"

I studied the holes in its head, a smaller one which was about the size of a dime and a larger, more cavernous one— the exit wound. "Because, otherwise, there'd be brains all over." I stepped over it and picked up the gun, checked its chamber. "There's still bullets in it."

She stared at me tentatively as I closed the chamber and gripped the weapon in both hands—neither of us saying anything. At last I nodded to the back door—the screen of which banged back and forth in the wind—and tried to brace myself. "You ready?"

She shook her head.

"Let's go," I said.

And then she was holding the screen as I inched forward and gripped the knob—turning it slowly, carefully, easing the door open. Stepping into a room which was dark as pitch; which reeked of cat piss and despair.

We worked well together, that much was clear; it was evidenced by how we swept and cleared the house so efficiently, Amelia opening the curtains (to let in more light) even as I scrambled to quick-check the rooms and closet spaces—finding a radio with batteries in it as well as some flashlights; not to mention a pantry full of food (mainly jars and jars of canned fish—salmon and snapper, according to the labels). Still, what I *didn't* find was any evidence of a non-electric power source for the lantern; something which seemed impossible—given the grid had failed shortly after the Flashback and the house itself was completely inert. Nor would this have gone unexamined—that is, if not for the discovery of the door; by which I mean the padlocked door to the tower itself, which we stumbled across at virtually the same instant—or so it seemed—having found it tucked away in a kind of antechamber in the furthermost section of the home.

"But, why the hell would he lock it?" I confess I was flummoxed.

Amelia frowned. "Why wouldn't he? He probably felt as though he were the only one that—I don't know, could be trusted with it. To maintain it. Especially after the Flashback."

She fingered a small hook next to the door. "That's odd—don't you think?"

I stared at the hook. It was the only thing that *wasn't.*

"It's probably on that corpse; the key, I mean."

She looked up at me fetchingly, her brown eyes—she said they were green—flicking up and down my body, once, twice.

"Now wait just a damn minute,"

"Now you wouldn't promise me a lighthouse and then fail to deliver, would you?" She ran her hands over my shirt and up the sides of my neck, cupping my face in her palms, tilting her head. "I mean, we *are* on our honeymoon—aren't we? And who knows what a girl might do if escorted to the top of that beautiful beacon with the waves crashing all around her and the seabirds—"

"Pterodactyls," I corrected her. "They're pterodactyls. And they'll peck your eyes out."

"Whatever," she rasped, and brushed my lips with her own. "What are you afraid of? That you'll catch the Ebola virus? Or maybe smallpox? The 1918 flu?"

"What I'm afraid of," I lowered her hands gently. "Is that we're going to lose the light and get stuck here. Like, all night." I looked at her sternly. "And I don't think you want that."

She picked at and adjusted my shirt collar, undeterred. "Why not? I mean, where else should we go? Back to Walmart? Back to those little settees in Home Furnishings, with their hard, hard little cushions—where you were such a gentleman, I might add, to just talk to me and assuage my doubts, and to not try so much as a—"

There was a sound, a kind of warbling yowl, a drawn-out, caterwauling, doleful cry, which rose up from the nearby trees and reverberated along the shoreline—where it was promptly answered by another, and yet another.

Neither of us moved.

At last I said: "That was a pit raptor."

Nobody said anything as the waves crashed against the rocks and the pterodactyls squawked.

"Out on the point? That's impossible."

"No, it's not. They're night hunters. They're just beginning their workday."

"But—"

"*Shhh.* Listen."

The sound came again—briefer, this time, more succinct, as though the animal was moving.

I looked around the room—my heart pounding, but there were no windows, no way to tell what was going on outside. "We've got to go. Like, now. Before—"

"But, don't you see? That's what I was trying to tell you. *We took the top down.*"

I froze, feeling as though the walls were closing in—like I might actually pass out. But then—then it just passed, I can't really explain it, and I was myself again (the "cool cucumber," as Amelia had described me), and what's more, I'd accepted it. Accepted that I had led us blunderingly into a bad situation because I had hoped, in some dim quarter of my mind—and this despite it being the end of the world itself—to make time with her.

Amelia. The girl I'd met in a ruined Walmart in Coos Bay while scrounging for a pair of shoes—again, while the sun was going down—as well as something to eat. I guess one didn't know whether to laugh or to cry. Either way, one thing had become clear. And that was that, for this night, anyway— we weren't going anywhere.

Now, you might ask: Didn't I find it odd that she'd be so adamant on sleeping separately—in spite of the cold and her earlier flirtatiousness—that we had to drag a bed into the antechamber? And my answer is: No. Not really. Rather, I just took it to mean she was establishing a boundary, and that the apocalypse itself couldn't turn her into something she wasn't—which, frankly, I respected. Besides, any man who knows anything knows the coin paid going in is the same earned staying out, which is to say Time, however scrambled it had become, was on my side, and I knew it.

More than any of that, though, was that I wanted to try out the radio, which I did, drinking scotch from the caretaker's stash and looking out the window—which framed the breakers and gathered pterodactyls like a picture—wrapped in one of the keeper's thick, filthy blankets. At which I was delighted to discover that the batteries were good and that it in fact worked— and so began scrubbing the dial; hoping, against hope, to catch something, anything (an emergency broadcast signal, a test tone, *anything*) but finding only static; until, suddenly, even as I was about to give up, there were a flurry of sounds—sounds such as I hadn't heard since before the Flashback—which, taken together, constituted a thing I'd thought no longer possible, a thing as extinct as the terrible lizards themselves, which I turned down immediately in order to keep all to myself, and soaked up as though fresh from the desert—marinating in it, breathing it all in, drowning.

Woah, Georgia ... Geoorrgia ... No peace, no peace I find. Just an old, sweet song, keeps Georgia, on my miiind ....

I think I must have sunk to the floor, sunk to it in a veritable puddle, spilling the bottle of scotch which clinked and sloshed, forgetting about the cold and the lantern and the pit raptors—which may or may not have still been out there—forgetting the lost country and its hopelessness.

I said just an old, sweet song, keeps Georgia ... on my miiind ...

Until it was over, and the instruments and back-up singers had all faded to nothing, and a voice came on—a new voice, a speaking voice; a *woman's* voice—and said, mellifluously, "And that was the immortal Ray Charles, with "Georgia on my Mind." And this—this is Radio Free Montana—with Bella Ray, broadcasting from Barley Hot Springs in what some used to call the Great White North—which was not intended as a compliment." She laughed. "So just trust in God and keep your powder dry; and stay with us here wherever you may be—whether that's a cold water flat in Devil's Lake, North Dakota, or a high-rise hotel in Miami-Dade—wherever you are out there in the Big Empty, we here at KAAR-RFM will try to have your back. And now it's back to the music and Patsy Cline, with "Walking After Midnight." Take it away, Patsy!"

I was up and moving down the hall almost before I'd realized it, double-timing it for Amelia's room, using one of the flashlights I'd found to see the way, knocking on her door (which seemed thick as a vault now that I thought about it and just sort of absorbed the sound, like solid rock).

Jesus, I remember thinking. I'd searched for a mere signal and found a whole community! It was like we'd gotten rescued from *Gilligan's Island;* escaped from the *Land of the Lost.* Like we'd come home from Oz itself. And I simply couldn't wait to tell her— although how the music hadn't awakened her was completely beyond me. I mean, surely—

But she didn't answer the door, which seemed impossible, not even when I pounded on it with my fists, which literally shook off paint peelings. "Amelia!" I shouted. "Amelia!" I pounded again and again. "Wake up, Amelia!"

Until at last I thought, *Fuck this,* and tried the knob— only to find it locked. At which I resolved to kick it in (fat chance), or find an ax (she could be dying in there!), and was backing away from it to try just that, when it occurred to me I was acting like a psychopath and a fool.

The fact was, she was a heavy sleeper, I'd seen it myself the previous night. And she was in the habit of wrapping the pillow about her head, which would have further blunted any sound. And that door—Jesus Christ.

I wandered back into the living room and turned off the radio, to conserve the batteries. It would just have to wait until morning, like digging the key out of the corpse's pocket. The fact was—everything was going to be all right. And with that I found another bottle of liquor—Jeppson's Malört, whatever the fuck that was—and settled in on the couch; after which the grandfather clock struck 8 and what looked a plesiosaur, only huge, like a small whale, leapt from the ocean—to snatch one of the pterodactyls from the orange-painted rocks.

"What, you've never wondered if you dreamt something or actually experienced it? Happens to me. And you said it yourself: you were shit-canned off that—what was it?"

"Jeppson's Malört," I said—still tasting it in my mouth, smelling it on my sweat. Still feeling as though it had been poured over my brain like bile. "Look, it wasn't a dream, okay?"

I stopped walking and stared at her—to emphasize my point—as seabirds swirled (there were no pterodactyls today) and the waves crashed. "Look, I know it's hard to believe, but I'm telling you: Someone is on the air." I gripped her shoulders—harder than I'd intended. "Radio Free Montana—that's what they call themselves. Broadcasting out of a place called Barley Hot Springs. Jesus, Amelia. Don't you see what that means?"

She placed her hands on her hips. "Have you listened to yourself?" She briefly put her face in her palm. "How would a signal even get from there to here, without—I don't know, a relay of some kind. What you're saying is *crazy,* Francis—can't you see that?" She shook her head as if in pity. "I mean, can't you?"

"I'm not crazy," I said, and took my hands off her. "I heard what I heard. And we've got to go there—like, now, today. While the sun is shining. I swear, I'll—" I looked back at the lighthouse and the old truck parked near our Jeep. "I'll go alone if I have to."

She picked up a couple pieces of driftwood, first one, then the other, looking exasperated. "Then why aren't they broadcasting anymore? Riddle me that, Francis. And why aren't you gathering wood for the fire? For that matter; why aren't you burying our friend?"

"There's maggots," I said—and started walking, finding it strange she hadn't mentioned the key. "I'm working up to it. And to hell with the fire. You're just trying to change the subject."

"Oh, I see. Well—isn't that what we came out here for? To gather wood?" She hurried to catch up with me. "Or would you prefer to freeze again tonight? You know: and to pickle yourself in Jeppson's Merlot, like—"

"Malört," I said, increasing my pace. "Besides, I don't plan on being here. And neither should you."

She stopped abruptly and called after me, "Then where are you going?"

I took a few more steps and then paused—but didn't turn around. "I was just walking—if you want to know the truth. Figured it would do us some good. But now—now I want to look at *that.*" And I pointed.

At the beach grasses which had been singed and lain down nearly flat—as if a burning helicopter had set down directly in their midst—and the saltbushes twisted into an insidious vortex. At the mounds and mounds of sand and other sediment which had been dredged up and redeposited—in an approximate circle—by some presently unseen force (a bulldozer, perhaps); or an object from space having made sudden, violent impact.

"What do you suppose it was?" asked Amelia, poking the ashy dirt with one of her sticks, stirring it around.

"I wouldn't do that," I warned. "Could be unexploded ordinance—you never know."

She gasped and moved back—although not very far—as I studied the point of impact, noting how angular it was, how geometrical (as if a giant arrowhead had been stabbed into the earth); all of which left me to wonder—had the object somehow been removed? Or was it still down there?

I scanned the area, looking for debris. "There's no wreckage—which is odd. So I doubt it was a satellite. No; I'm afraid there's only two possibilities, really. Bomb or meteorite. And I doubt very much it was a bomb."

"Or *is?*"

"Or is."

She didn't say anything, only continued staring into the dirt.

At last I said, "What is it?"

"Nothing ... it ... it's nothing." She seemed dazed, confused. "It's just that ... it all seems so strange now. I mean—that we ever had use for such things. For bombs. That we could spend so much time and effort and money ... just to kill each other."

She looked out at the ocean and the billowing clouds, the whirling seabirds, the distant pterodactyls. "That we could make such ugliness and pain—such sheer terror—and in such a beautiful world. I mean, *look* at it, Francis. Can you honestly say that it's not better off without us? Or that, even if there are other people, we're not better off without them?"

I must have looked confused. "What the hell are you talking about?"

She turned to face me; her dark eyes close to mine. "Give me one reason, Francis. Give me one reason why we shouldn't just stay here, forever—you and I, alone. Give me one reason why we shouldn't restore the lighthouse and defend it and kill anyone who comes close; why we shouldn't go so far as to kill them first—just kill them where they sleep—and stop the threat before it even begins. Tell me now why they're worth saving, and why we shouldn't finish what *they* started," She nodded briskly at the sky, "What they instigated with the Flashback but failed to complete. What can be completed still—"

And I kissed her, suddenly, completely—I'm still not sure why, maybe because I thought she was breaking down and that doing so would be the only way to snap her out of it, to shock her back to her senses. All I know is that she responded almost immediately and we stayed like that for some time, kissing not as children lost in a storm—which is how it had felt that first night when she'd pecked me on the lips before retreating to her own settee—but as something akin to red hot lovers: thirstily, intensely, primally (but not base), the Bogie and Bacall of the apocalypse.

After which I said, "Maybe you shouldn't be alone tonight."

And she said: "Not yet." And then kissed me again.

Until the moment (and the day) had passed and we'd agreed to stay one more night, and she'd retired by 8 pm to the antechamber while I drank vodka on the couch, shortly after which a plesiosaur breached the froth like a glistening killer whale—and snatched a pterodactyl from the orange-painted rocks.

I'm not going to lie; I hadn't really expected to find it—the key—regardless of what I'd expressed previously; so, imagine my surprise when I searched the corpse's stained pockets—managing, somehow, to keep a tenuous grasp on my breakfast—and touched a crenulated edge.

Bingo, I remember thinking, not lastly because it seemed to absolve Amelia—whom I'd come to suspect had taken it and not told me—but also because it would allow me to test something; something I'd been thinking about a lot since discovering the strange crater. One of *many* things I'd been thinking about.

I peered up at the lantern as the rain fell and the clouds drifted, as the melancholy of the day hung over everything like a shroud. *Tell me now why humanity is worth saving, and why we shouldn't finish what They started. What They instigated with the Flashback but failed to complete. What can be completed still.*

The words sat on my stomach like poached eggs. Absolved her? Perhaps. But not explained anything.

I gazed along the beach: at the desolate breakers and the gray tide rolling in, at the vortex of saltbushes about a half mile away—flies buzzing my face as I did so. I wasn't ready for this shit. For burying the lighthouse keeper. Then I started walking (wondering, as I went, what the weather was like in Montana, and if they had children there—and if so, were they happy and well-provided for?) ... until at last I came to the crater; where I quickly noticed something which should have been obvious the day before (but somehow hadn't been), and that was that it was incredibly close to the road itself—and that, indeed, they were separated only by a sandy embankment. An embankment, I soon realized, which still had drag marks in it—as though someone had unearthed whatever had fallen and pulled it up to the road.

I looked back the way I'd come—the rain pelting my jacket, the wind buffeted my hair.

As though someone had loaded it onto a truck; and then driven it—not bothering to pass "Go" or to collect $200—back to the lighthouse at Granite Point.

"Amelia?" I knocked on her door gently but firmly. "The Jeep's all ready to go. Also, I—I buried the keeper. I mean it's pretty shallow, but ... it'll have to do."

I waited a moment to see if she'd answer. When she didn't, I added: "And there's something else. Something I want to show you."

Still no answer. Only the breathing of the ocean, the ticking of the grandfather clock. I knocked again.

"Amelia? *Hey.* You there?"

That's when I knew. That's when I knew she'd had the key all along—had it since before I'd even discovered the antechamber; since she'd found it on the hook next to the lighthouse door—and that she must have planted it on the keeper only recently, possibly even the previous night.

And then I was turning the knob and the door was opening—just swinging in as easy as could be—and my shadow had fallen across her bed which was piled with blankets and clothes; after which, sweating and trembling, I looked at the lighthouse door—and saw that it was lazed open.

And began to move toward it.

I saw it even before I saw her—a spearpoint-shaped thing, an impossible thing, a thing blacker than black yet giving off light—which levitated straight as an arrow at the center of the Fresnel and somehow caused it to turn, to warp, to change its shape and then back again, to be at once physical yet abstract. Nor was it the size of even the largest lightbulbs but rather tall as a man, with no surface features whatsoever—like one of those cars which has been painted Vantablack and so absorbs all incidental light—a thing as perfect as it was paradoxical, and which had no color of its own yet somehow radiated multitudes.

A thing beyond which—out on the catwalk—stood Amelia: barefoot but wrapped in the keeper's bathrobe; facing away from the black light and myself; facing the sea which rose up and crashed on the rocks.

I circled around toward her but paused, gripping the doorframe. "H-Hello? Amelia? What—what are you doing out there? Are you okay?"

She didn't respond, only continued facing the sea (and the seabirds, which swirled like moths), her hair whipping and lashing—pulsing and glowing—appearing as though it were on fire as I crept onto the catwalk and approached her with caution. As she dropped the robe from her body—revealing herself to be completely nude—and I reached for her shoulder, slowly turning her around.

At which she said, "Careful, it'll eat your eyes," and looked up at me with eyes that had become black glass—like black, interstellar voids—and yet, *not,* because they were also full of light; full of pulsars and quasars and nebulae and supernovae; of blue giants and red dwarfs and white fountains and stellar flares—and colors which could not be defined much less comprehended—hues I should not have been able to see but could!

All of which was the moment I looked at the clouds and understood—and knew at once what the queer object was—for it was nothing less than one of the strange lights in the sky; nothing less than one of the architects of the Flashback itself— one that had fallen to Earth like a shooting star and been recovered by the lighthouse keeper after the Collapse (and which he had then placed inside his Fresnel). One that had gotten into Amelia and was in her even now, whispering to her, I realized—even as I backed into the lantern house and she quickly followed—guiding her. Compelling her toward some end I hadn't the ability to imagine.

"You see it—I can tell you do," she said, having followed my gaze; having focused on the lights in the clouds, on *them*—whose colors were the same as those in her eyes. "You see it and yet do not fully understand it." She looked at me and tilted her head; began touching my lips, tracing them as though they were art. "Let it in, Francis. Let it in as I will let you in—here, now, in every way."

She lowered to her knees—smoothly, silkily—sliding her hands along my body, unfastening my pants. "They have work for us." She pushed up my shirt and began kissing my stomach. "Do it with me, Francis. Do the work. You said it yourself—they're in Montana. Take me there."

And then she was gripping me and taking me into her mouth, moving her lips up and down, as I put her head in my hands and looked at the thing, the anomaly, the perfect, black arrowhead which somehow emanated light, and which showed me things even as I looked at it—dreadful things, horrible things—images in which people were being murdered by their own trust and generosity; visions in which I saw an entire community lain to waste. Until I could take it no more—for it was the future I saw—and tore myself away: yanking up my trousers and hurrying for the hatch, clambering down the spiral staircase which pulsed and flashed with light, bursting into the antechamber and down the hall into the living room.

Where I snatched up a bottle of whisky and began drinking it raw and undiluted. Where I crumbled to the floor and moaned, wondering what to think or do.

They call it the golden hour, that period of time right before sunset when the sky glows orange and the shadows lose their edges, and the world becomes, for the space of about 20 minutes, something elevated and painterly—ephemeral, even sublime. That's how the world felt as I sat on the rocks and watched the waves crash and spume—*sublime.* A thing of such grandeur and beauty that we couldn't help but to stand in awe. And yet, at the same time, weren't we part and parcel? Weren't we built of the same materials—the same *substantia primae*—and woven into its fabric like threads? And—that being the case—weren't we special too?

"You know it's funny," said Amelia, her voice sounding distant, muted, as though it were coming from a thousand miles away, "but somehow I knew you'd be here."

I looked up as she sat next to me—having put on a jacket like myself—and looked out at the sea, which crashed and breathed. "You always were more thoughtful than you let on," she said. She leaned into me with surprising intimacy. "More dutiful, more decent. It was the first thing I noticed about you."

I didn't say anything, only gazed out at the water and the swirling pterodactyls—one of which glided in for a landing.

At last she said: "It doesn't have to be this way, you know. We could pretend we never came here ... that nothing ever happened—even go our separate ways, if that's what you want."

I looked at my shoes—the ones I'd found at Walmart—and tried to smile. "You'd just come back. Back here, I mean. It—I think it's a part of you now. Part of your makeup."

Neither of us said anything as the birds squawked and wheeled and the sun sank toward the sea.

"Maybe. But does it matter? You'd be long gone. And who knows, maybe I can learn something from them. Something that ..." She trailed off; her face suddenly ashen.

"I'm sorry," I said, and gripped the gun. "But I—I can't let you do it. And I think we both know why."

She looked at me somewhat blankly before getting up slowly and walking to the edge of the breaker. "And so you're just going to casually blow me away, is that it? Just air me out, as they say?" She laughed, but when she turned to face me her eyes were full of compassion, not malice. "And you think you can really do that? Just whiff me out like a match?" She shook her head. "No you can't, Francis. I know you better than that—or I'd never come with you in the first place.

Please. Put down the gun. You're not a murderer. Not even they could turn you into one. You know that."

I stood but kept the pistol trained on her, moving toward her slowly, closing the gap between us. "I'm not just going to stand by while you—while you kill the people of Barley. I—I'll never do that, Amelia. I'm sorry. And if that means ... If that means—"

"Shhh," she said. "Listen to yourself." She held her hand out between us. "Give me the gun, Francis. Please. You don't want to do this, I know. Give it to me."

I shook my head, trying to resist. There was something about her now; something about her eyes. Just a hint of strange color—a hint of *them*—which made them oddly hypnotic, oddly compelling. "I don't—I can't—"

And then she leapt forward—suddenly, violently—snatching the gun from my hand, shoving me from the rock—*hard*—turning it on me even as I got to my feet—my head bleeding from the fall.

"Well now—how the times change." She cocked the weapon decisively. "And to think it wanted me to kill you and I refused!"

I raised my hands even while avoiding her eyes. "Now, just—settle down, okay? Nobody's going to kill anybody. All right?" I took a step backward—focusing on the gun, on its 9mm barrel. "I mean, we're two for two—right? I spared you ... and now, hopefully, you'll spare me."

She didn't respond, only continued sighting me, her lower lip trembling.

At last she said, "It's crazy, isn't it? Pointing guns at each other—as though we've somehow been enemies and not friends." Her eyes began to well up markedly, profusely. *"I've never wanted to hurt you, Francis.* But you have to understand, that—I'm no longer alone. That there's something else inside me now, and that it's vying—"

I stepped forward suddenly and she jerked the gun to track me.

"It's all right," I said. "It's all right. It's just that—"

And that's when it happened: that's when the silver and black plesiosaur breached the water like a mirage—its needle-teeth flashing and its dark neck glistening; its great flippers raked back like the wings of a plane—and snatched her from the rocks as though she were a doll. That's when the two of them seemed to hang briefly in the air—painted redden gold and burnt orange by the sun; rendered exquisite for a single fleeting instant—before crashing back to sea with a mighty smack and spray—and vanishing completely in its rough, roiling waters.

By the time I headed out the next day, the sun was at 12 o'clock and I'd fashioned two markers—one for the keeper and one for Amelia—both of which I'd planted atop breakers so they wouldn't be swept away. And then I'd made a sign—a sign for future travelers—which I'd hemmed and hawed over considerably before finally scrawling across it: GO TO BARLEY HOT SPRINGS IN MONTANA. STAY AWAY FROM THE LANTERN. Nor was it lost on me that the strange anomaly—who's very purpose had been to perpetuate the Flashback and thus usher men from the earth—would now be used to connect us; and to offer survivors hope. And I supposed that in the Big Empty, that was as good as it got.

And then I was off—having locked the tower door and disposed of its key—driving through Charleston and Barview and Coos Bay, following Tremont Avenue until it merged with Route 101, driving the Oregon Coast Highway all the way to Tillamook and beyond.

Because the windows were bulletproof, it all had to come out through the main entrance, and that included the grand piano in the Entrance Hall—which we wheeled recklessly against the doorframe before upending it with a huff and shoving it down the stairs, where it sounded briefly, chaotically, as it impacted each step. By then I was leaning on one side of the door while Fiona leaned on the other, looking on: at our friends as they started busting up the instrument below with bats and feet and sledgehammers, but also at the overgrown North Lawn of the White House and its spitting, crackling bonfire; at the tricked out Hondas and Toyotas as they continued pouring onto the field and bringing more—more beer kegs and more gasoline, more children of the Flashback, more us.

"Look at it, big sister," I said, finding her already staring at me in the flickering semi-dark, "It's like poetry, I swear."

"Green Room," she answered calmly, seeming almost to smolder. "And stop calling me that."

My eyes flicked up and down her body—something they'd been doing a lot of lately—but I don't think she noticed. Of course she was right; a lot had changed since our first burn—not the least of which was my voice—and calling her that no longer seemed appropriate. She, too, had changed—becoming less like a big sister (or even a mother) and more like an equal, even if, at 19, she still had a good 4 years on me.

"Okay, babe," I said, winking at her. I kicked the pedestal and candelabra next to me over with a resounding crash. "So let's do it."

And we went to work, Fiona pulling down the pictures and the red and green curtains while I took my bat to the china cabinet—smashing the glass as though it were a thin layer of ice, sending shards of it flying, bludgeoning the green plates and gold leafed vases like piñatas, like the shattered skulls of imagined enemies, until 243 years of history lay a glistening wreck at my feet—just so much broken detritus to be burned with the rest; just so much dust and memory to be erased and finally forgotten. At which I looked at Fiona and she looked back, smiling, her teeth large and slightly crooked, carnivorous—because it was a pleasure to burn, an ecstasy to burn.

By the time we rejoined the party, the bonfire was licking at the boughs of the maple trees and the staging had been erected for Calvin's speech—staging he was already ascending, gripping the rungs with one hand while holding a rolled up document—or documents—in the other, the firelight reflecting off his glasses.

"So what's he going to talk about?" I asked Fiona, heaving one of the two chairs I'd brought onto the fire—its red upholstery going up like dry paper, creating plumes of black smoke.

"How should I know? He's barely said two words to me since North Carolina." She pitched the framed pictures she was carrying—one of a dude she'd called Jimmy Carter—onto the roaring heap. "Look, Leif. I know he's something of a hero to you ... but you don't know him like I do. And I'm telling you, his heart's no longer in this. The Burning. It hasn't been since Georgia. At least."

I threw the other chair onto the pyre. "But it was his idea in the first place—wasn't it? Isn't that what you said—"

"I've said a lot of things," she snapped, and used her whole body to throw the second picture. "People change, Leif. At least some do. Others just get old."

I paused, thinking about that. Had something happened between them, like a fight? What did that mean, 'Others just get old?'"

"Okay, wild children, listen up!" cried Calvin from the top of the platform—and waved the rolled up documents to get everyone's attention. "Hear, hear! You're having *way* too much fun."

It took a minute but eventually the car stereos and loose chatter diminished and the silence reasserted itself—or nearly so, for the fire continued to crack and to pop and to roar like a veritable furnace.

"But then, why else would God have invented adolescence—if not to have fun?"

Hoots and cheers, whistles and applause.

"And that we have had. From Austin to Baton Rouge and Jackson to Montgomery, from Atlanta to Raleigh and Norfolk to Richmond ... to come at last to Washington, and the seat of Old Power itself. To come at last to the very pinnacle of what we set out to do—which was to loot and burn every vestige of what had come before; every deed and every banknote, every binding contract and article of law, and to cede them back to whatever chaos must ultimately rule our lives."

He looked out over us, his friends, his people, and seemed to reflect. "And yet I wonder—what remains of the old world and the old laws to douse and burn? I mean, besides these ..." He lifted the rolled papers above his head, inciting raucous applause. "These relics of a bygone age— which Leif and Fiona have so brazenly liberated? Well, I tell you, there is one thing—but we'll save that for later, when they return ..."

I looked at Fiona and she looked back. Were we going back to the Archives?

"For now, let us commend these, one U.S. Constitution and one Declaration of Independence, to the fires of a New World—a world as young and savage and beautiful as we are, for it has yet to see even its 30th month, just as we have yet to see our 30th year. And afterward, afterward, I'll have a special announcement. Right now it's time to party; and to dance on the grave of that which is old and dead—and which never served us anyway. *Salud!*"

"*Salud!*" echoed the crowd, raising their plastic cups.

And then he was unfurling the documents and dropping them into the fire, which hissed and popped and seemed almost alive, and Fiona and I were shoving our way through the crowd—both of us, I think, wondering where we were being sent, and more importantly, what this 'special announcement' might be.

"Babe," said Calvin, descending the ladder, and I looked away as he and Fiona embraced (briefly), I'm not sure why.

"Got another job for you two—if you're up to it."

"If we're up to it," said Fiona, and laughed, at which there was an awkward silence I didn't understand. "I know: You want us to take a group of bad apples and put down the Norsemen. Am I right?"

The Norsemen were the older group who's territory we'd violated in order to access the White House and National Mall—and who were bound to cause us trouble if we didn't leave soon.

"Wrong. I want you to go to the National Museum and liberate the Star-Spangled Banner—the flag, not the song—and bring it here to be burned."

Fiona shot me a glance. "He's a vandal, Leif, not a fighter."

"I'm not a killer, if that's what you mean," he retorted, then turned away and watched the fire, hands on his hips. "Nor will I let any of us be. I mean, if I've said it once I'll say it again: this isn't about bloodshed. It's not even about rebellion. It's more about ..." He paused—as though saying anything else could only lead to regret.

"I thought it was about nothing," said Fiona, softly. "That that was its beauty—it was wildness for the sake of wildness. Passion for the sake of passion. Isn't that what you said?" She laughed with surprising bitterness. "Different context, I guess."

"It was about filling the nothing," he said, still facing away. "And letting go. Until ... But then—you haven't had to think about any of that ... have you? No one's made you king."

"And cue the Messiah Complex," fumed Fiona, which I took as my cue to leave; to give them space—to let them hash it out, whatever it was—after which I wandered over to one of the kegs and filled a cup, reckoning that next to a roaring fire wasn't the best place to keep beer—because it tasted like piss, literally. Nor did I stop at one but downed three in rapid succession, wondering what Calvin had meant by 'filling the nothing' and 'letting go,' and about being king—not to mention starting a sentence with 'until' ... but never finishing it.

And I guess I must have stood there for a while, because I distinctly recall watching the same group of teens—their arms laden with destruction—moving back and forth between the fire and the White House—the fucking White House!—to the point that I began feeling shitty about what we'd done; and even a little sick to my stomach. But then Fiona returned jingling Calvin's keys and we were firing up his Mustang convertible, and the next thing I remember she was piloting us down 14th Street NW past buildings with Doric columns (now choked in prehistoric ivy) and a pair of grazing stegosaurs and at least one giant millipede; all the way to Constitution Avenue and the National Museum; which I took special note of only because I was trying not to look at her body—something she noticed, I'm sure, but didn't seem to mind—because she just glanced at me beneath the blood red sky and smiled—toothily. Carnivorously.

It was the sort of thing you had to actually *see;* up close, personal—as up close and personal as the glass would allow, anyway—to fully appreciate; to fully understand that this was *it,* the flag that inspired the national anthem, the actual Fort McHenry garrison flag, a thing more than 40 feet high and maybe 30 feet long, laying at an angle in a climate-controlled black room, or a room that *had* been climate-controlled, until the Flashback, until the lights had gone out from Anchorage to Miami.

"Oh, say can you see," I sang, moving my flashlight over the material, which was tattered and torn, "By the dawn's early light ..."

241

I grinned and trailed off, letting the silence take control, letting the room buzz, and we just stood there.

"What so proudly we hailed," sang Fiona at length, her voice cracking a little, "at the twilight's last gleaming." She took a breath in the dark. "Whose broad stripes and bright stars ... through the perilous fight ... O'er the ramparts we watched—were so gallantly streaming ..."

Then, together: "And the rocket's red glare, the bombs bursting in air, gave proof through the night ... that our flag was still there." We both took a breath. "Oh, say does that star-spangled *ba-anner* yet wave ... o'er the *land* of the free ... and the *home* ... of the ... brave."

And again there was a silence, as perfect and deep as anything I'd ever experienced, either then or since.

"Fuck," I said.

"Yeah," said Fiona. "Fuck."

I looked at the sparse starfield illuminated in her beam.

"They're all gone," I said, and lowered my flashlight. "Everyone who ever touched this. Those who first sowed it; those who stood in its shadow. Those who built this building to preserve it—all gone."

"Yeah," whispered Fiona. "It's just us."

"I don't know, big sis—I mean 'babe.' But do you ever wonder if—like, we're doing the right thing?"

"No."

"Okay. Well. Why is that, exactly?"

"Because there is no right thing. I mean, maybe there was ... before the universe just—went bugfuck. Before everyone just vanished. But now? What's right and what's wrong, Leif? I mean, what could possibly make any difference—one way or the other?"

"I don't know. It just seems that, like—"

"You're sounding like Calvin; don't go there. Because, I'm telling you, he's not who you think he is. Not anymore. He's—"

"Evolving?"

"Aging. Just aging. There's a difference."

"It's going to happen," I said. "We can't stay teenagers for—"

"Can't we?" She shook her head. "Maybe you don't see yourself ... but I do. See you, that is. And let me tell you— *you're a fire."* She touched my hand where it gripped the sledgehammer. "And fires need to keep moving, keep consuming," She raised my arm gently, assuredly, until I dropped my flashlight completely and took the hammer in both hands. "... or they burn out."

And then I swung, harder than I ever had before, harder even than when I'd destroyed the china hutch, punching a white crater into the glass as big my head, causing cracks to spread out in rings, like a contagion, I thought, or a cancer, until I swung again and the head of the hammer smashed clean through, enough so that I had to fight to pull it back out, after which Fiona joined in and we smashed through the glass together, not all at once but blow after blow, until the bitter shards lay all around us and we fell to the flag's faded cloth, kissing and groping each other with abandon, unfastening and working off each other's clothes, fucking like it was the end of the world, which of course it was— consuming each other like paper in fire.

It goes without saying that I was driving too fast; I was 15 and had just gotten laid. Add to that my inexperience—and a spike strip laid across the road—and, well, you probably have some idea how we ended up in the fountain of the Ronald Reagan Building with Old Glory folded up and sticking out of the trunk. All I know for certain is that we were both injured, Fiona seriously—to the extant that the blood from her head had fouled her left eye and she couldn't stop shaking; which is how I noticed the figures approaching us from behind (I saw them in the rearview mirror when I removed Calvin's doo-rag, to stop her bleeding).

"Fiona, listen—we—we gotta get out of here. Can you walk?"

"What is it?" she asked, weakly, deliriously, looking around like a blind person (which I suppose she was), bleeding profusely.

I squinted at the figures—there were more of them now—saw long beards and jackboots; rifles, riot gear, motorcycle helmets to which horns had been attached.

"Norsemen," I said. "Lots of them. Hold on."

I threw open my door and went around, noticing how exposed we were, how exposed the entrance to the building was.

"I'm going to put you across my back, okay? Just hang on."

"Okay."

"Here we go—"

And then I heaved her across my back and we went, hustling up 14th Street NW even as the Norsemen opened fire and the pavement sparked all around us—all the way to something called the M.I.M. Museum, the door of which I kicked in awkwardly before carrying Fiona up a flight of steps and laying her before a giant mural, after which I collapsed against the nearby wall—the window of which promptly exploded.

"Fuck!" I cursed, lying flat on my stomach, then crawled through the glass to Fiona where I shielded her lithe body with my own.

"It's okay, we're okay," I said quickly, even as she started to hyperventilate. "We're fine. They don't know we're not armed—they don't know we're not armed. They're not going to come in. Not yet."

I wrapped her in my arms and held her tight, even as the other windows were blown out and glass rained down. And then, just as suddenly as it had begun, it was over; at least for the moment—after which I lifted my head, slowly, cautiously, and listened.

Nothing. A squawk of a pterodactyl, maybe, way off in the distance.

"Leif?" managed Fiona, groggily. "Are you there?"

I squeezed her tightly, stunned that she couldn't feel it. *"Shh-shhh,"* I said, stroking her hair, which was matted with blood, kissing her forehead.

At last a voice called, "We just want the girl. Give us the girl; vacate the House and the Mall, and we're done here. All right?"

I held Fiona close trying to still her trembling—realizing, in the process, that I was trembling myself. *"Shhh*—it's okay," I said, finding her hand, enveloping it in my own. "Everything is going to be okay."

"Aww, you're sweet," she said, her voice faint, papery. "But it's not. It never has been. You know that. Even before the Flashback."

"Shhh," I repeated, and diverted my eyes to the mural, which depicted, in stark black and white, seemingly all the atrocities human beings had ever committed—most of which I was unfamiliar with, the Holocaust and Hiroshima being obvious exceptions.

"They're right, you know," she said, softly, having followed my gaze. "The lights in the clouds. The shapes ... in that beautiful borealis, that came with the Flashback. They're right about us."

But I only stared at the painting, at the depictions of medieval torture and Mayan beheadings, at the lifeless, flattened cities and mounds of emaciated corpses, like driftwood; at the piles of skulls and perfect, white tombstones extending forever.

"... Right to have—how would they say it? To have 'cancelled' us." She laughed a little, which became a series of jagged coughs. "And Calvin ... Calvin is wrong. About you. About me. About everyone."

She shifted her head slightly, looking at the whole mural. "We ... we were *meant* to burn."

I angled my head to look at her; at the dark, smoldering eyes, the large, slightly mis-aligned teeth, even as she exhaled in a long, rattling breath, and just shrunk—like a bag with all the air sucked out; like a marionette lowered to the floor in an unrecognizable heap. After which I pressed my cheek to her own and just stayed that way, although for how long I couldn't possibly say. All I know is that I was 'awakened' by gunshots, by the *crack-crack* of small arms, followed by screaming; screaming and the instantly recognizable growls of dinosaurs—big ones, by the sound of it—which itself gave way to silence ... at which I knew, with a mixture of relief and anger (because it was too late for Fiona anyway), that the Norsemen were no more.

By the time I'd walked all the way back to the White House and the North Lawn—carrying Fiona's body on my shoulders—Calvin's announcement was well underway, although it came to an abrupt halt when I appeared near the scaffold and laid her at its feet; after which there were gasps followed by a hushed silence—that is, save for the ubiquitous crackling of the fire.

When at last Calvin spoke, he did so as someone who had already resigned himself to the harsh reality of her death, asking only if she had suffered, to which I responded, "No," and then inviting me to join him on the platform, which I did, climbing the rungs and taking his offered hand until we stood together over the crowd and the roaring pyre and he had turned to address his audience again.

"And so it goes," he said, simply, giving the moment time to breathe, allowing everyone to catch their breath, until someone unexpectedly shouted, "How did she die?" —at which he turned to me, humbly, impotently, I thought, and indicated I should step forward; which I did, stepping to the very edge of the platform and looking down at the flames and the upturned faces, liking the way it felt, liking the way it made my blood race and seemed to snap everything into focus, liking the sense of power and purpose.

"Norsemen," I said, bluntly, after which, having been a student of Calvin since before puberty, meaning I'd idolized him and observed him carefully in the hopes that I might one day be like him, I let the moment breathe—until, finally, I added, "They laid a trap ... and we blundered into it. And then they issued an ultimatum: Leave now. Leave, or die."

"Fuck them!" barked someone almost immediately, and was quickly joined by others—all of whom felt that retaliation should be swift as it was lethal.

"We outnumber them five to one! I say we do it now, while it's dark, and we have the element of surprise!"

At which Calvin quickly tugged me back and we changed places, so that I was standing behind him as he said, "Now wait just a minute, gang, just hold that line of thought. Because, see, the thing is, we *are* in their territory. All right? They warned us and we— well, we rightfully ignored them, because, as you say," He pointed at one of the teenagers, "We outnumbered them. By about five to one, as you say. But that's because we—we had a *job* to do. We had to come here and ... and burn what remained of the Old World, the old ways. But the Burning is done, don't you understand? We've done what we set out to do, we've burned it *fucking all!*"

He looked left and right quickly, as though to fan the flames—taking them all in, seeking to build momentum. When no one spoke up he said, "And that's why I think it's time to ... to consider a new way. A new paradigm, as they say. A new, well, a new purpose. A way—"

"Our purpose is to burn!" shouted someone near the front, an expression which was met with cheers and sustained applause, and at least one horse whistle.

"Yes! Yes, it is!" Calvin shouted back, and hastened to add, "And so you have! So you have. And so very, very brightly, I might add. But there comes a time when ... when Time itself—begins to *mutate.* When your mind and your body begin to change, to *evolve.*"

"It's called getting old!" someone shouted, and was met by laughter.

"It's also called adapting; just bending ever so slightly so that instead of blowing you over the wind becomes an *ally,* a source of energy, and a renewable one at that. What I'm saying is ... the Burn is over. That the fields have been thoroughly cleansed and prepped. And that it's time to ... to build again. It's time to re-learn farming, irrigation, how to brew beer, for God's sake! Because the keg—the keg eventually runs out. And that's because what we're doing here isn't sustainable. It—it never was. *But.* But. You wanted a leader ... and somehow you found me. And so it was up to me in those first dark days to lift you up and to bolster your spirits, to channel your energy, to keep you busy and just get you through it." He sounded fatherly, patriarchal. "To help you let go of what was—and will never be again."

He turned toward me suddenly, I don't know why. "So ... no. There will be no retaliation. Not against the Norsemen, nor any other group. And there will be no more destruction." And then he held out his hand—I'm still not sure why—and I just looked at it; wondering if he knew, somehow—if he had intuited it. That Fiona and I had lain together; that I was beginning to doubt his wisdom and his leadership, just as she had. That's when I noticed his hand was shaking slightly, as I had seen the hands of the very old and infirm do, and when I looked to his face I could see it— the age, the wear and tear, the lines just beginning to form around his eyes and his mouth, the hint of darkness just above his cheeks. But then he shook his hand as though urging me to take it and I did—grasping it firmly, assuredly— and we pulled each other into an embrace, a right bear hug, slapping each other on the back, seeming to acknowledge what we had in common, which, I was beginning to suspect, was a penchant for leadership. And Fiona.

But then I lifted my gaze over his shoulder—following the billowing embers, as I recall—and saw that great and terrible borealis in the sky and the dark shapes within it; saw the lights which shifted and bled in and out of each other and the alien colors which were not colors at all as we knew them but rather facets of some strange and inconceivable prism, and knew, even before I looked, that I would see those same colors in the eyes of the children below—the lost children, the children of the Flashback—just as I had seen them in the eyes of the dinosaurs which now ruled the earth. And more, that if

I were to look, I'd see them in my own. And that's when I slid the shard of glass out of my back pocket (the one I'd kept as a keepsake after making love to Fiona) and, clasping it in both hands—so that it cut me deep before anyone else— drove it into Calvin's lower back.

At which Time stopped. It didn't mutate; it didn't evolve and transform—it just stopped; for I, and I alone, had stopped it. And then I was jerking Calvin against me, violently, brutally, again and again, sinking the shard deep into his flesh, using it to impale his spine, until he began coughing up blood—which gurgled darkly in the twilight and for the briefest of moments made one giant bubble—before releasing him completely and letting him fall backward into the fire, where he impacted like a fresh log, causing embers to explode upward, and began screaming—hideously, obscenely. Briefly.

"Salud!" cried everyone below at once, raising their fists in solidarity, even as I looked at the sky yet again and considered what I saw there, and what I had seen of myself; as I considered what I had seen in the M.I.M. Museum and in Fiona's dying eyes.

You wanted a fresh start, I said to them, the lights, the shapes *within* the lights. *You wanted to cleanse away the old. Let us help you.*

And then I looked at my friends, at my people, my *tribe,* seeing the Flashback in their eyes and knowing, at last, that this was its final expression; that we were meant to burn and to be burned, to end everything we'd ever touched; to end it all and to finally end ourselves. To just walk into the fire and close the book for good. To fertilize the fields for whatever was to come next.

To burn and to burn brightly.

To burn and to be burned, briefly.

It was a pleasure to piss on the world—piss on the Flashback. To stand at the edge of the W. Rosemond Avenue Bridge like you were mounting Gaia herself and let it pass: the Session Premium Lager or Pabst Blue Ribbon or Miller High Life (depending on the night); the Blue Moon or Genesee or Carling Black Label—which sat on the stomach like eggs. To just piss on the whole catastrophe—defiling it right back—as the Charger grumbled and spat and its stereo played AC/DC's "Ride On"—bluesily, smokily, *loudly,* because that's how we rolled.

"It wasn't there last night, I'm sure," I said, finishing up. "I mean, something that size—one of us would have noticed, doused or no. Don't you think?"

"Beats me," said Clinton. "I'm just here for the lols."

I approached the large, metal sign (which had been hung from the opposite side of the bridge before we'd lifted it off and turned it around) and reread it.

ATTENTION!
ALL REFUGEES

CAMP **HOLY CROSS**
NOW ACCEPTING INTAKE

EXTRACTION OCCURS
EVERY OTHER DAY AT
DAWN, ON THE BRIDGE

NO GUNS • NO ALCOHOL
NO TOBACCO • NO DRUGS

"Might explain the helicopter we've seen flying around," he added.

I stared at the sign and its crude block lettering. "Yeah. Maybe."

A chattering sound caused me to look at the car: *"Hey!"* —at which compies scattered explosively—like scurrying field mice—their pale, upheld tails bobbing.

Clinton laughed. "I told you—it's that beef jerky. They can smell it from a mile away."

"'Carnivore Candy,'" I said, repeating the brand, and chuckled. We went to the car and got in—and I buckled my seatbelt. "Take it easy this time, yeah?"

"You got something to live for?" He put in the clutch and gave it a rev, which sputtered and crackled. "Unless, of course, you want to join the monastery."

I just laughed. "You saw the sign."

He chuckled and put the car in gear. "I saw it."

And we went—glass packs rumbling, bass thumping, guns and ammo rattling—like we were going to war. Like we were riding into battle and never coming back; which, in a sense, we were.

They needed to go, I decided, peering over the scope at the windows of 24 Taps Burgers and Brews—and fired; the AR 15's muzzle flashing, making a fiery cross; the glass shattering and raining down—like sparkling glitter.

"The bus," said Clinton, his voice piqued with excitement, and laughed. *"Hit the bus."*

I aimed at the STA coach and fired—raking it with bullets, obliterating its windows, blowing its windshield out as we passed.

"Here," said Clinton. He reached behind him and groped for something—came up with a package of red-stemmed bottle rockets. "It'll save on ammo."

I took the package and looked at it. "What are we saving it for; the Afterlife? We'll need *two,* one for you and one for me."

"Well, who says you get to have all the fun until then?" He glanced at the road and then back to me. "So—switch it up."

I steadied the rifle between my legs and reached for my knife. "Sure, I guess." I slit the package open and removed a rocket. "I'm going to miss the Nunnery, I know that." I slid the stem into my empty beer bottle. "Especially ... you know."

"*Alexa.*" He scoffed at the idea. "Dude; she isn't going to miss you. Your toilet paper, maybe. The antibiotics ... But you, as a man? Forget it."

I guess I must have shrugged. "Yeah, well." I reached for the lighter and held it to the fuse. "Over there—iguanodon by the Dodson's clock. Corner pocket."

"But that's—"

And then he was ducking, ducking and covering his head with an arm, as I pointed the bottle at his window and the fuse sparked, hissing. As the paper projectile launched without warning and bounced off the window frame; then ricocheted about the cab like a bullet, like a punctured gas cylinder—sizzling, screaming, colliding against glass, careening off the seats and the dashboard even as Clinton pulled the car over and ratcheted the break. As we piled out of the doors and the rocket burst: flooding the cab with white light, showering the pavement with sparks.

"*Just—holy-fucking-Christ,*" gasped Clinton. He jumped up and down—doing the bug dance. "Are you insane?"

I laughed even though I could hardly breathe—then steadied myself against a tree. "No, no. Just—I'm just *really* a shitty shot." I looked at him through my bangs. "Sure you don't have anything to live for?"

It was, of course, an attempt at levity. A way to lighten the load—lessen the burden—to laugh, even, at what the world had become, what we'd decided to do. At making that decision bearable. Instead, I think, it came across as a challenge.

"Oh. I see." He looked me square in the eyes. "So—it's a joke, then. Is that it? The pact, the promise—"

I started shaking my head.

"No?"

He went to the car and shut it off—curtly, decisively, even as I attempted to dig out. "Look, Clint—"

"Shhh," he whispered—and held up a finger. "Just listen."

"Look—"

"Do it."

I did it; scanning the broad, empty avenue and the dark, silent buildings, the cars scattered helter-skelter, the stark, tumbling debris. "I don't hear any ..."

But I *did* hear it. The emptiness. The vacuum (or nearly so). The sound of the iguanodon foraging even as a pterodactyl squawked somewhere in the night and a newspaper skittered, crab-like, across the street. The sound of the world after people; after cities. A concrete veldt.

"Listen," he repeated—and gestured expansively. *"Look.* Look at those cycad bushes, those stands of palms ... see how they crowd the evergreens, the so-called natives? And look there; at that bus driver—see how the tree has simply, amalgamated him? And what's that—that ghostly light?" He looked at the sky and the clouds shot through with green; at the hovering lights—which glimmered and pulsed. "Only our 'friends'—whoever, *whatever* they are. Only that *force;* that phenomenon—as indifferent as Nature herself—which has selected us for extinction; for the trash bin of history." He stared at me feverishly, intensely. "As though we never existed. As though the millions, the *billions,* who have been vanished—the husbands and wives and children, the entire families—*the whole fucking cities!*—had never been born at all."

He took a step back, smartly, crisply—as though to punctuate what he was saying. "And you think that's worth living for? Or that I would want that? Or even—"

"Look, forget it," I said, and went to the car. "It was a fucking joke." I got in and slammed the door—turned the key enough to power the stereo. "Let's go!"

He hesitated as AC/DC played "Squealer"—then shouted over the music: "We check out at dawn, asshole. Just like agreed. Because I *ain't* doin' Hell alone."

"Okay, okay, just shut the fuck up, would you?"

And he got in—lighting a cigarette before shutting the door, fetching us each a warm Genesee (which I snatched and twisted open), putting the car in gear as I flicked the cap away and saw her for the first time: the Girl on the Dinosaur—and a predatory one, at that—the Girl in the Custom Saddle. The girl crossing Stevens Street at Sprague—just as cool and calm as could be.

The girl I tried to follow until we rumbled up Riverside Avenue and she disappeared behind First Interstate Bank; though not before she looked at me and smiled, I swear. Not before I'd fallen in love with her; a ghost, an eidolon. A figment of my imagination.

"Dude; what's with you, anyway? You've been quiet since we left downtown."

I crawled over and between the markers, clenching the rocket stem in my mouth—focused strictly on the task, serious as a bayonet to the throat.

"Like, *whatever,* man," Clinton added.

I stopped and spat the rocket out. "Look. You're the boss of this particular thing—okay? So you like to lob fireworks at your ex-girlfriend's house; *fine.* I don't ask questions. I'm just—I'm just concentrating on the job."

I took the rockets from my back pockets and gathered everything into one hand; then scrabbled to our usual spot—a horizontal slab they called a stele (in this case dedicated to someone killed in Iraq), and began setting up. "How do you know she's even alive?"

"I told you; I saw her at the fairgrounds, before the Guard caved. She was right there in the soup line. Didn't see Loverboy, though—guess he must have gotten himself vanished." He rolled onto his side in the tall grass and started planting rockets. "She's alive, all right. Alive and home; with a trunk full of weed, I bet."

He paused, glaring at the house. "I know that bitch."

I finished my rows and took out my Bick; followed his gaze.

"Looks pretty quiet," I said.

"Yeah." He readied his lighter. "But we can fix that."

And we started flicking; lighting up the rows with grim precision, setting off a hail of sparks and hisses, retreating into the grass as first one then another then another *piffed* and launched—screaming into the air; whistling toward the target, exploding like grenades on its roof and in the bushes. Turning the suburban street into a warzone.

Laughing and carrying on as the carnage unfolded and at last subsided; the smoke drifting, the embers settling. Patting ourselves on our scrawny backs for another mission accomplished; even as shots rang out and something whizzed past—a blunt thing, a humorless thing. Something which struck a granite tombstone deeper in the cemetery and punched a dollar-sized crater in it.

And then we were scrambling: crawling as fast as we could—double-timing it toward the car as still more shots rang out and echoed along the streets; as bullets pocked the mausoleum and cut the air like knives. Until we reached the Charger and leapt to our feet, throwing open the doors—even as raptors gathered and encircled the car—at which I lit a string of M-80s and threw them into the group; and the fireworks exploded like dynamite, reverberated like shotgun blasts. At which the animals scattered in perfect unison and we peeled from the lot—en route to the Nunnery, I suppose. En route to *Alexa.*

En route to the last shag of our lives.

"And you're sure of it," said Alexa, lying on her side, staring at the wall. "You're sure it hadn't been there before?"

I stared at the trailer's water-damaged ceiling and the spider scurrying along one of its yellow-brown wrinkles, feeling as though I might nod off, bordering on dream. "I'm sure of it. It looked new, for one. Like it had just been painted. And it was *clean.*"

I rolled to face her and her dirty brown hair tickled my nose. "Like it had been wiped down; like someone had cared enough—was *comfortable* enough—to make an impression." I rubbed my hand back and forth on her thigh; and she allowed it. "Like it had come from somewhere else. A different reality, a place completely outside the Flashback. A clean, well-lit place."

She shocked me by putting her hand over mine. "A clean, well-lit place ..." She pulled the sheets up and yawed around to face me, looked me in the eyes. "Do you mind if I ask you something? Something personal?"

I shook my head, afraid that she was going to ask me what I did *before*—before Time got scrambled, like a sausage and egg breakfast—which wasn't much.

"What's your name?"

I must have blinked, remembering what she'd said about "transactional intimacy" and "professional boundaries," and not getting too comfortable with one another. "Preston," I said—tentatively, hesitantly, and swallowed. "Preston Stokes."

"Preston Stokes," she repeated, and seemed to think about it. "No—no, that's not you. It's too ... Preston's a soldier's name—or a wealthy industrialist's. You're more of a ..."

I raised an eyebrow, like Mr. Spock. I thought it might make her laugh.

"Lucas. I'm going to call you Lucas." She kissed me suddenly. "And you can call me Lana; which may or may not be my real name." She kissed me again—just a peck, but it may as well have been the world. "Lucas and Lana."

"Lucas and Lana," I repeated—and smiled. "There it is."

And we chuckled—not very merrily, not for very long—until she diverted her eyes and the silence resumed.

At last, she said: "We'd never fit in, you know." She swallowed moistly, viscously, thickly. "In their clean, well-lit place. In their chapel full of rules and edicts. Not anymore. Not since we've become ... who we've become."

I couldn't help but to notice that she was looking at the clock; and followed her gaze. We were over-time.

I got up and put on my trousers—peered between the curtains at Clinton, who was outside smoking a cigarette (he'd finished early and was waiting for me). "Yeah—well. I doubt it's even legitimate. They're probably, like, fucking cannibals—or something." I yanked on my T-shirt. "Ain't *no one* thriving in this."

She laughed at that as I turned to go. "No, I don't suppose." She sat up and gave me *the Look*—even while letting the sheets fall. "See you next time? Lucas?"

I paused in the compartment's doorway—remembering the pact, remembering what it was we were going to do. "If I've anything to trade—of course." I looked her straight in the eye. "But then—no one's thriving in this. *Lana.*"

And I left—quickly, abruptly—having said something I'd always wanted to say (even though it was a complete and total distortion). Because, in actual fact, there really *was* someone who was thriving—the Girl on the Dinosaur. The Girl in the Custom Saddle.

If, that is, she even existed. If I hadn't just made her up out of whole cloth.

If I hadn't gone stark-raving mad—like the world, like Time itself.

I gripped the door handle fiercely—I had to grip something, and it was right there—as Clinton took the curve; the Charger leaning precariously, its tires chirping and squealing—like chicks falling from the nest.

"Jesus, what *is it* with you?"

He just smiled, gripping the wheel, focusing straight ahead. "I'm enjoying my last few hours on this earth—that is, if you don't mind?" He gave me a harsh look. "Maybe you should do the same—instead of looking so goddamn serious about everything." He fished around behind his seat; but didn't seem to have any luck. "Hello? Earth to Preston. Can you beer me?"

I fetched him a Black Label as we careened down the road—popped its cap. "Look, I'm going to say it again: Don't you think we should at least check it out?"

Clinton laughed as we skidded through an intersection—then floored it again. "Listen: You want to live with a bunch of old ladies and spend your life raising Dutch barns—fine. It's no skin off me. But I'm voting with my feet and checking out of this shit-show. *This* morning." He swerved to avoid a cycad tree and almost lost control—but quickly recovered. "And I'm gonna do it in a blaze of glory."

"Fine," I said. "That's fine." I studied his face as he focused on the road. "So drop me off at the bridge and have at it—all right? I want to see what it's about."

And then we were sliding, or the ass-end of the car was, skidding to a halt at the corner of W. 7th Avenue and S. Inland Empire Way—in fucking Spokane, Washington—after the Apocalypse, after the time-storm. Then we were sitting there under the freeway overpass and staring at some art on a concrete column; the engine idling, rumbling and sputtering, the wind blowing hotly as AC/DC sang "Down Payment Blues."

"Explain it," said Clinton, looking as though he'd just as soon kill me as look at me. "Tell me why you'd rather live—like that, like a prisoner, like a monk, than to just dash the cup to the ground and be free. Free of all this," He indicated the cycads and the overgrown sidewalks—the moss-covered bridge, the carcass of a small dinosaur. "Free of them." He indicated the sky.

I looked at the art on the overpass and thought about it—at its gay, vivid colors and depiction of a flying bird, which was coming in for a landing; and at the Sunset Boulevard Bridge—which had stood since 1913 and stood still: its arches suffused with purple, for the sun was rising in the east, its streetlamps glinting gold.

"It's just that ... maybe it doesn't have to be this way. This—this hopeless. This primal. Maybe we can tame it again, civilize it. Maybe we can do more than just survive all this," I looked at him across the cab. "Maybe we can thrive."

He started to speak but paused; unsure if I was having him on or not—gauging my sincerity. "And—what? You think ..."

"I don't know what I think," I said, and looked at the art—at the bird coming in for a landing and the gay, vibrant colors. At the graffiti which hadn't the power to overwhelm it. "I know *that's* still here—I know that. And I know ... that there's others out there; others who want to help. I didn't before, but ... now I do." I watched as he lit a cigarette and took a deep drag; blew bluish-colored smoke out the window. "And ... and I guess that's changed everything. You know I mean?"

And he just looked at me. And I looked back; hopeful, expectant.

He started tittering.

"I couldn't get it up with Mercedes—can you believe that?" He leaned closer, snorting and puffing, snickering through his nose. "Not even when she went down. I mean, I was like, I guess I'm a shower not a grower, baby!" And he *laughed.*

I must have just looked at him. There beneath the overpass, near the Spokane River and the Sunset Boulevard Bridge, as the sky began to lighten and the pterodactyls began to chatter. There in our hometown—which hadn't really changed so much (except for the cycads and the odd dinosaur).

There in the 'Kan; the Lilac City, the Easy Valley, which hadn't really changed at all.

"I'm sorry," said Clinton—and seemed genuinely saddened, genuinely sympathetic. "But it's 9 am, dude. And that's a sight past dawn."

I watched the skies, watched the road, waiting for the *chop-chop* of a helicopter, waiting for signs of a truck.

But there was nothing; not so much as a whisper, not even a flock of birds. Just the blue dome of sky and a smattering of clouds; the hot, yellow sun; a distant column of smoke. There weren't even any insects.

"It's not too late," said Clinton. "And there's plenty of rounds yet. Hell, we could even put it off until tomorrow, if you want." He looked at the car, which gleamed in the sun. "I'm kind of liking this sunshine, if you want to know the truth."

I shielded my eyes and scanned the horizon— shook my head. "No. No, thanks. I—I'm just going to wait here ... for a bit. You—you go on along. Really."

"Dude—"

But I just stared at him, the wind jostling my hair.

He moved toward the car but paused, facing away. "The gas'll all be gone soon; there won't even be any left to siphon." He lifted an arm as though he were going to make a point; then slowly lowered it, let it dangle. "It'll all be degraded—completely useless."

He swiveled around suddenly. "Do you at least want a gun?"

I shook my head.

"Yeah ... it figures." He got in the car and shut the door. "Well—we had some fun. Guess that's as good as it gets."

And then the engine leapt up with a rumble and he was gone; taking it easy until he rounded the far corner, opening it up as he hit the straightaway. Vanishing from sight amongst the various structures and trees.

That's when I heard it: the *chop-chop* of a helicopter— coming on fast from the eastern horizon; thundering overhead before circling once and touching down. That's when I saw the men clamber out and rapidly approach: their faces healthy, their orange jumpsuits clean and bright—and realized, too, that they were unarmed. Unarmed and, my God, *smiling*.

"Is it just you? Are you the only one?" The man had a French accent but flawless enunciation. "There is no one else?"

I raised my hands as they inspected and frisked me. "No. I mean, there was, but—"

"And you've no weapons at all? No needles? No paraphernalia?"

"No—"

"Then let's go. I'll explain everything en route." And to the others he said: "Let's go, let's go, let's—" He trailed off abruptly.

"What? What is it?" I had to shout above the rotors.

"Over there—there's—there's someone else." He barked at whoever it was: "Come on, lassie! There's raptors here and about, you know!"

And then we all climbed in: first Alexa and myself, then the man with the French accent, and finally the men in the jumpsuits—and began to climb. Then we began lifting into the sky even as Alexa turned toward me and told me she'd seen Clinton; seen him drive right off of a cliff, that is.

Seen the Charger burst into a ball of flame and become a tumbling wreck that exploded over and over and seemed to have been full of fireworks. Seen it become a black and red coffin that no one could have escaped—much less survive, at least while trapped inside.

A "proverbial horror show," is how she'd described it; at which I simply pulled her close and held her tight, looking out the window, looking for the smoke. At which I didn't see any but at last saw something else—something beautiful, impossible. Something I showed Alexa, who gasped and said, "You see it too? You actually see it? The Girl on the Dinosaur? *That* girl, right there, crossing the Sunset Bridge? But I thought only—"

At which I kissed her; kissed her hard and kissed her long; kissed her like a sailor returning from war. Kissed her for the future, which I could almost taste.

The End

If you enjoyed this work of fiction, please consider leaving a review at your point of sale. Thanks!

Wayne Kyle Spitzer is an American writer, illustrator, and filmmaker. He is the author of countless books, stories and other works, including a film (*Shadows in the Garden*), a screenplay (*Algernon Blackwood's The Willows*), and a memoir (*X-Ray Rider*). His work has appeared in *MetaStellar—Speculative fiction and beyond, subTerrain Magazine: Strong Words for a Polite Nation* and *Columbia: The Magazine of Northwest History,* among others. He holds a Master of Fine Arts degree from Eastern Washington University, a B.A. from Gonzaga University, and an A.A.S. from Spokane Falls Community College. His recent fiction includes *The Man/Woman War* cycle of stories as well as the *Dinosaur Apocalypse Saga*. He lives with his sweetheart Ngoc Trinh Ho in the Spokane Valley.

www.ingramcontent.com/pod-product-compliance
Lightning Source LLC
Chambersburg PA
CBHW020907160726
47993CB00005B/1851